"Who t
her expression

"Well, she's no~~t who she~~ *said* she was," Baldwin replied.

Pointing to his laptop, Galanter said, "Hang on. There's one more thing." He fast-forwarded the video, and another car came into view. Two more people jumped out of this car, both males, coming to the assistance of Alicia Colbern's unmoving attackers.

Definitely Feds, Baldwin decided as he absorbed what he had just seen, *but who*? It certainly was possible that the CIA, FBI, or some other group from the vast alphabet soup of government agencies had taken an active interest in Colbern—one of the 4400—but none of them had approached NTAC. Background checks had been run against the returnees and a few had even turned up criminal records, but those mostly were for minor infractions. Of course, the review had only been comprehensive with respect to those who had been taken more recently. Information on returnees taken more than thirty years back had been of varying quantity and detail, and a few had come back with no results whatsoever.

Adjusting his holstered Glock so that it sat more comfortably on his right hip, Baldwin said, "We can put some feelers out to other agencies, but something tells me that's a dead end even before we get started. Whoever was after Alicia Colbern, they wanted to do it on their own terms, and to hell with us."

THE 4400®

WET WORK

DAYTON WARD &
KEVIN DILMORE

Based upon *THE 4400* created by
Scott Peters and René Echevarria

Pocket Star Books
New York   London   Toronto   Sydney

Pocket Star Books
A Division of Simon & Schuster, Inc.
1230 Avenue of the Americas
New York, NY 10020

This book is a work of fiction. Names, characters, places, and incidents either are products of the authors' imagination or are used fictitiously. Any resemblance to actual events or locales or persons, living or dead, is entirely coincidental.

First Pocket Star Books paperback edition November 2008

POCKET STAR and colophon are registered trademarks of Simon & Schuster, Inc.

For information about special discounts for bulk purchases, please contact Simon & Schuster Special Sales at 1-800-456-6798 or business@simonandschuster.com.

Cover design by Alan Dingman

Manufactured in the United States of America

10 9 8 7 6 5 4 3 2 1

ISBN-13: 978-1-4165-4321-3
ISBN-10:   1-4165-4321-X

DEPARTURE

JUNE 1992

ONE

SHE STARED THROUGH the scope, her body still absorbing the rifle's recoil as she watched the back of her target's head explode in a crimson rain.

There was almost no wind, and the angle she had selected provided her an unobstructed view between those few trees at the edge of Federal Hill Park's expansive open field. At this range, the shot was child's play, the single round entering the man's forehead just above his left eye. He had turned at the last possible instant as she pulled the trigger, placing the round slightly off its intended mark, but the results were the same, as Sheik Miraj al-Diladi dropped limp to the stage behind his podium, dead before he had even begun to fall.

From her concealed sniper's nest two hundred yards away, Lona Callahan continued to peer through the scope, watching the scene around the raised dais as the audience scattered. Most ran away or simply dropped to the ground in search of protective cover, but a few rushed to the platform in the hopes of aiding the fallen al-Diladi. The body already was surrounded by assistants or other members of the cleric's entourage, some of them looking around and pointing in all directions in attempts to determine the origin of the shot. They would have little luck with that, owing to the rifle's silencer. Lona did not normally bother with that particular accessory, but her proximity to the target had made it necessary. She would have preferred a greater distance between them, but the site of al-Diladi's rally coupled with the constricted geography in this part of south Baltimore had forced her to carry out her assignment from a closer range.

Ignoring the distant cries of fear and terror echoing across the park, she instead focused her attention on the rapidly expanding pool of blood beneath al-Diladi's head. The single shot was the result of weeks of planning combined with Lona having gotten herself into position more than an hour before the cleric was scheduled to speak. She had observed the gathering of people swell about the large open field at the center of Federal Hill Park, and had watched through her scope as al-Diladi's entourage arrived and inspected the dais before allowing him to step out of his limousine. Training the rifle's crosshairs on his head from the moment he settled behind the podium, Lona waited until al-Diladi began speaking to the assembled audience to verify that he would remain in place. From there her training and experience took over as she drew a single, calming breath and released it an instant before her finger squeezed the trigger. The rest had taken care of itself.

Satisfied, Lona rose from her prone position on the dining table she had used as her platform, rolling to her feet and flipping away the dark green nylon poncho she had used to cover herself. The poncho worked in concert with the lack of light in the apartment as well as her black Lycra bodysuit—with its matching hood to cover her head and face—to make her all but invisible to any casual observer who might cast a furtive glance through the partially open window. Situated six feet from the window, the table had allowed her to set up her shot without exposing her position. Sticking one's rifle barrel through an open window was the stuff of amateurs.

Just ask Lee Harvey Oswald.

Moving with practiced efficiency, Lona disassembled the rifle, returning the components to their padded carry case. The Dragunov was not her preferred weapon, but it had proven more than adequate for this assignment. She would not use it again, of course; it would be disposed of once she was away from here. Her hands were protected by thin latex gloves that would prevent the transfer of fingerprints or skin particles as she worked.

Completing the collection of her other equipment, Lona glanced at the watch on her wrist. Three minutes since she had taken the shot. She could hear the faint sounds of sirens approaching, eighty seconds ahead of the schedule she kept in her head. *Impressive,* she conceded, even though she had factored in a greater level of efficiency for first responders to the scene.

Time to go.

There already was a police presence on hand, owing to

the nature of the park gathering. Sheik al-Diladi had been a controversial figure, a prominent Muslim cleric who had taken polarizing stances on a number of issues in recent years. Decrying extremist groups who carried out terrorist acts in the name of Islam, al-Diladi had long been a vocal advocate for harmony and tolerance—not only in the Middle East but also between that embattled region and the West. He should have been the ideal ambassador to usher in a new era of peace, and to most of the world that was exactly the image he projected. Indeed, the park gathering today was but the latest stop on a multicity tour through the United States, with al-Diladi bringing his message not only to Muslim followers but anyone else who cared to listen.

However, Miraj al-Diladi presented an entirely different persona to the world's leading intelligence agencies, many of which had been investigating his alleged ties to many of the very terrorist groups that were targets of his public denouncements. It had taken years to gather evidence sufficient to justify any sort of retaliatory action against the divisive cleric, after which the Central Intelligence Agency finally had taken the bold step of putting such sanctions into play.

Enter Lona Callahan.

Still wearing her mask and gloves, Lona reached into her bag and extracted a pair of white running shoes, which she donned over the black stockings she wore to cover her feet. That accomplished, she picked up the red backpack containing the rifle and her other gear and slung it across her back before taking a last look around the run-down apartment to ensure no sign of her sniper's nest remained. She knew better than to close the window—doing so in the moments after the shooting might attract unwanted attention. The table in the dining area was returned to its former forlorn state, stacked with the magazines, unopened mail, and empty pizza boxes she had gathered for just that purpose. Every apartment in the building that faced the park would be searched, she knew, but investigators would find nothing. Lona had rented the room two months earlier under an alias, and when that name was scrutinized along with every known detail of the assassination in the days to come, the world's intelligence and law enforcement entities ultimately would come to the same conclusion.

The Wraith had claimed another victim.

Lona smiled beneath her hood at the thought of the melodramatic moniker bestowed upon her by the media, dating back nearly a decade to when she had committed her first high-profile assassination. It had been another political leader on that occasion, the fascist dictator of a small South American country believed to be assisting Colombian drug cartels in their efforts to smuggle cocaine into the United States. His murder—also carried out with the use of a sniper rifle—was broadcast live on state-run television and picked up by intelligence services around the world, to say nothing of the international media. No clues or worthwhile evidence had been found to suggest a suspect or a motive for the assassination; it was as though the leader's killer were a ghost, and the papers and news networks had taken it from there.

Pausing at the door, Lona listened for signs of movement in the hallway. She heard nothing and stepped into the narrow, dimly lit corridor on her way to the stairwell. It was empty, as well, and she descended the steps two at a time, waiting until she had moved from the fourth to the second floor before finally removing her hood and sticking it in a side pocket of her backpack. As she walked, she reached up to ensure her blond wig was still in place to conceal her red hair.

It was not much of a disguise, but Lona always had operated on the principle that less was more. Large dark sunglasses could pique curiosity, as would long coats with collars pulled up around the face or any one of a dozen things a Hollywood assassin might do when leaving the scene of a crime. The goal was to blend in, appearing as ordinary and part of the landscape as possible. With that in mind, Lona had chosen the simple black exercise suit with white piping, the same sort of unremarkable outfit worn by women running the streets and parks all over the city.

Encountering no one before reaching the first-floor landing, she entered a passageway that would take her to a door leading into an alley behind the apartment building. Now she removed her latex gloves, knowing they would attract attention. This, Lona knew, would be the critical part of her exfiltration, the time when she was at her most vulnerable. Police would at least be in the beginning stages of setting up cordons and blocking off streets with the hope that the shooter was still in the area and that they might block or hinder an escape. One key advantage she possessed was that, as a woman, she would not draw immediate suspicion from casual bystanders. However, with law enforcement already in the area, the possibility of her being seen or even stopped by an alert police officer was not to be ignored.

Careful not to use her hands, Lona pushed open the door and stepped outside. The sounds of police sirens now were louder, and she could hear frantic shouts in the distance. She had exited via the door at the midpoint of the long, narrow four-story building, placing her roughly sixty yards from the street that separated the apartment complex property line from the western edge of the park. The alley itself reeked of urine, stale beer, and overfilled Dumpsters sitting too long in Baltimore's June sun, but it had the virtue of being void of other people.

Adjusting the pack on her back, Lona started up the alley heading west, away from the park. From here, it would be a simple matter to turn north at the alley's far end and walk two blocks before crossing the street to the nearby Maryland Science Center. She would proceed north to Harborplace, a waterfront marketplace boasting restaurants, bars, and retail shops as well as a significant tourist presence. There, she would lose herself in the crowd before making her way to the parking garage east of the market and the car she had staged there for her getaway.

Lona was almost to the mouth of the alley when the uniformed police officer came around the corner.

Damn it.

The cop barely had time even to register her presence before she launched herself at him, striking him in the face with the heel of her hand and feeling cartilage snap. He was a big man, dark-skinned and well muscled, but the blow had taken him completely off guard—and now she had the edge. His eyes screwed shut in pain as he reached for his broken nose, blood already streaming from it and staining his dark uniform shirt. Not giving him any quarter, Lona lashed out with a roundhouse kick, her foot slamming into the side of his face and driving him to the cracked pavement.

He grunted once before falling still, and Lona quickly reached for his neck to verify that she had not killed the man. Finding a pulse, she breathed in relief as she regarded his prone form. With rare exceptions when no other alternatives presented themselves, Lona always had prided herself on not killing anyone but her designated marks. It was an odd ethical code for an international assassin to possess, but it was one she embraced. The cop's strength and training may well have allowed him to give her a decent fight, and while she still was sure she would have beaten him, the scuffle would almost certainly have drawn the attention of a passerby. Instead, the police officer, whose metal name tag read "Jenkins," would be fine once his nose and pride healed. More important, Lona found it unlikely that he had gotten even a fleeting glimpse of her face. He would be unable to identify her or even to offer a description of her to a police sketch artist.

Glancing around to ensure she remained unobserved, Lona headed once more out of the alley but stopped again, this time responding to an abrupt sound from behind her. Turning, she searched for the source of the odd drone that seemed to be echoing through the alley, but saw nothing.

It seemed mechanical, wavering in pitch as it increased in volume with each passing second, growing to the point that it drowned out every other sound. Lona sensed discomfort in her inner ears before a wave of dizziness washed over her. She reached toward the apartment building's brick façade for support just as an intense light appeared above her. Looking up, she shielded her eyes, seeing nothing but the light. Air rushed around her and Lona felt as though something had reached down to take her in its massive grip. The odd drone had dissolved into the howl of wind all around her and as the ground disappeared beneath her feet, she was swathed in the feeling that she might be flying.

Then, Lona saw . . .

TWO

THE APARTMENT WAS too clean, Tom Baldwin decided. Not too neat or tidy, at least not if the kitchen and dining area was any indication. It was simply too *clean*. His gut told him that something about the room was off, but he had no idea yet what that might be.

Way to crack the case, Agent Uncertainty.

"Maybe she shopped every couple of days," he said, holding open the door to the kitchen's off-white refrigerator and examining the unit's contents, which were uninspiring to say the least. A half-gallon plastic jug of milk of the two-percent variety that to Baldwin always tasted watered down, two cartons of leftover Chinese food, and three bananas appeared to be among the most recent additions. Baldwin glanced at the milk's expiration date, noting that it was a week in the past. "Assuming she even ate here at all, that is."

"What are you trying to say, Agent Baldwin?" asked

Ted McIntyre, the senior agent on scene, from where he stood next to the apartment's pair of windows. "Are you formulating a theory?"

Baldwin rolled his eyes as he closed the refrigerator. Special Agent in Charge Theodore J. McIntyre was many things, among them a veteran member of the Bureau as well as Baldwin's immediate superior. He also was a colossal, patronizing prick, which seemed to be a trait required for climbing the FBI advancement ladder. "Not yet. Right now I'm just making notes."

"Well, here's something to note," McIntyre said, motioning for Baldwin to join him at the windows. "What do you make of this?"

The left window was closed and covered by a grungy yellow roller blind, whereas its companion was open a third of the way and propped up with a standard wooden twelve-inch ruler. Its blind also was pulled down, but only enough to cover the closed portion of the window. Baldwin found it odd that the window was open at all, given the laboring of the dilapidated air-conditioning unit mounted on the wall to his right.

Bending down so that he could look through the open portal, Baldwin observed that the sight line was directly across Federal Hill Park. A few trees lined the way and at points their branches obscured his view, but he still was able to see the raised dais and podium on which Sheik Miraj al-Diladi had been standing when he was shot. Even from this distance, he could make out the thin lines of yellow police tape around the platform. Uniformed Baltimore police officers as well as plainclothes detectives from the department's Homicide Division moved about the area, presumably canvassing the park grounds for evidence.

"Two, maybe two hundred twenty yards away?" Baldwin said, pointing through the window. "Pretty easy shot for someone who knows what they're doing. If they were using a scope, it'd be a piece of cake." He shrugged. "We're still not sure yet where the shot even came from." Looking around the room again, he added, "The walls are made out of Kleenex. If this was the sniper nest, the shooter would've had to use a silencer to avoid rousing the neighbors."

McIntyre nodded, validating his protégé's observations while not showing any outward signs of being impressed. "If the shot did come from the front, which is what Baltimore PD is telling us for the moment, that narrows down the angles. And this building is one of the better prospects." He paused, taking a moment to kneel down so that he could get his own view of the park through the window. "So, Agent Baldwin, what's your gut telling you? Just another pissed-off guy with too much free time and too few people skills? Or, somebody we know?"

"Hard to say at this point," Baldwin said, knowing what his supervisor meant.

The Wraith?

Known only by the sensationalist nickname for nearly a decade, the otherwise unidentified international assassin was a logical suspect. Indeed, the FBI's Behavioral Analysis Unit had picked al-Diladi's visit to Baltimore as a possible target for the mysterious shooter, and twenty-seven agents had come up from Washington to supplement the local field office as the date for the cleric's arrival drew closer. In keeping with the notorious killer's methods, no hints or any sort of advance warning had been detected in the days leading up to the rally. Now, in the aftermath of al-Diladi's murder, there also was a notable lack of evidence being found to justify pointing the finger at the Wraith, and Baldwin was nowhere near being ready to make that kind of speculation. Junior FBI agents two years out of the Academy did not normally posit such theories—not if they wanted to become senior agents.

Over the past several years, the Wraith had been linked to dozens of killings all over the world. Political leaders and powerful heads of business as well as known and suspected terrorists numbered among those believed to be victims of the assassin, about which virtually nothing was known but who appeared on the Most Wanted lists of nearly every intelligence and law enforcement agency on the planet. A global manhunt had been under way for years with no success. While leading theories pointed to a professional, contracted killer, no clues or leads as to his or her identity or location had been found. Likewise, no information regarding any potential employers had surfaced. Every avenue of inquiry reached a dead end, every question asked begat yet more questions, and investigators assigned to the case had long ago found themselves chasing their tails.

Maybe I should've brought my running shoes, Baldwin mused.

The June heat and humidity was forcing its way through the open window and threatening to overpower the inadequate air conditioner. Reaching up to wipe sweat from his forehead, McIntyre asked, "What do we know about the renter?"

Consulting the memo pad on which he had been scribbling several pages of hurried notes since his arrival on the scene, Baldwin replied, "Name's Jennifer Black. Single, been living here a couple of months." Though he was certain he had not read or heard it before today, he felt that there was still something odd about the name. "The detective running the investigation for Baltimore Homicide, Pembleton, gave me a quick background check he'd run on her when I asked. No record, nothing from DMV, and he's still trying to track down job info and all of that. I've already relayed everything back to the office and called in for the whole nine yards." He glanced at the watch he wore on his right wrist. "Should have something by the time we get back."

"And this is the broad we think beat up the cop downstairs?" McIntyre asked. "What's his name? Jenkins?" Shaking his head, he added, "Man, that guy's buddies are going to give him hell for the next year."

Suppressing his own chuckle, Baldwin shook his head. "No way to be sure without an ID. Officer Jenkins says he only got a glimpse of whoever clocked him before his nose was broken, but he's pretty sure it was a woman. Blond hair, black running suit, white shoes, wearing some kind of backpack." All-points bulletins already had been issued for police to detain anyone matching the woman's description but Baldwin knew that was a long shot. Other agents were canvassing the apartment building, but only a few of the other residents had ever seen the person living in this unit.

Still, they were able to verify that a slim blond woman lived here, alone, and kept mostly to herself. It all was adding up to a big fat zero, Baldwin knew, something for which McIntyre's superiors would have little enthusiasm. That in turn would translate to more chewing out from McIntyre to his subordinates, Baldwin included.

While this was by far the most high-profile case to which he had been assigned during his brief FBI career, Baldwin was one of hundreds of agents assisting in the investigation. As such, he was only slightly less removed from the upper echelons of the case's chain of command than the janitor who cleaned Ted McIntyre's office each night. As a junior agent, it was likely that he soon would be given another assignment, perhaps even sent to a different field office elsewhere in the country, long before this case either was concluded or fell into limbo as leads dried up and no further evidence presented itself. In the meantime, Baldwin knew that other, more experienced minds were at this moment sifting through every flimsy piece of evidence collected in the wake of al-Diladi's death. Would any of that lead to a suspect, perhaps even the mysterious Jennifer Black?

What is it about that damned name?

The question rattled around in his mind as he scrutinized his notes, circling where he had written down the name with his pen. What was it that bothered him? He ran his free hand through his hair, sighing as he felt the first hints of fatigue teasing the edges of his mind. The letters seemed to dance on the paper in his hand, as though trying to convey something more to him.

Jennifer Black. It was simple, unassuming, unremarkable. On a list of names, it would possess nothing to distinguish it from . . .

A list of names.

"Son of a bitch," Baldwin said, beginning to scribble on the notepad. When he looked up again, McIntyre was staring at him, a perplexed look clouding his features.

"What?" asked the senior agent.

"Jennifer Black," Baldwin said. "That's the name on the lease, right?" He held up his notepad for McIntyre to see. "Scramble the letters around, and look what you get."

His scowl deepening, McIntyre shrugged. "Ken F. Jacelbrin. So what?"

Baldwin grunted in mild irritation. "Nineteen-eighty-nine. The hotel in San Francisco where they found that CEO drowned in the pool? The guy who ripped off his company's retirement funds, whatever the hell his name was? There was a Ken F. Jacelbrin registered at the hotel on the night of the murder, but he disappeared before he could be questioned."

It was more than a little satisfying to watch McIntyre's face go slack and his eyes dawn in realization. "Jesus. You've got to be kidding me. He's a she, or she's a he?"

"Maybe," Baldwin replied, shaking his head and feeling his heart beginning to race as he recalled the relevant data from one of the Wraith case files he had studied months earlier. The name was listed among the handful of registered guests from that night who had been sought out for questioning but never found. Follow-ups were attempted, but he had read nothing in the files detailing any results from those efforts. As for the Wraith, since no conclusive evidence identified the assassin's gender, it was logical to assume he—or she—might use both male and female aliases to preserve his or her anonymity.

Could this be it? Had the person who killed that corrupt businessman three years earlier actually rented this very apartment and murdered Miraj al-Diladi, to say nothing of at least two dozen others and perhaps more around the world? If so, had a relatively inexperienced agent, the same guy who had given up a sports scholarship to study criminal justice before applying to the FBI, just stumbled onto an innocuous clue that might well be one of the very few solid leads in this case?

Don't get ahead of yourself, rookie.

As though reading his mind, McIntyre said, "Let's not get too excited. When we get back to the shop, run both names and see what the computer spits out. Go back to the 'Frisco file and pull out whatever they have on this Jacelbrin guy. Let's find out if he's really a ghost. Add whatever you find to the new file you're going to start on Jennifer Black." Almost as an afterthought, he added, "Nice thinking, Baldwin."

Nodding in appreciation for the unexpected compliment, Baldwin reminded himself to keep his enthusiasm in check. If the Wraith's past was any indication, the trail he was about to follow with this new information likely would lead to yet another dead end. The assassin—he or she—had spent many years covering his or her tracks. Baldwin doubted he would get so lucky as to trip over some loose end left unattended. That sort of thing only

happened in the last ten minutes of TV crime dramas.
Then again . . .

For a moment, Baldwin allowed himself to consider the possibility that, somehow, the Wraith finally had made the key mistake that would lead to his or her eventual downfall, and that it was he who had chanced upon it. Most long-term cases were solved in a similar fashion, after all. Might this bit of happenstance be just what was needed, and possibly even end up as a defining moment in the career of an up-and-coming FBI agent?

Only time would tell.

RETURN
AUGUST 2004

THREE

NEAR MOUNT RAINIER, WASHINGTON

WHITE LIGHT FLOODED her vision and the wind howled in her ears. She felt neither heat nor cold and, though she was not in pain, every nerve ending tingled as if ready to overload. Voices echoed in her head, and she was certain she heard other cries of confusion and fear from all around her. There was no immediate sense of movement, but Lona Callahan still felt as though she was falling.

Then the light and the noise faded, replaced in the space of a heartbeat with an abrupt silence.

Gone were the narrow, dirty streets and dilapidated buildings of old Baltimore, and replacing them were snow-covered mountains to either side of her. Looking around, Lona realized that she was standing on the sandy shore of a massive lake. There was a chill on her exposed skin and she could see her breath, all of which was inconsistent with summer on the Atlantic coast. Judging by the topography, Lona guessed she was somewhere in the Pacific Northwest—Washington State or perhaps Canada.

And she was not alone.

Hundreds, *thousands* of other people—men and women of varying ages and representing every ethnicity she might immediately recognize—milled about wearing expressions of bewilderment that no doubt mirrored her own. No one spoke, each person seemingly stunned into astonished silence. An elderly woman to her left stumbled and nearly fell before Lona caught her by the arm, holding her steady until she regained her balance. They made eye contact and Lona found herself offering what she hoped was a small smile of reassurance. She did the same thing with a young blond girl who also stood nearby. To her credit, the child seemed calm and composed, as though at peace with or at least accepting the bizarre situation she and the others faced.

Lona was cold. Folding her arms across her chest in an attempt to warm herself, she looked down to see that she still wore the Lycra running suit—but something was wrong. With a start, Lona realized she was no longer wearing her red backpack. It was nowhere to be found, having somehow disappeared along with its damning contents. Reaching up, she felt that her blond wig also was gone, her natural, short red hair now revealed. What had happened to her?

A dense fog surrounded her and the group, but as the wind pushed it away Lona became aware of dozens of other people standing farther up the shoreline. She recognized police and military uniforms, as well as the portable video camera equipment wielded by field journalists. Helicopters, some carrying law enforcement and others bearing news reporters, descended from the dusky, overcast sky and hovered directly over the odd assemblage.

"Where am I?" Someone called the question out from behind her, and Lona listened as a chorus of similar queries began to fill the air. She then noticed some people had moved away from the water and toward the party of onlookers. A number of police officers responded by fanning out to form a line, holding up their empty hands in an attempt to keep the group corralled on the beach.

Near the center of the line, a lone woman stepped forward. She was slender, her fair complexion contrasted by dark hair pulled into a knot at the back of her head, and dressed in black pants with the hint of a red sweater visible beneath her long coat. She stared at the group with amazement rather than fear, though Lona also saw the uncertainty in the woman's eyes while at the same time sensing her intelligence and strength. Was she in charge? Might she have the answers to the hundreds of questions being shouted in ever-increasing volume by the people around her, or even those harbored by Lona herself?

A police officer handed the woman a bullhorn, and she aimed it toward the crowd. "Ladies and gentlemen," the woman called out, holding up her free hand in a gesture for everyone to focus their attention on her, "my name is Diana Skouris. Please just stay where you are and our people will do everything they can to assist you."

She was making it up as she went along, Lona decided. Skouris—and by extension everyone with her—had no idea what was going on here, who Lona or any of these people were or how they had come to be here, wherever this place might be. As the woman, likely some variety of federal agent, issued instructions for anyone in need of medical attention to step to the front of the group, someone beside her repeated her directions in Spanish. Police officers started moving into the crowd, some carrying notepads and pencils, while others cordoned off the beach from the area beyond it by deploying bright yellow caution tape. Everywhere, men or women in civilian attire, most likely plainclothes police or other government agents, were yammering into cellular phones, undoubtedly reporting to superiors or requesting additional personnel and equipment. Meanwhile, reporters and camera operators jockeyed for key positions along the yellow tape, each of them vying for the best angle on the beach and the bizarre collection of people currently crowding it. Whatever was going on, it was quickly evolving into a massive effort.

With as casual an air as she could muster, Lona allowed herself to blend back with the rest of the group while forcing herself to remain calm. Though her true identity was known only to a precious few individuals—to the best of her knowledge, anyway—she saw no need to take unnecessary chances. What she needed now was information. Once in possession of that vital data, she could formulate a plan for what to do next.

Yes, she decided, *that was it. That felt right.* Already she could feel her inner calm reestablishing itself, her instincts quelling as experience and training took over. She had long ago grown accustomed to working on her own, armed only with her skills and wits and without benefit of support from her handlers or even her most trusted allies.

Until she determined otherwise, this was just like any other mission.

FOUR

3,085.

The number rolled about in Lona's mind, intruding upon and obscuring her other thoughts. Since the moment a federal agent had assigned it to her six days ago, the series of digits had dominated her life. Of the 4,400 men, women, and children who had appeared on that beach—from thin air, if the agents and the news reports were to be believed—she had been number 3,085 to receive a cursory, preliminary interview.

It had happened while she and the rest of her fellow "newcomers" still stood on the beach, and Lona quickly had realized that one of the benefits of being examined so late in the process was that the agents had been able to refine their questions in order to improve efficiency. By the time she sat down in front of the young, freckle-faced man with the bad haircut and poor fashion sense even for a government employee, one who obviously had tired of this task at least three or four hundred sessions ago, the routine seemed practiced and even complacent. Lona had provided a name, Social Security number, and date of birth as well as what she believed to be the current date, and where she had been on that date. Those last data points had at first seemed odd, even taking into account the fact that she most likely was missing at least some portion of time since the mission in Baltimore.

Instead, it gave birth to the other number dominating her thoughts: 12, being the years that had passed since her apparent disappearance. It had taken Lona several moments to fight the initial, automatic denial that had arisen in response to hearing such an outlandish assertion. Indeed, she still found it difficult to believe, even after nearly a week of being inundated with evidence to support what she had been told. Still, try as she might, Lona was unsuccessful in recalling anything that might have happened between her last seconds in Baltimore and her abrupt appearance at that mountain lake. So far as she could tell, the transition had been all but instantaneous, yet twelve years seemed to have passed in that blink of an eye.

Her story was not unique. According to the continuous news broadcasts, each of the other "returnees," as she and the others now were being called, was someone who had vanished from locations around the world and—as incredible as it sounded—from different points in time, some as far back as fifty years. Most were listed as missing persons, mysteries that had remained unsolved and in many cases all but forgotten as the years passed.

And now, all of them had been collected together, waiting for someone, anyone, to figure out just what the hell to do next. Hopefully, this also entailed finding out what had happened to them in the first place.

Following the initial interviews at what she had learned was Highland Beach, near the base of Mount Rainier in Washington State, Lona and the other returnees were transported by military convoy to a government building on the outskirts of Seattle, only to be placed in what was politely described as a "quarantine ward." None of the returnees were permitted to leave the ward, nor had they been afforded the opportunity to contact relatives or friends. The agency responsible for overseeing the quarantine had been gathering information on next of kin during the more extensive interview processes currently under way. Though Lona had no family, she still had what she hoped would be a viable plan for notifying a trusted friend when her time came.

As for the ward itself, with its cinder-block walls and high concrete ceiling, all of which were painted in a bland, depressing shade of beige, to Lona the new accommodations resembled a fortified bunker or fallout shelter or, perhaps more accurately, a prison. It was an illusion that only strengthened as Lona took in the dozens of returnees around her, each dressed as she was in matching utilitarian khaki work shirts and pants.

Segmented into several long barracks rooms with adjoining lavatory facilities, the ward's primary feature was the large dayroom at its center. Dozens of tables were arrayed about the massive room, affording the returnees a place to eat their meals and play cards or other games, as well as read the stacks of newspapers and magazines that were being provided by the crateload. Many of the returnees spent that first night devouring the publications and watching the news on the room's clusters of televisions.

Though the majority of the broadcasts were dominated with reports, updates, and conjecture about "the 4400," Lona also had managed to learn a few other interesting bits of information. In the time she had been gone, President Clinton had served two terms, after which his wife was elected to the Senate, and President Bush's son now held his father's former office. The United States had suffered a horrific terrorist attack on its own soil three years earlier, taking thousands of lives and triggering protracted conflicts in Afghanistan and Iraq. A second space shuttle, *Columbia,* had been lost in flight, everyone and everything appeared to have a "website" as well as a cellular phone, and three additional *Star Trek* television series had come along.

Interesting times, indeed.

Of the news programs currently devoting extensive coverage to the mystery of the 4400, it intrigued Lona to see that more than a few were holding debates as to the rights of the returnees. The idea that they might be incarcerated illegally was countered with the not unreasonable position that the 4400 could be carrying some kind of contagion or, as one agent had suggested, that they might even be brainwashed sleeper soldiers coerced by a rogue government or terrorist organization. No matter how seemingly bizarre, such possibilities had to be investigated before the enigmatic group could be released.

Many of the journalists on the different screens were asking the same questions as the returnees themselves: Why? For what purpose had they been taken? Who was responsible? Theories about that also had filled the airwaves, each sounding more fantastic and ridiculous than the last, and many of which were undoubtedly fueled by the spectacular event that had heralded the arrival of the 4400. The immense ball of light, first believed to be a massive comet on a collision course with Earth, was now believed to be an artificial construct, though its origins remained unknown. Implausible hypotheses involving alien abductions and interrogations, along with all manner of obscene experiments on the part of the supposed extraterrestrials, were being given serious time and attention on what Lona would have thought were reputable news programs.

In fact, she had come to the conclusion that the very concept of reporting the news seemed to have been supplanted by the sort of sensationalist tripe that at one time had been the purview of supermarket tabloids. It was a concept she found annoying, considering the sheer availability of information that now was possible with the expansion of cable television and the Internet. Still in their infancy in 1992 so far as commercial and public interests were concerned, the Internet and the World Wide Web now offered the casual user a seemingly limitless supply of information on any imaginable topic. Indeed, Lona and the rest of the returnees had been given access to the Internet via a row of computer stations—each of which was both more compact and more powerful than the bulky desktop model she once had owned—though it quickly became obvious that only a small segment of the 4400 possessed even rudimentary personal computer skills.

For her own part, she had considered using the workstations to seek out news regarding any developments in the worldwide hunt for her alter ego, which surely would have been stymied for at least a time following her disappearance. Had someone finally discovered the Wraith's true identity? The closest she had come was archived newspaper articles from the day of Miraj al-Diladi's assassination, where she had read that the killer was never apprehended. She had not delved deeper, wary of her efforts being monitored by NTAC personnel and triggering any unnecessary alarms.

"Alicia Colbern, Returnee Number 3,085, please report to Interview Room 1."

The voice on the intercom repeated the instructions, echoing over the dayroom's background noise and pulling Lona from her reverie. Looking up from where she sat reading a newsmagazine, she saw a door open at the room's far end, its sleek metallic surface emblazoned with a large black "1." A young man, a returnee, exited the small room, seemingly agitated by whatever had taken place during his own session.

I guess it's time to start finding out how much they really know.

Making her way across the dayroom, Lona stepped through the doorway, entering the cramped cubicle that resembled the type of visitor's station found in most prisons. A sheet of thick glass divided the room, and on the other side she saw a tall, lean man regarding her. She guessed him to be in his early to middle forties, with blue eyes and dirty blond hair cut short in a style consistent with law enforcement or certain branches of the military. He wore a dark sport coat and slacks with a light blue pullover shirt, and Lona noticed the slight yet still perceptible bulge of the pistol holstered at his right hip beneath the jacket. Though he attempted to offer a welcoming smile, Lona noted the tightened line of his jaw and even anguish in his eyes. Whatever had happened between him and the previous interviewee, it appeared to have affected him on an emotional, perhaps even personal level.

I wonder what that means?

"Please, have a seat," the man said, his voice filtered through the speaker grille connecting both halves of the room. He gestured toward the chair that was the lone furnishing on this side of the divider and Lona did as asked, edging closer to the narrow ledge that served as a table or desk facing the glass shield. The man took the chair opposite her, clearing his throat. "My name's Tom Baldwin. I'm one of the lead investigators assigned to figure out how all of you came to be here and, hopefully, why you were taken in the first place." Shaking his head, he released a small, humorless chuckle. "Piece of cake, right?"

He said nothing else for a moment as he opened the manila file folder he had brought with him and began jotting something down on the first page. Observing this in silence, Lona noted that Baldwin was left-handed. The folder's cover was labeled with her name—or, rather, the alias she had provided during that preliminary interview at Highland Beach—and was embossed with the logo of the agency he represented, the National Threat Assessment Command, or NTAC, as she had seen it abbreviated. Lona had no reason to recognize the agency or its parent organization, the Department of Homeland Security, as both groups were formed in the aftermath of the catastrophic terrorist attacks of 2001 and given the specific mission of defending the United States from similar or even deadlier future assaults.

"I know that you're probably anxious to get out of here as quickly as possible, Ms. Colbern," Baldwin said after he had finished studying the folder's contents. "I hope you'll understand that you're being kept here for your protection as well as the public's, until such time as we can verify that you're not carrying anything harmful, like . . ."

"An alien disease?" Lona finished, smiling as she cut him off. Leaning back in the chair, she folded her arms across her chest.

Despite his apparent earlier gruff mood, Baldwin smiled at the joke. "Something like that, I suppose." She could see the skepticism in his eyes. The agent did not believe that the 4400 had been abducted by extraterrestrials, and it was obvious he was having trouble accepting that the returnees all were people taken from different points over the preceding decades. Like most investigators, Baldwin maintained the hope a logical explanation would be found, if only he searched long enough and hard enough to find it.

"We're in the process of determining everyone's identity along with attempting to notify any next of kin." Looking down at the folder once more, he asked, "It says here that you have no family. Is that correct?"

Lona nodded. "I'm an only child and an orphan raised by foster parents. They both died when I was in college." It was part of the cover identity she had established for Alicia Colbern, one of the dozen aliases she had crafted above and beyond the set of alter egos provided by her handlers. Offering an alias to the NTAC agents was easy, particularly since she had been carrying no identification at the time of her apparent abduction. Alicia possessed everything so as to present the appearance of a genuine person—a Social Security number, a driver's license, a home address in Tampa, Florida, even a carefully crafted employment and education history.

The only hitch would be the fingerprints and photograph collected by NTAC as, thanks to her given profession at the time of her abduction, they would match nothing on file within any known database anywhere in the world save one. While the United States government's vast intelligence apparatus surely had grown larger and more powerful in the twelve years since her disappearance, her file would almost certainly remain inaccessible except to a select few individuals. Because of those people and the power they wielded, Lona held no illusions that the story she was weaving would stand up to prolonged scrutiny. Instead, she was gambling that she and the rest of the

4400 would be released before any of her former superiors learned that she was sitting all but gift-wrapped here in NTAC's quarantine center.

She watched him studying her file again, and this time his brow knit in apparent confusion. "According to your preliminary interview, you disappeared on June 7, 1992."

"That's right," Lona replied. "I was jogging on my lunch break. You know, getting out of the damned cubicle for a while. Next thing I know, I'm standing on that beach with everyone else." She had no way to know how or if her different identities were listed in any missing persons reports. All of that would depend on how her disappearance was handled by her support network when it became obvious that she would not be returning home. In the meantime, the date she had given Baldwin corresponded to the day she had left Wyoming for Baltimore to complete her preparatory activities prior to the arrival of Sheik Miraj al-Diladi in the city. Until such time as she was able to make contact with her web of lifelines, she would have to continue improvising her backstory as it related to her abduction. In order to keep things simple, she opted to go with the battle-tested method of incorporating as much truth into her undercover story as possible. "Is something wrong?"

Shaking his head, Baldwin answered, "No. I mean, it's just that . . ." He sighed, frowning as he wiped the side of his face. "I'm sorry, it's nothing. I'd just remembered a case I was working in June 1992, is all."

Had he been in Baltimore that day, perhaps working for the FBI or some other local law enforcement agency?

She made a mental note to research that information at her first opportunity, once she was well away from this place.

"Do you have anyone you'd like us to call?" Baldwin asked, putting aside whatever was bothering him. "A friend, co-worker, or other emergency point of contact?"

There was only one option, of course, only one person Lona could trust, assuming that person was still alive and not in prison. "Yes," she replied. "There is someone. Would you be able to deliver a message when you make the call?"

Baldwin nodded. "Of course. I'll see that it's taken care of as soon as possible."

Sooner the better, Lona decided. The time to act was fast approaching. If she was to be successful in the coming days, she would need a plan.

FIVE

FALLS CHURCH, VIRGINIA

IT TOOK NICHOLAS McFARLAND until the second iteration of his cellular phone's custom ringtone before he awoke. Rolling over, he tried to untangle himself from the bedclothes while reaching for the phone. He succeeded only in knocking it from his nightstand to the floor.

"Damn it," he muttered, still groggy from sleep and groping for the errant phone as it continued to ring, its backlit display screen illuminating the room.

Beside him in the bed, his wife, Linda, rolled away from him and pulled her pillow over her head. "Have I mentioned lately how much I hate that phone?" she muttered.

"Not since dinner," McFarland replied, though he doubted his wife heard him, as he already could hear her breathing returning to its normal sleep rhythm. Smiling at her practiced and enviable ability to tune out both him and the demands of his work, he flipped open the phone's cover to find that he had received a text message. It carried a priority alert and instructions to log in to his secure electronic mail account as soon as possible. "ASAP," of course, was a Company euphemism for "Get your ass in gear."

Grabbing his robe from where it draped across the foot of the bed, he glanced at the bedside clock, grunting in irritation when he saw the time. Being roused in the middle of the night was part of the job, of course, but that did not mean he had to like it.

He exited the room as quietly as possible so as to avoid further disturbing Linda, and closed the door behind him. Once in his study, he reached for the encrypted laptop computer sitting atop his desk, selecting the icon that activated his email. Accessing the account required a log-on ID and password cipher that changed once every twelve hours, and it took his still sleep-fogged mind an extra moment to recall the current keyword. He ran one hand through his close-cropped hair before wiping grit from his eyes, waiting for the laptop to synch up with the secure workstation in his office at the headquarters of the Central Intelligence Agency in Langley, Virginia.

Then, he wiped them again when he got his first look at the email staring back at him from the computer's plasma display. He frowned as he read the subject line. That had to be it, McFarland decided: he was seeing things.

Lona Callahan?

He had no trouble recalling the name, of course. One of the most brutally effective freelance operatives ever employed by the Agency, Callahan had performed all manner of critical assignments during the 1980s and into the

1990s, most of which were illegal actions and remained classified to all but a handful of individuals. Numerous law enforcement agencies around the world, working jointly under the general supervision of the FBI and MI5, still had open case files on Lona Callahan, though of course her true identity remained a mystery to them. So far as they and the rest of the world were concerned, the person they sought was still known only as "the Wraith."

Callahan's employment as a contracted agent had begun after she accepted an assignment given to her by another case officer, who had taken it upon himself to solicit the services of freelance operators to perform various covert activities for which the Agency could enjoy the option of denying responsibility. Callahan, at the time a relative unknown in the murder-for-hire business, had used the underground mercenary networks to contact the handler. Her first assignment—a test as much as it was a legitimate mission—had been to carry out an assassination in South America.

Upon completion of that task, payment was made to her through a Byzantine series of electronic funds transfers, arranged by Callahan with the same artful knack she had at protecting her anonymity and location while at the same time shielding the Agency from culpability. This bizarre employer-employee relationship had existed without incident for nearly nine years, during which Callahan saw her handlers face-to-face only on rare occasions, even after McFarland was briefed into the situation and devised the Wraith persona to cloak her activities.

He regarded the photograph attached to the email,

which depicted the strikingly beautiful woman he had met only once. Her dark red hair cut in a short, feminine style that bared the back of her neck, she stared out from the photograph with piercing emerald green eyes that seemed bottomless, as though offering any onlooker an unobstructed view into her soul. There was a relaxed set to her slender jaw, and while it appeared as though she had attempted to affect an expression of anxiety and perhaps confusion—likely a simple feat when this picture was taken in the NTAC quarantine center—McFarland recognized a familiar determination in her expression. Yes, indeed, this was Lona Callahan.

"I'll be damned," he said aloud, shaking his head.

Though she had successfully carried out the assassination of Muslim cleric Sheik Miraj al-Diladi in June 1992, Callahan had failed to contact her handler following that mission. FBI agents and police officers on the scene in Baltimore had found no forensic evidence to connect her to the assassination. As no reports of her being captured or killed had ever surfaced, McFarland and the others responsible for issuing her assignments eventually had come to believe that she simply had walked away, giving up her dangerous, enigmatic existence in order to enjoy whatever luxurious lifestyle could be purchased with the several million U.S. taxpayer dollars she had banked over a decade's time. Extensive search efforts had of course been conducted, with agents tracking clues all over the world, but Callahan had proven most proficient at concealing all traces of her real life.

Christ, he thought. *To this day, I'm not even sure that's her real name.* Bearing that in mind, it did not surprise him when all attempts to find her had failed.

Now, it appeared that a reason for her disappearance was finally being offered, as incredible as that explanation might be. Lona Callahan had not, as previously believed, been living a life of utter luxury thanks to the sizable fortune she had amassed as a government-sanctioned gun-for-hire. Instead, she apparently was one of the 4,400 people who had appeared from within the monstrous ball of light that had descended from space to hover above Mount Rainier in central Washington State a week ago. McFarland, along with what he suspected was the rest of the world, had watched the remarkable story unfold each day on the news, at once intrigued and mystified as details regarding the strange visitors began to emerge. While he still held many doubts as to the veracity of the reports coming from NTAC—that these people had all "returned" after being abducted at different points in time stretching back more than six decades without having aged so much as a second from the time they originally disappeared—he was unable to counter the wild notion.

He also had kept abreast of NTAC's ongoing investigation into the 4400, thanks to the interagency background checks currently under way. In addition to verifying identities through the returnees' own statements, fingerprints, dental records, or DNA where applicable, discreet inquiries also were being made to every law enforcement entity on the planet, attempting to ascertain whether any of the so-called displaced individuals appeared on any Most Wanted or terror watch lists. Lona Callahan had provided a false name and background—one that did not appear in any of the files McFarland and his peers had kept on her—and her fingerprints were not on record anywhere in the world save for one highly classified database at CIA headquarters in Langley. It was only a matter of time before the match was made, and though the results of that search were not forwarded on to NTAC, a preprogrammed series of alerts was set into motion, including the notification of McFarland himself.

According to the information provided by "Alicia Colbern" to NTAC, she had disappeared in June 1992, though she had given a different location. This, along with other information she had given, offered just enough truth to withstand a great deal of the government scrutiny it would receive. Fortunately for her, and for McFarland, Homeland Security's resources and access to classified information held by other intelligence agencies were still not as far-reaching as originally had been envisioned during that department's conception.

McFarland flinched when his phone rang again. Irritated at his own reaction, he reached for the phone, guessing at who might be on the other end of the line and certain it would be one of two people. He was right.

"Hello, Lynn," he said, pleased at his powers of deducing the all but preordained. "How's the weather down in San Antonio?"

"Nick," replied the voice of Lynn Norton, McFarland's longtime friend and onetime fellow CIA deputy director, "I just got a ciphered email. Is this for real?"

Nodding though Norton could not see it, McFarland

said, "So far as I can tell at the moment. Naturally I'll be seeking independent confirmation, but her fingerprints were a match." As he spoke, he was careful to avoid mentioning specifics, mindful of the fact that he and Norton were conversing on an open phone connection.

Through the phone, McFarland heard the other man exhale in disbelief. "All this time and she's been getting probed by aliens or some other such damn thing? It's crazy. What are you thinking?"

McFarland paused, ignoring the sudden gnawing urge he felt to smoke a cigarette and instead reaching for the crystal carafe perched near the corner of his desk. "Bringing her in, of course," he said as he poured himself a glass of water. Indeed, it had been on his mind from the first moment he had eyed the email report. Given she had been gone for twelve years without having aged a day or lost so much as an iota of her previous skills, conditioning, or experience due to atrophy over such an extended period, Lona Callahan could once again be an invaluable asset. There were all manner of difficult, hazardous, and just plain illegal assignments for which an operator of her proven talents would prove ideal. She might be useful for another decade, at least, assuming she was not captured or killed or did not disappear again, either of her own volition or that of some as yet unknown third party.

Norton asked, "Who else knows about this?"

"Other than you and me? Only Fred, as soon as he reads his email," McFarland replied, referring to their mutual friend and another retired senior Agency executive, Frederick Morehouse. Like Norton, Morehouse also had left government service years earlier for the higher pay and arguably lesser stress of the private sector, though he had soon grown weary of the corporate world and opted to retire altogether. At present, he was spending his golden years golfing and doting on his grandchildren from his farmhouse in Atlanta. "Beyond that, there's no one else who knows the specifics." There once had been a fourth member of the informal cabal who assisted in coordinating Callahan's assignments and support network, Michelle Davenport, but she had died as a result of breast cancer nearly a decade ago.

On the phone, Norton coughed. "So, what do we do?"

Taking a long drink of water from his glass, McFarland replied, "For the moment, nothing. She knows to maintain her cover until such time as she's contacted via proper protocols." Her actions to this point had been consistent with an agent operating in a hostile situation under deep cover and dependent upon outside forces to initiate the extraction. McFarland was certain Callahan would sit tight within NTAC's quarantine ward and bide her time. "Besides, so long as those people are being held in isolation, it's Homeland Security's game. We have no jurisdiction, and going in there making a fuss over her will only arouse their suspicions. She knows what to do, and she'll be fine. Until then, we've got some work to do in order to be ready."

Norton laughed. "We? I'm retired, pal." In truth, he was the chief executive officer of a booming defense contractor in San Antonio, which at present was competing against larger though more controversial outfits to provide services and supplies to the United States military as it continued its protracted operations in Iraq, Afghanistan, and other Middle East hot spots. After a moment, he added, "I know, I know. Once in, never out. Blah, blah, blah. What do you need me to do?"

"I'll be in touch soon," McFarland replied. "Count on it." If nothing else, he would need a trusted confidant who also was well aware of Callahan's history and capabilities. As much as he hated to admit it, twelve years was a long time.

I've got a hell of a lot of catch-up reading to do, and pretty damned quick.

The phone conversation ended, but McFarland suspected his old friend and colleague had no intention of returning to bed. Both men had invested much in time, energy, and money in the contracting and support of Lona Callahan during her years of service. As he sipped his water, McFarland was already imagining the myriad uses to which she could be put in short order.

Lona, Lona, you wayward child, he mused. *Welcome home.*

REINTRODUCTION

OCTOBER 2004

SIX

LONA CALLAHAN COULD feel the energy coursing through the dayroom, which at this moment seemed cramped as it played host to all of the 4400 as well as several NTAC agents. It was the first time that all of the returnees had been assembled in such fashion since their initial appearance on Highland Beach. During the ensuing weeks, NTAC agents had opted to work with their quarantined pledges individually or in smaller groups, striving to understand the remarkable and still-unexplained event that tied together these thousands of people from scattered parts of the world as well as different points in time.

So, Lona decided, for everyone to be gathered here in this manner on this day probably meant that something interesting was about to happen. She found it more than a bit telling that the televisions, which heretofore had been allowed to run constantly since the beginning of the quarantine, had been shut off without explanation late the previous evening. Obviously, the rest of the world already knew whatever it was NTAC was not telling the 4400.

Were they being transferred to another, more secure facility? The notion of being moved through covert means to a secret location had played on Lona's mind, but she discounted the idea almost as quickly as it had come. Relocating thousands of people without attracting attention in a world enveloped by constant live news coverage was a ludicrous proposition at best. Still, Lona had to admit that the sudden desire to control the flow of information to the returnees was more than a bit unsettling.

I guess we'll find out soon enough.

A small dais was staged at what had been designated as the front of the massive room, and atop it was positioned a podium with a microphone. The front of the podium was adorned with a gold seal bearing the NTAC logo, and behind it stood a man in his late forties or perhaps early fifties. He was thin, almost gaunt in Lona's opinion, his brown hair lightly peppered with gray. His dark suit was offset by a plain white shirt and unimpressive blue tie featuring a generic geometric pattern; the typical attire of a mid-level government supervisor. He presented the appearance of a man in that precise position and carrying the requisite level of responsibility, who had with much reluctance grown into a life of long hours, little recognition, and no hope of advancement. Lona figured him for a divorcee, with two or more kids who were the primary reason he stuck with an unfulfilling yet secure career, providing some measure of stability and at the same time keeping him from crawling too far into the bottle, which likely had become his best friend in recent years.

I wonder how the past few weeks have changed his lot in life.

"Ladies and gentlemen, if I may have your attention for a moment," the man said into the microphone, raising his hands in a gesture for the audience to quiet down as his voice was piped through the dayroom's sound system. He waited a few beats before continuing. "For those of you who don't know me, my name is Dennis Ryland, and I'm the director of the NTAC offices here in Seattle. To keep a long story short, I'm the one tasked with overseeing your investigations and hopefully finding some answers.

"I'd be lying if I said I understood what all of you must be feeling as you think about returning to a world that . . . that's moved on without you in many respects." He paused, and while Lona could see that Ryland was speaking from notes, she thought he might also be trying to add something else to his prepared remarks, perhaps even trying to inject some bit of humanity into the proceedings. Like the 4400 themselves, he and everyone who worked for him found themselves in uncharted waters.

Leaning on the podium, Ryland said, "While I regret the need to keep you here these past weeks, I hope you've come to understand that this wasn't done with malice, but instead because we simply didn't know if we might be dealing with some form of contagion that you may have acquired from . . . wherever it is that you were taken. I'm happy to say that none of the tests conducted to date have found any evidence of infection of any kind." A collective murmur of relief rippled through the assemblage.

"We have no reason to keep you here any longer," Ryland said after the commotion died down. "Therefore, it's my pleasure to tell you that once we've arranged some new required protocols, you will be released from quarantine and permitted to go wherever you wish."

Applause erupted throughout the dayroom, echoing off the cement walls, with hugs and handshakes shared along with pats on the back and various other gestures of support and newfound camaraderie. Despite her preference to maintain some form of detachment from her fellow 4400s, Lona found herself participating in the emotional exchange. They all had come through an inexplicable ordeal, but it seemed that they would finally be allowed to take that first step toward regaining at least something resembling a normal life.

Even as she hugged an elderly woman who had all but started crying, Lona caught the expression on Ryland's face. The NTAC director was doing his best to maintain a neutral composure, but she could tell that he was not happy with this new development. Obviously, the mystery surrounding her and the rest of the 4400 was one that had dominated his every waking moment since their abrupt arrival. Lona had no doubt that Ryland and his agents would rather be left to continue their investigations while she and the others remained in quarantine, as it would only be that much harder to track the returnees once they scattered to the four winds.

Pesky things, those civil rights.

Sarcasm aside, Lona had kept apprised of the ongoing legal debates surrounding the returnees thanks to the televisions in the dayroom, and knew that the American Civil Liberties Union, various other advocacy groups, and the public at large had been tirelessly lobbying for the release of the 4400. The ACLU even had filed several lawsuits on behalf of the families of numerous returnees. Lona suspected that such pressure was now too much to ignore, particularly given the rather important fact that there was no evidence of wrongdoing on the part of any returnee, which included very few prior criminal records. In the end, the government had but one response to the ceaseless public outcry.

Waiting for everyone to once more settle down, Ryland gestured with his hands for the group to again give him their attention. "Now, I'm sure it's crossed your minds that this isn't as simple as sending you on your way. Even as we speak, a comprehensive program for relocation and acclimation assistance is being readied that will offer whatever aid you require as you return to your private lives. At the same time, we remain committed to learning everything we can about what happened to each of you."

That was a tall order, Lona knew, as did everyone else in the room. For the past six weeks, NTAC had been expending uncounted man-hours and other resources toward finding out what or who was behind the abduction and return of the 4400. No clues had been found, with many pundits on the television news programs decrying the likelihood of any explanation presenting itself in the near future. Indeed, as most people seemed to believe that an extraterrestrial intelligence was responsible, nothing less than a gigantic alien spaceship landing on the White House lawn would be enough to satisfy the questions seemingly harbored by everyone.

Interestingly, while many of her fellow returnees seemed almost consumed by the question of why they had been taken and returned, Lona herself had realized some weeks ago that the mystery did not seem as much an issue. Naturally she had thought and wondered about it, but rather than fall into despair over her abrupt displacement from her previous life, instead she found herself at ease with her surroundings and the reality of the "new world" awaiting her outside the quarantine center. In fact, she found herself almost serene when considering the notion. Of course, Lona was forced to concede that—unlike many of the others—she was fortunate to have been taken from a point in time not so far removed that her return presented her with reentering an all but alien world. Making up for lost time after twelve years would be far easier than attempting to overcome a fifty-year gap, to be sure.

Ryland continued his remarks for several moments, outlining how the United States government had pledged to assist the returnees during the coming transition, such as with job training in order to provide updated vocational skills, health and unemployment insurance, help in finding homes or providing rental vouchers, as well as aiding in the location of surviving relatives and friends for those returnees for whom a next of kin had not yet been notified.

"What if we have nowhere to go?" one man asked. "I've

been gone forty-eight years. My wife's dead, and no one's been able to locate my daughter."

"You may stay here as long as you need or want to until you can get back on your feet," Ryland replied. "It's not our intention to turn our backs on you, now or ever."

More instructions followed, detailing how returnees would check in at weekly intervals with regional NTAC offices wherever they decided to relocate. Ryland reiterated the government's position on solving the mystery surrounding the returnees, soliciting the assistance of the 4400 themselves if they perchance learned anything on their own that might aid in the investigation.

"The out-processing will take a few days," he added, "but we expect that everyone will be free to go by the end of the week. In the meantime, we hope to make your last few nights with us as comfortable as possible, and my people stand ready to assist you in any way as we prepare for your departure. I'll be happy to take questions for a few minutes, but before I do, I just want to thank you all for your cooperation and your patience. I know it hasn't been easy for any of you, but I promise you we'll see this through together."

Hands shot up across the dayroom. Most of the questions dealt with contacting friends and family members, but Lona already was tuning out those conversations. Instead, her thoughts were turning to her own next steps. Given the amount of time that had passed since she and the other returnees entered quarantine, Lona found it impossible to believe that any of her former handlers did not know she was here. No visitations had been permitted, but she had to believe that her unusual status would by now have attracted some sort of attention. Was NTAC's security cordon so tight that even her superiors were prevented from contacting her? If so, that umbrella would shortly be lifted, at which time Lona would have to be ready, but even that concern could not weigh down the growing excitement she was feeling.

Soon, she would be free.

SEVEN

"GOOD LUCK."

The NTAC agent behind the counter smiled as he spoke the words, but to Lona Callahan the salutation sounded scripted if not outright forced. She supposed she should not blame the young man, as he likely had offered that same set of well-wishes to hundreds of people throughout the morning.

She collected from him the packet of information and vouchers prepared for her by the NTAC team responsible for processing the 4400's release. On top of the packet was a laminated blue card and matching lanyard, and on the card in bold white print was her quarantine number: 3085. Families or close friends of individual returnees—thousands of whom were at this moment waiting outside the NTAC building or even inside the reception lobby—had been given a matching card in the hopes of facilitating reunions. Lona could see the logic behind the protocol, given that in many cases, relatives would be a generation or more removed from a returned family member, possibly having grown up not knowing the missing person. Not for the first time, Lona was thankful that her absence had been comparatively short, making her forthcoming acclimation far easier.

It also helps that there's no family waiting for me.

With nothing left to keep her in the quarantine center, Lona smiled and nodded her thanks to the NTAC agent before picking up the small shoulder bag containing her paltry few possessions. She proceeded through the indicated exit door, walking with other returnees who also had finished their processing. Exchanging smiles with several of the people around her, she noted the mix of anxiety and excitement in their expressions.

Yes, they were free, but what waited for them beyond the beige cinder-block world that had been their home these past weeks? How much had really changed while they were away? The advances in technology were intimidating, but what else would be different? Would the world truly embrace the 4400? Several of the news programs had ceaselessly debated that topic, with opinions split on whether the returnees would be welcomed or shunned. NTAC, as part of its processing procedures, had informed each of them that it might be best if they did not "advertise" their true identities—at least until they got themselves settled wherever it was that they might be going—in order to avoid possible discrimination or other trouble caused by fear or ignorance.

Lona reached the lobby, where armed NTAC agents in paramilitary uniforms stood near the row of glass doors, controlling access to and from the building. Within the high-ceilinged foyer, dozens of people in groups of varying sizes were greeting returnees, and she noted the range of reactions being displayed: tears of joy from a wife as she was reunited with the husband she had lost three years earlier; uncertainty from the adult grandson of a woman thought lost decades ago; friends and former comrades in arms of a man who disappeared during combat in Vietnam.

The interactions were as varied as the people themselves, and along with those Lona saw other people in situations similar to hers with no one here to greet them. In several instances next of kin had not been located, while in other, more extreme cases relatives or friends had refused to come, perhaps due to fear or denial. Lona even knew of one or two instances where returnees had learned that their spouses had moved on after losing all hope of ever again seeing their loved one, harboring no wish to reopen those closed chapters of their lives.

Lona could not help feeling pangs of sadness as she listened to such stories. These people had been taken from their lives without warning or explanation, and now were being asked to cope with the incredible reality into which they had been plunged without even the support of people they once had loved or called friend. It was a challenge that would test even the strongest of wills and constitutions. Some returnees would persevere and ultimately triumph, and she was certain she fell into this camp. Others likely would spiral down wells of despair and depression. How would NTAC handle those crises when they arose?

Leaving behind the procession of reunions taking place in the lobby, Lona made her way through the last door separating her from the outside world. She took her first steps outside the building that had been her home for six weeks, and could not help stopping to take in her surroundings. She recalled the drab, overcast day that had heralded the arrival of the 4400 at Highland Beach, and smiled now at the warmth of the midday sun on her face. Thinking on it, Lona realized that it really was the first time she had seen the sun in twelve years. She shook her head at the latest in the string of surreal thoughts that had occupied her mind during the past weeks, though as before she found herself not needing to dwell on the bizarre nature of her situation as had many of her fellow returnees. She was here and it was now, and there was nothing she could do to change this new reality. Better to concentrate on moving forward.

There's too much to do now.

A throng of people crowded the front lawn of the NTAC office complex, with returnees as well as families and friends engaging in their own reunions, pleasant or otherwise. A row of police officers manned a barricade at the outer edge of the lawn, beyond which stood others— representatives of media outlets from around the country and even the world as well as hundreds of interested onlookers who had just come down to see what the fuss was all about. Lona scanned the faces she could see from this distance and recognized no one, but that of course did not rule out the possibility of someone observing her from a covert position. Gut instinct told her that was the case, but a cursory check of nearby vehicles as well as the windows and doorways of surrounding buildings offered no evidence. Still, Lona found herself almost counting on the possibility, if only to finally end the question of whether her former handlers even knew she was here.

Hitching her bag higher on her left shoulder, Lona decided against facing the gauntlet of reporters, police, and other onlookers cramming the main courtyard, opting instead for a more circuitous route away from NTAC. She spied a narrow path between the side of the building and a row of high hedges, using the well-groomed shrubbery to mask her movements as she made away from the assemblage. Similar landscaping afforded her additional cover until she was well away from the worst of the crowd, and in short order she was away from the government buildings and traversing a sidewalk that seemed to be leading her toward an industrial area on the outskirts of downtown Seattle. Rows of low-rise buildings and warehouses lined both sides of the street, and the few pedestrians she saw appeared to pay her no notice. She nodded to herself, pleased that she had selected a casual outfit from the massive wardrobe donated to returnees by various charitable organizations. Without the khaki shirt and utility pants such as she had worn in quarantine, she put forth the appearance of just another nondescript citizen, possibly on her way to work or school.

Lona caught sight of the sedan after walking less than two blocks. It was dark blue, without decorative embellishments of any kind save a trio of antennae affixed to the car's trunk, a dead giveaway even if she had not seen the government license plates. It had been sitting parked along a side street as she crossed an intersection, and she heard it pull forward and turn to follow her after she walked past. Lona kept track of it thanks to its reflection in the windows of various storefronts, and she was able to see that the car held two occupants—a man and a woman—each wearing sunglasses. The woman also wore an earpiece with a coiled wire running behind her right ear. *Agency,* Lona decided.

The car accelerated a bit, just enough that the driver could guide the vehicle past her until it pulled alongside the curb farther up the street. Lona kept both hands visible as both front doors opened and the occupants climbed out. The man, his brown hair cut short in a military style, wore tailored gray slacks and coat over a white dress shirt and red tie, while the woman sported a dark blue pantsuit with a white silk blouse and blond hair pulled back into a tight bun. Each sported bulges beneath their left arms, and Lona caught a glimpse of the woman's weapon—a Glock, most likely—as she pulled herself from the car.

"Ms. Callahan?" the woman asked, much to Lona's surprise. So far as she knew, only five people besides herself in the entire world could connect her face with her real name, and this government lackey most definitely was not one of them.

As though sensing Lona's apprehension, the woman reached into the right side of her jacket and extracted a thin wallet, opening it to expose what Lona recognized as standard-issue identification for employees of the Central

Intelligence Agency—or a masterful forgery, at the very least. "My name is Deborah Wright, and this is my partner, Richard Malick," she said, indicating the man who was coming around the back of the car. "We're with the CIA. Deputy Director Nicholas McFarland has sent us to make sure you're brought in safely. Our authorization protocol is Alpha Omega Three Nine Five Five."

Despite herself, Callahan blinked as she heard McFarland's name and the recall cipher. It was one she herself had selected as part of her planning for her last assignment. She was to have provided the code upon successful completion of the mission, notifying her handlers that she had reached a safe location and would soon be in contact for further instructions.

Recalling one of the challenges she had drafted for use as secondary verification, Lona asked, "I'm sorry, but I'm late meeting my husband at the theater."

To her surprise and relief, the male agent replied, "The matinee's sold out, but the manager has set aside tickets for the evening show, if you're interested."

Lona nodded, satisfied. Her suspicions had been correct all along, and her former superiors did indeed know that she had returned. They obviously had been waiting for an opportunity to make contact that would preserve her cover while she resided in quarantine. Now that she was out in the open, Nicholas McFarland doubtless viewed this as an opportunity to conduct a long-overdue debriefing, and it was likely he was considering the potential of having her once again in his arsenal of covert weapons. To make that happen, she would first need to be brought in. So far as these two agents knew, they were acting to protect a valuable Agency asset.

They were wrong.

"I still can't go with you," she said. "As I said, I'm late for another appointment."

Holding up her left hand, Agent Wright shook her head. "I'm afraid that's not possible, Ms. Callahan. We have our orders." Both agents' right hands were moving for the weapons concealed beneath their jackets.

In one easy motion, Lona slipped the bag from her shoulder and flung it at Wright. It struck her in the right arm, spoiling her attempt to draw her pistol and giving Lona all the time she needed to close the distance separating her from Agent Malick. She reached him just as his own Glock cleared its holster and she slammed the heel of her hand into his nose. Malick yelped in pain, staggering backward and dropping the pistol. Lona kicked the weapon away before retreating a few steps, aware that Wright had drawn her gun and now was aiming it at her.

"Freeze!" the agent snapped, leveling the pistol so that its barrel pointed directly at Lona's chest. Lona had been on the business end of enough guns not to be panicked. To her, it was simply another tactical condition to be negotiated and conquered. She felt no anxiety, but instead sensed a strange, warm glow beginning to envelop her body. It seemed somehow soothing, for reasons she could not explain, coupled with a sudden awareness that she was in supreme control of the current situation.

She stepped toward Wright.

"Stop!" the agent ordered, her jaw tensing as she realized

Lona had no intention of obeying her orders. Lona felt the warm glow around her intensify, and watched Wright blink as she pulled the trigger. The sound of the gunshot was deafening in the confines of the narrow street, and Lona flinched in anticipation of the bullet striking her.

Instead, the bullet stopped.

It seemed to hang in midair, less than two feet in front of her. Feeling her mouth fall open in shock, Lona stared at the suspended round and noted that its motion had not been arrested, but instead reduced to an incredible degree. She noted the slow rotation of the bullet as well as its agonizingly slow advance toward her. As for Wright, the woman also seemed to be struck motionless, her determined expression frozen on her face even as she remained in her firing stance.

Unsure of what was happening but realizing that her own ability to move had not been compromised, Lona stepped around the bullet before closing on Wright. She was two paces away when the agent began to move again. Her face twisted into confusion and fear as she realized Lona was nearly on top of her, by which time Lona grabbed her weapon arm and jerked the pistol up and away. Spinning her body around, she flipped Wright over her hip and slammed her down onto the sidewalk. The agent cried out as Lona yanked the Glock from her hand.

Lona turned in time to see Malick lunging for her, blood streaming from his broken nose. He was too close for her to use the gun, so she dodged back and to her right, working for some maneuvering room in order to defend his attack. The warm glow again washed over her just as

Malick closed to within an arm's length, ready to strike, and in that instant his body slowed almost to a stop. He simply hung before her, impossibly balanced on the ball of one foot and with his right arm and fist extended in mid-swing. His expression was one of rage, his eyes wide and with spittle hurling from the corners of his mouth, each fleck hanging in the air before his face.

What in God's name is going on?

Lona, still able to move, let her instincts and train-ing take over as she lashed out at the agent, catching the side of his head with her fist. Time sped up again and he crumpled from the force of the blow, dropping to his knees and grunting in new pain. Lona followed the attack with another, kicking Malick in the face and sending him flipping to the ground on his back, where he lay still.

Her breath was coming in rapid, deep gasps now, and Lona realized she had broken into a seemingly instanta-neous and drenching sweat. Putting a finger to her throat, she searched out her pulse and found it racing. She felt as though she had just run three miles at a full-out sprint. Whatever had just happened, her body was paying the price for the abrupt, unexplained exertion.

Lona heard sirens now as well as the revving engines of approaching cars—backup units, she guessed. Even with the echoes carrying across the confined street, she could tell that vehicles were approaching from multiple direc-tions. She felt her grip tighten on the Glock she'd taken from Agent Wright, and anticipated the coming fight even as she began scanning the street and the surrounding buildings and alleys for some avenue of escape.

Another engine caught her attention, this one higher-pitched and much closer, and Lona turned in time to see a motorcycle explode from an alley a block up the street. Its rider was dressed in black leather with matching helmet, and seemed to be in complete control of the street machine as he angled it toward her. Lona raised the pistol to aim at the newcomer, but the motorcyclist kept coming, only slowing when the bike was within twenty feet of her before skidding to a halt. Ignoring the gun pointed at him, the rider reached up and removed his helmet.

No, not his helmet. *Hers.*

Dark brown hair fell out of the helmet, cascading down around the woman's shoulders. Brilliant cobalt blue eyes stared back at Lona, eyes she had looked into on countless occasions and instantly recognized.

"Reiko?" she breathed in disbelief.

"Come on!" called out Reiko Vandeberg, her voice tinged with a hint of the German accent she never had been able to suppress. Lona saw new lines around the woman's eyes and mouth, but she still looked as radiant as the last time she had seen her, twelve years earlier and before Lona had left for the assignment in Baltimore. How was she here, now?

You called for her, fool. Think!

"We have to go, Lona! Now!" Reiko shouted, donning her helmet once more and revving the motorcycle's engine. With one hand she reached for Lona, her eyes visible and pleading through the helmet's face shield.

Lona had figured attempting to contact her assistant and lover would be a long shot, thinking that Reiko had to

have moved on with her own life in the years since Lona's
disappearance, and assuming law enforcement agents had
not caught up with her. Instead—and as she always had—
Reiko had come through, arriving when called, this time
in response to the summons Lona had issued with the assistance of that NTAC agent, Baldwin.

The cars were close now. Movement up the street
caught Lona's attention and she looked up to see another
dark sedan turning a corner and heading straight for them,
a flashing blue globe atop its roof. From behind her, she
could hear another car closing in. Time was running out.

Jumping forward, Lona swung one leg over the seat of
the motorcycle, her hands slipping around the comfortable
curves of Reiko's torso just as the other woman gunned
the bike's engine. The back wheel spun, laying a streak
of melted rubber upon the street before gaining traction
and propelling the motorcycle forward. Lona held on,
her hands gripped tight around Reiko's waist as the other
woman leaned into the bike's handlebars, guiding the machine back down the alley.

What had happened back there? The question screamed
in Lona's mind. How had she been able to do the things
she had done? Had something been done to her and if so,
who—or what—was responsible?

No answers were forthcoming. With nothing to do save
hang on, Lona pressed the side of her face into Reiko's
back, closing her eyes as her lover drove them into the hive
of activity that was downtown Seattle.

EIGHT

SEATTLE, WASHINGTON

WELL, TOM BALDWIN thought as he stood within the cordoned section of street less than a mile from NTAC, *this didn't take long.*

Police tape was draped across both lanes of the street, and uniformed officers had been placed at intersections two blocks away in all directions, tasked with rerouting traffic away from the area. A few dozen onlookers stood beyond the tape, curious as to what might bring law enforcement to this part of town in the middle of the day. More than one person had inquired as to the location of any bodies, walking away in apparent disappointment when none were revealed. The air stunk of diesel fumes from passing trucks that had become trapped along the narrow thoroughfare, unable to escape from between buildings lining each side of the street. Heat radiated from the asphalt, reflecting the rays of the afternoon sun. Only outside for a few minutes, Baldwin already was starting to sweat.

Admit it. You came back because you miss this crap.

"She left her bag behind," said a voice from behind him, and Baldwin turned to see his partner, Diana Skouris, walking toward him. She held an olive-drab shoulder bag in one hand and a familiar-looking manila envelope in the other. The envelope was stamped with the NTAC logo and carried a stark white label with a bar code, and Baldwin recognized it as the packet of information and vouchers supplied by NTAC to each returnee who had elected to leave quarantine.

"Alicia Colbern," he read aloud from the label stamped on the envelope. The name was familiar, though for the moment he could not place it. Opening the packet, Baldwin extracted the laminated blue card adorned with its owner's assigned number, in this case, 3085. "She's out of quarantine less than half an hour and somebody tries to mug her?"

"Don't look at me," Skouris said. "You're the detective." A small smile tugging at the corners of her mouth, she waved one hand to indicate the scene. "So, detect something."

Baldwin could not help chuckling at that. Though he and Skouris only had been partners since shortly after the arrival of the 4400, it had taken little time for the duo to develop not only a pleasant working relationship but also the friendly ribbing banter that Baldwin always had believed was a vital component of solid, comfortable teamwork. Despite their disparate backgrounds—he a former cop and FBI agent, she a scientist specializing in microbiology and epidemiology at the Centers for Disease

Control before coming to NTAC—in short order they were learning to merge their strengths, experience, and perspectives into an effective collaboration. Egos did not enter the equation, instead set aside for the good of the mission being accomplished. Though he was not yet ready to admit it to Skouris herself, Baldwin already considered her among the best partners with whom he had been paired.

Returning his attention to the business at hand, Baldwin placed his hands on his hips as he studied the scene. "I thought you said we had security camera footage?"

Skouris nodded. "Galanter's on his way with it now," she said, hooking her thumb over her shoulder toward the three-story building behind her. With its faux-brick façade and large tinted windows through which Baldwin could almost see the security gates designed to prevent anyone from gaining entry, the building housed a branch office of a large regional bank. According to the preliminary report Baldwin had received, it was fortunate happenstance that the incident had taken place within range of the stationary video camera that was part of the automated teller machine built into the structure's front wall. The bank manager already had reported that the camera had not captured the entire incident, but perhaps it would be enough to give Baldwin and Skouris some initial clue as to what had happened here.

"Ryland warned us that there would be people who might act out against the 4400," Baldwin said. "Could it be something like that?"

Crossing her arms, Skouris replied, "We've both read

the reports about certain fringe groups who consider them a threat." She shrugged. "It's certainly not impossible."

Baldwin considered the notion. During the weeks the returnees had spent in quarantine, local and national news broadcasts had covered rallies and speeches staged by a few such groups. The leader of a religious cult based in Kansas had even likened the 4400 to a plague sent by God as punishment for society's acceptance of continuing moral decay, which in his mind included homosexuality, premarital sex, and the instant replay review rules in professional football.

I may have to give him that last one, Baldwin mused.

"Agent Baldwin? Agent Skouris?" a voice called out from behind them, and Baldwin turned to see David Galanter, one of NTAC's computer and electronics forensics technicians, emerging from the bank with a laptop computer cradled in the crook of his right arm. Having compressed his stout frame into a wrinkled pair of khaki cargo pants along with an equally disheveled blue dress shirt and a garish, multihued tie that made Baldwin wish he could go color-blind on cue, Galanter presented—as always—the appearance of someone who selected his daily attire from piles of discarded clothing destined for charitable donation or the trash. What the man lacked in fashion sense, he more than made up for with formidable technical skills, which was all Baldwin cared about at the moment.

"You've got the tape?" he asked as Galanter stepped closer, noting the disapproving frown on the other man's face as he asked the question.

"It's all digital in there," the tech replied, holding up the laptop in his beefy right hand. "Got it all right here, what there was of it, anyway." Without waiting for instructions to do so, Galanter opened the portable computer and tilted the screen so that Baldwin and Skouris could better see it. Baldwin recognized the familiar features of a common audio/video software presentation application, with a video file opened and paused in the playback window. "I've got it queued up to just before Alicia Colbern enters the frame for the first time. There's no audio, but I don't think you'll need it."

Galanter pressed the control to restart the video, and Baldwin watched a dark blue or black sedan pass across the camera's view. It stopped before moving completely out the frame, its rear fender and trunk still visible. Then the now-familiar woman with the short red hair, Alicia Colbern, appeared, wearing gray slacks and an off-white pullover shirt with long sleeves and carrying a knapsack slung over her left shoulder. She stopped walking as two people, a male driver and a female passenger, exited the car.

"Antennae," Skouris said, pointing to the car's trunk on the screen. "Cops?"

Shaking his head, Galanter said, "Wait for it."

Baldwin sighed in minor frustration, but let it slide as the video continued to play. On the screen, a conversation seemed to be taking place between Colbern and the two new arrivals. With one look at their attire, Baldwin knew there was no way they were beat cops or even plainclothes detectives. "They're wired," he said. "Check her right ear."

"Feds?" Skouris asked.

Before Galanter could answer, the sedate scene on the monitor dissolved into chaos, with Colbern flinging her knapsack at the female. The man was reaching into his suit jacket, presumably for a gun, but Colbern was on him, striking him in the face and causing him to stumble away from the curb, dropping his weapon in the process.

"Jesus," Baldwin breathed, and that was all he had time for as Colbern turned toward the woman, who had drawn her own sidearm and assumed a firing stance. Baldwin saw the recoil as she fired the pistol from nearly point-blank range—and *missed*—followed by an apparent defect in the video as Colbern seemed to close the distance that separated her and the other woman in the blink of an eye, disarming and subduing her with what he recognized as practiced efficiency in hand-to-hand combat.

"It has to be a glitch," Galanter said, as though anticipating the question. "I'll check it out when I break down the whole thing back at the lab." Baldwin said nothing as he watched the man Colbern already had wounded move in for another attack, which she defeated with more astonishing speed and agility, laying him out on the sidewalk in scarcely a few heartbeats.

"Who the hell is she?" Skouris asked, her expression a mixture of shock and confusion. On the monitor, Colbern paused over her handiwork for a few moments, staring at something offscreen. Then she ran across the frame and out of sight, leaving the security camera to linger on the fallen forms of her apparent adversaries.

"Well, she's not who she *said* she was," Baldwin replied.

Pointing to his laptop, Galanter said, "Hang on. There's one more thing." He fast-forwarded the video, bypassing what essentially was nearly a minute of still-life footage before another car, also a dark sedan, came into view. Two more people jumped out of this car, both males, coming to the assistance of Colbern's unmoving attackers.

Definitely Feds, Baldwin decided as he absorbed what he had just seen, but who? It certainly was possible that the CIA, FBI, or some other group from the vast alphabet soup of government agencies had taken an active interest in one of the 4400, but none of them had approached NTAC. Background checks had been run against the returnees and a few had even turned up criminal records, but those mostly were for minor infractions. Of course, the review had only been comprehensive with respect to those who had been taken more recently. Information on returnees taken more than thirty years back had been of varying quantity and detail, and a few had come back with no results whatsoever.

"Galanter," Baldwin said, waving toward the other man's laptop, "go back and see what else you can dig out of that. License plate, a clear head shot for the facial recognition databases, whatever you can find." He was doubtful that anything useful could be gleaned from the low-quality video, but that was why people like Galanter were in the computer labs in the first place.

The tech nodded. "We're on it, boss." He smiled as he gathered his equipment, no doubt enthused by the challenge of prying something of worth from the video footage.

As Galanter left, Skouris looked to Baldwin. "What do we do?"

Baldwin shrugged. "Not much, at least not for the moment." Even with the 4400 released from quarantine, it was not as though NTAC's workload had diminished to any significant degree. With the returnees heading for different locations around the country, the regional NTAC offices were responsible for monitoring those who opted to settle within their areas of responsibility. The Seattle office would be keeping tabs on nearly eighty returnees who had elected to stay in the area, along with more than a hundred who had chosen to live in the quarantine center until they got themselves a better handle on their current situation. Most of those people had been taken decades ago and had no apparent remaining family, thus they had so far been unsuccessful in locating someone with whom they could connect from their former life. In addition to handling weekly updates from each of the returnees, the NTAC investigative teams would continue to investigate the puzzle of why the 4400 had been abducted—and returned—in the first place.

"We can put in a call to the regional office wherever she's headed," Baldwin continued. "Florida, I think it was. Ask them to let us know when she checks in."

"*If* she checks in," Skouris countered. "I read her file, Tom. It says she was an accountant in Tampa. How many accountants do you know who can disable two armed opponents without breaking a sweat?"

"No argument here." Adjusting his holstered Glock so that it sat more comfortably on his right hip, Baldwin said, "We can put some feelers out to other agencies, too, but something tells me that's a dead end even before we get started. Whoever was after Alicia Colbern, they wanted to do it on their own terms, and to hell with us."

It was a mystery, and Baldwin hated mysteries. In this line of work, the unknown and the unexplained had a way of conjuring further problems, which in turn might evolve into warnings and alarms before blowing up in your face, or biting you on the ass.

"Maybe we let them out too soon, after all," Skouris said, and Baldwin saw the doubt in her eyes.

Baldwin grunted in disagreement. "We had no right to keep them, Diana."

"Not because we think they're a threat," she replied, "but maybe for their own protection."

This was not the first time the topic had been debated. There was nothing for them to do save abide by the instructions they were given, and at the time the decision was handed down, Baldwin had deemed it a waste of time and energy to question the orders.

Now, however, he had to wonder if Skouris was right all along.

Yeah, Baldwin decided, *I really do love my job.*

NINE

NICHOLAS MCFARLAND STARED at the report in his hands, reading it for the fourth time and still not believing any of the words printed on the page.

"She *initiated* the confrontation?" he asked, feeling his jaw tighten in confusion. "Even after you verified your identity?"

From where she stood before the deputy director's desk, her right arm in a sling thanks to the separated shoulder she had received as a result of her scuffle with Lona Callahan the previous day, Agent Deborah Wright nodded. "Yes, sir. There was no question she understood the protocols. She issued the correct challenges and recognized the expected responses."

"We explained why we were there, sir," added her partner, Agent Richard Malick, "and she appeared to comprehend that." Reaching up, he touched the X-shaped bandage adorning his broken nose. "She simply wasn't interested in coming with us."

"An understatement, by the looks of things," McFarland replied, sympathizing with the bruises on Malick's face and the heavy swelling around his eyes. Wright also sported other souvenirs of their altercation, in the form of scrapes and abrasions along the side of her neck and face. In all honesty, McFarland was baffled that the two agents were even still alive, given that she had killed in self-defense on more than one occasion. To the best of his knowledge, however, such actions had never been taken against American intelligence or law enforcement personnel.

Thank God for small favors.

Malick shook his head, "She knows her stuff, I'll give her that. I've never seen *anybody* move that fast."

"She was a blur," Wright said, her brow furrowing, "like she anticipated when I was going to fire and ducked out of the way just in time. Damnedest thing I ever saw."

"Well, I for one am happy you missed," McFarland said, reaching for the ashtray on his desk and retrieving the smoldering cigarette there. "I ordered you to bring her in alive." Before Wright could say anything, he raised his free hand. "I know you were defending yourself, but next time find a way that doesn't involve your pistol." Bringing the cigarette to his lips, he inhaled long and deep in defiance of four or five regulations prohibiting smoking anywhere on the premises. He did not smoke at home, mostly due to his wife's demands that he quit altogether. Linda knew he indulged at work, and in truth he had reduced the number of cigarettes he smoked during the day to less than five, a drastic change from the two packs per day he had puffed up until just three months ago. It was only during the longer, more stressful days that McFarland tended to backpedal on his promise to rid himself of the habit once and for all.

Days like today, for example.

"This doesn't make any damned sense," he said, more to himself than either of the agents. "She had to know we were trying to bring her in." Granted, debriefings in the past had been held at locations of Callahan's choosing, and usually only with McFarland or one of the other handlers cleared to oversee her activities. Regardless, this situation was markedly different, which McFarland would have expected Callahan to recognize, for her own safety to say nothing of operational security. Even after her twelve-year absence, some things still needed to remain secrets.

In her case, he reminded himself, *pretty much everything will have to stay classified. Forever.* If the details of even one of Lona Callahan's Agency-approved missions ever were to see the light of day, Lynn Norton, Fred Morehouse, and McFarland himself, the surviving officers responsible for overseeing her activities, would likely go to prison for the rest of their lives.

"She could've thought we were trying to neutralize her," Malick suggested after a moment. "It's been twelve years. Maybe she figured you had no further use for her."

Rising from his high-backed leather chair, McFarland grunted his disagreement as he made his way around the oversized mahogany desk and across his spacious office to the set of three bay windows that formed his office's outer wall. "Don't take this personally, Malick," he said, pausing to take another drag from his cigarette, "but I'd have *you* killed before her. We invested far too much time and resources into cultivating her. Even though she was a freelance asset, she never failed to come through on any mission she was given. She may have been a mercenary, but she was a damned loyal mercenary, even if it was only to the money we were paying her."

"Besides," Wright added, "it may have been twelve years for us, but for her that was all yesterday." She paused, frowning. "Or six weeks ago. Whatever."

McFarland nodded. Whether six weeks in quarantine or six seconds separating her from 1992, he felt that it surely could not have been enough time to convince Callahan to desert her benefactors, and in such violent fashion.

Still, the agents had raised an interesting point. After twelve years, Callahan likely deduced that her support network was gone, and she would have been correct. It had been disbanded years earlier, after it was assumed that she either was dead, captured by a foreign government, or simply had opted for "retirement." All that remained of her original chain of command was McFarland himself, and the files he kept buried in the deepest, darkest hole he could find.

Standing before the windows and looking out over the wooded terrain surrounding the CIA Headquarters complex, McFarland shook his head and released a tired sigh. The leaves had turned weeks ago and many of the trees already were shedding, draping the forest floor with an immense, vibrant quilt. Fall always had been the season he welcomed with anticipation. It was his favorite time of the year, which often brought with it change and new opportunities or challenges.

Yeah. That's one way of putting it.

"Well," he said, stepping away from the window, "for whatever reason, she broke contact, and who the hell knows where she's gotten to by now. What about this motorcycle rider who picked her up? Do we know anything about her?"

Wright shook her head. "A woman, but the images we pulled from street cameras didn't match anything in our databases. She's a ghost."

"Damn," McFarland hissed between gritted teeth. "It has to be someone she knew before, somebody she managed to contact while in quarantine. Find out from NTAC who she listed as next of kin or someone to notify." He knew it was a fruitless suggestion that likely would lead to a false identity and a dead end, but the lead had to be followed even if it ran straight into a brick wall.

Reaching for the ashtray on his desk, he ground out the stub of his expended cigarette before retrieving a fresh one from his desk's center drawer. He could almost feel Linda's disapproving scowl as he lit up, but right now that was the least of his problems.

"Speaking of NTAC," he said after taking the first drag on the fresh cigarette and blowing a plume of smoke into the air above his head, "what do they know? Your report said you were picked up by a security camera. Do we have containment on this?"

Malick, uncomfortable in the smoke-filled room if his eyes were any indication, replied, "The camera caught the bulk of our fight with her. NTAC's investigating, but they don't have much to go on. I checked the footage, but it didn't have a good shot of the bike she left on. No way to run a license plate."

"We'll just have to deal with that when it comes up," McFarland said, dragging on his cigarette. The presence of his agents on the security camera footage was inconvenient, but not alarming. That could be handled, or simply ignored. Without actual evidence, NTAC would have no claim to another agency interfering with their admittedly unusual mission. "Where's NTAC on locating her?"

Wright replied, "She's good at covering her tracks, that's for damned sure. They put in requests to their Southeast Region office to check out the Tampa address she left, but even if it's not a fake, she's been gone twelve years. Whatever's there has probably been sold a couple of times since she was . . . abducted." She shook her head, exhaling between pursed lips. "I still can't bring myself to buy that story."

"Even if NTAC follows Alicia Colbern far enough to learn it's an alias," added Malick, "there's nothing beyond that for them to examine without outside assistance."

If and when NTAC came to the CIA asking for such aid, McFarland would be able to handle the situation without attracting undue attention from his superiors and all while keeping the other, upstart organization at arm's length. "The question now is: What do we do about Callahan?"

He had squandered the one opportunity to make contact with her. Any further attempts would have to be initiated from her end, assuming she was interested in such discourse. Had the uncertainty surrounding her disappearance and return unnerved her to the point that she felt she needed to retreat to a safe haven? Even if only long enough to get her bearings in a world that had passed her by? Perhaps while in quarantine, Callahan had decided not to return to her former life, choosing instead to fade into obscurity, if indeed such a thing existed for her or any of "the 4400."

It would not be so simple, McFarland decided. Unlike the futile efforts to locate her in 1992, now he knew she was out there, somewhere. Technology and intelligence resources had advanced tenfold in the time since her original disappearance, and would play a large role in tracking her down, no matter how far she ran or how deep she tried to hide.

It might take time, but one way or another, Lona Callahan would be found.

TEN

LA GRANDE, OREGON

As it had uncounted times before, the intense light washed over her, warming her skin. Wind howled in her ears, drowning out her cries for help. Only as the light faded could she discern the clouds parting beneath her, and as she plummeted through she saw the brown-green matte of the earth hurtling toward her. She flailed but found nothing to arrest her headlong descent, and when she screamed she heard nothing as the ground raced up to meet her.

Lona awoke, her body snapping to a sitting position. Her right arm, extending from the bed so that her hand rested on the nightstand, swept away a water glass and the cheap digital alarm clock positioned near her head. She flinched as water pelted the side of her face and the glass fell to the carpeted floor. The clock landed on one edge, hitting its power switch and flooding the room with the staccato beats of a hard rock ballad she vaguely remembered from her days in college.

Cursing, Lona reached for the clock's power cord and yanked it free of the outlet behind the nightstand, returning the room to blissful silence. Blinking, she cleared her sleep-blurred vision and took in her surroundings, realizing she was alone in a king-sized bed. Though the suite's furnishings were opulent, their color and arrangement as well as the generic artwork hanging on the walls reminded her that she was in a high-end hotel rather than an apartment or house. An ornate, cherrywood armoire was positioned across the room at the foot of the bed, its doors opened to reveal a dormant television as well as a small refrigerator. The door to the bathroom was closed, muffling the sounds of the shower. A thin slice of daylight streamed between the curtains on the far wall, promising a sunny morning, and Lona relaxed as the memories of the previous day returned.

I wonder what McFarland's thinking now, she mused, pulling aside the sheets and rising from the bed.

It had been a simple matter to evade the pathetic attempt at pursuit. Assuming the people Lona had put down were actual CIA agents, she supposed it made sense that there would not have been a stronger Agency presence. So far as they and McFarland were concerned and despite the passage of time, she would still be considered an operative in need of retrieval and debriefing. They would have no way of knowing that returning to her former life was now the furthest thing from her mind.

Sorry about that.

The journey to their current and very temporary safe house had taken until well after dark the previous evening, owing to Reiko's choice to avoid the direct interstate route and instead utilize secondary roads and other off-beaten paths. Upon their arrival, Lona learned that Reiko already had booked the room for several days and had checked in two days earlier under an alias, one Lona did not recognize from their years working together. She saw no need to question Reiko's decisions, trusting that her friend had developed her own approach to stealth as well as a requisite support network in the years since Lona's disappearance.

Moving to a freestanding mirror situated in the corner of the room, Lona stood before it and examined herself. Dressed in a T-shirt and pajama bottoms as provided by Reiko from one of two suitcases sitting in the closet, Lona noted the dark circles beneath her eyes. Though she had slept for nearly eleven hours since arriving at the hotel, she still felt some lingering vestiges of the fatigue that had gripped her the previous day, following her fight with the CIA agents.

What did I do?

That question had gnawed at her throughout the ride from Seattle. She had replayed the encounter in her mind over and over, each time coming away with more questions than answers. Was what she experienced nothing more than illusion, or perhaps even hallucination brought about by something given to her while in quarantine? Lona had not once received any sort of inoculation while in NTAC's care, but that did not rule out something in her food or drink. Though she was familiar with various effects of psychotropic drugs—either from recreational use or deliberate instances during early training so that she could become familiar with the sensations and learn how to operate despite an impaired condition—she could not discount the possibility of new substances that produced no noticeable effects.

No, Lona decided. It could not be that simple. The expressions on the faces of the agents she had fought were of shock, confusion, and fear. Whatever it was she had done, they had witnessed it. If that were truly the case, then how had she done it, and what were the effects on her body?

Behind her, she heard the water shut off in the bathroom, and a moment later the door opened to admit a billowing cloud of steam. Lona smiled at that, recalling how Reiko always had preferred showers that seemed on the verge of scalding her skin. She smiled again when Reiko herself stepped into the room, wearing a terry-cloth bathrobe and drying her long brown hair with a large towel.

"You're awake," she said, returning the smile as she made eye contact. "How did you sleep?"

"Like a baby," Lona replied. "Best sleep I've had in weeks. Sure beats the army bunks they gave us."

Once again, she felt the familiar tug of desire upon seeing her longtime friend and lover. Though there had been warm embraces and kisses of reunion as soon as opportunity presented itself during the trip from Seattle, Lona had sensed Reiko's discomfort. It was understandable, of course. From Lona's point of view, only seven weeks had passed since she last had seen Reiko—one week spent in Baltimore in preparation for the Miraj al-Diladi assassination and then the time spent in NTAC quarantine. For

Reiko, it had been twelve years, and it was obvious that she had moved on after enough time passed and it became apparent that Lona would not be returning. Though Reiko had not said as much, Lona was certain that there was someone else and she had taken steps to respect Reiko's situation.

As if sensing Lona's own uneasiness, Reiko said, "I still can't believe you're here." Continuing to work on her damp hair with the towel, she moved to sit at the edge of the bed. "When you didn't come back after Baltimore, I was sure you'd been captured or killed. For a while I just laid low and waited for someone to kick down my door."

It was more hyperbole than anything else, Lona knew. During her employ with the CIA, she had taken steps to insulate her partner from anything to do with the Agency. So far as the United States intelligence apparatus was concerned, Reiko Vandeberg had never existed, and from everything Lona had been able to determine, that was still the case.

"For a while," Reiko added after a moment, "I even thought there might have been someone else. Eventually, though, I decided that you'd never do something like that without telling me. So, that left you either being dead or in prison somewhere." That was when the smile returned. "I was stunned when I got the message via that old phone number. I was sure it had to be a setup, the CIA or someone else you'd pissed off having finally found a connection to me." She dropped the towel to her lap and reached out to clasp Lona's left hand in both of her own. "By then the news channels were going day and night about you and the others, and I sat there for days until I saw your picture on the screen. Even then I was scared to call." With one hand, she reached to stroke the side of Lona's face. "My God, you haven't aged a day since the last time I saw you."

Lona covered Reiko's hand with her own, sighing at the intimate touch as she nodded in understanding. The story of the 4400 would be a remarkable notion to absorb, with thousands of people across the world being reunited with friends and family members believed missing or dead. She still had occasion to doubt what had happened to her, despite all the evidence with which she and the rest of the returnees had been inundated since their return.

"And yet you came," Lona said, feeling Reiko squeeze the hand in her lap. Still, Lona could sense the other woman's anxiety.

"I've done more than that," Reiko replied. "After you disappeared, I took care of your assets, at least the ones I knew about. I'm sure there was more that you kept secret, for your own protection or to insulate me." Shaking her head, she used one hand to offer a dismissive wave. "Anyway, the house in Wyoming is waiting for you. I even had your Mustang in for a tune-up."

Laughing at that, Lona said, "Would you believe that the entire time I spent in quarantine, I never once worried about the house or any of those other things?" It was odd, she knew, but something had told her not to concern herself with such things as whatever material possessions she might have owned prior to her disappearance. There were more important subjects to ponder.

The brief moment of quiet was shattered at the sound

of a cell phone ringing somewhere on the other side of the room. Reiko blinked at the summons before lurching from the bed and crossing to where a pile of her clothes lay strewn across a chair. She retrieved the phone, looking at its digital display as it continued to ring before she glanced back toward Lona. "It's . . . I mean . . . I have to take this," she said, moving toward the suite's other room. Lona sat on the bed, listening to the bits and fragments of Reiko's half of the muted conversation filtering back into the room. It was not hard to guess who was on the other end of the line.

"No," she heard Reiko snap after a moment, the single word delivered with more force than anything she had said to that point. "It's not anything you did. I told you why I had to do this. Yes, I *do* love you, but this is . . . look, I can't do this now. No, you can't . . . I'm *not coming back.* Good-bye, Carmen."

Lona felt her heart jump as she heard Reiko sever the conversation, waiting the additional moments until the other woman appeared in the doorway, tears streaming down her cheeks.

"Reiko?" she asked, her voice barely a whisper.

Wiping tears from her eyes, Reiko drew a deep breath. "It's okay. I do love her, but the truth is that I never stopped loving you."

The odd warmth Lona had felt the previous day in Seattle once more washed over her body as she rose from the bed. In scarcely the blink of an eye she was across the room, her pulse racing and again feeling perspiration moisten her skin.

Her eyes widening in shock and confusion, Reiko gasped at what Lona knew she must have seen. "How did you . . . ?"

Lona shook her head, pushing aside the question and instead focusing her attention on the woman who had not allowed the years to diminish the love or desire that had guided her to Seattle. Her hands found their way through the folds of the robe and to the bare skin concealed beneath, and her lips sought out Reiko's, reveling in the contact for which she had yearned these many weeks.

For now, the questions could wait.

REEMERGENCE

JULY 2005

ELEVEN

CIA HEADQUARTERS
LANGLEY, VIRGINIA

BRIAN HICKS KNEW that in the wars against terrorism, drugs, and various other flavors of tyranny, some of those fronts were fraught with danger and even more than a touch of mystery and intrigue. Around the world, soldiers equipped with state-of-the-art battlefield armaments and training were engaging America's enemies and fighting the good fight. Elsewhere, covert agents wielding the latest gadgets and weapons as well as wits honed through hard-won experience were hunting evil masterminds bent on destroying his country's way of life.

Then there was him, Brian Hicks, who like everyone else on this floor made his contributions from the supposed comfort of a drab gray cubicle. His arsenal consisted of an ergonomically designed office chair, a computer, a phone, a desk, and cabinets crammed with reports, charts, and maps he was certain no other human being would ever read.

Anything to support the "war effort," blah, blah, blah.

This was not the career Brian had envisioned when he was first approached by a recruiter for the Central Intelligence Agency while still a student at Florida State University. Until that fateful day, he had anticipated continuing with his studies and earning his degree in computer information systems, eventually going on to earn obscene amounts of money at some big IT company. This, of course, was before the reality of outsourcing such jobs to overseas companies or just those U.S. firms with a significant global presence that could afford to transfer that kind of work to employees in countries earning a fraction of the "bloated" salaries paid to their American counterparts. While still in college, Brian had believed a lucrative career in the private sector awaited him.

All of that had changed the day the quiet man in the dark suit arrived on campus, bringing with him a surprisingly thick file that seemed to hold every byte of information pertaining to the life of Brian Hicks. Contained within the file were statements from all manner of people in his life, including his parents, friends from high school, teachers he had long since forgotten, and former employers. The recruiter appeared to know the most mundane details, such as the books he read, the movies he liked, or the porn he downloaded from the Internet. He even knew about the spring break weekend in Daytona Beach during his junior year culminating in the night spent with that crazy redhead from Michigan State who had ended up in a bunch of those *Girls Gone Wild* videos. The Agency man had a statement from her, too.

Long story short, the guy in the suit knew *everything*.

He also had been aware of Brian's love and apparent gift for computers. He had visited the websites Brian created, first as school projects and later as a means of helping to defray the cost of his college tuition. The recruiter also had recounted a few shady incidents from Brian's past, such as the occasions he hacked online retailers in order to secure assorted electronics and video games while making sure that those purchases were recorded on other customers' invoices.

Interestingly, the Agency had seemed not at all interested in those dealings, except to the extent that they showcased Brian's technical prowess. The recruiter's pitch for his employer was enticing, filled with examples of how Brian could utilize his talents to contribute to America's ongoing battles with old as well as emerging enemies. With computers permeating nearly every aspect of modern civilization—including intelligence gathering as well as crime and terrorism—the need for specialists who could navigate and even wage war within the "virtual" world created and supported by these machines continued to grow. It all seemed so exciting when Brian entered the service of the CIA two years ago, the ink still fresh on his college diploma, but reality had wasted little time in asserting itself into his choice of career.

Sucker.

The bulk of Brian's days were spent tracking computer transactions of various types—electronic mail, online purchases, funds transfers—as assigned to him by case officers and other upper-level supervisors within the Agency's ever-expanding Directorate of Science and Technology. Most of the information he sought was routine and unexciting, so far as he was concerned. He also knew that somewhere else in the building, other analysts sifted through the data he and his peers collected, searching for patterns and commonalities that might point to individuals deemed worthy of further scrutiny for one reason or another and about which Brian never learned anything. If ever the tired, threadbare cliché of "Need to Know" applied, it did to Brian Hicks and others at his level.

However, on rare occasions during the course of his seemingly endless games of virtual hide and seek, something interesting reared its ugly head. Like today, for example.

Brian was eight or nine screens deep into a series of transactions from New York to a bank in the Cayman Islands, with many of those transfers believed to be part of a larger effort to funnel money to several groups suspected of planning acts of domestic terrorism. He had traced through more than half of the fifty-six transfers he was assigned as part of a larger case file when an alert-window abruptly popped up on his screen. Frowning at the small gray box, which displayed a status message regarding a funds transfer unrelated to his current search, Brian's confusion only deepened as he read the case number appended to the message. It was one he did not recognize.

"Hello?" he asked aloud, though there was no one around to hear it. The number the alert referenced was not associated with his current task, nor any that he could remember having recently worked. It took several minutes of scanning archived emails and case-related directories on his workstation before he found a match, though instead of satisfaction at finally making a connection, Brian only felt more confusion.

The case file in question was thirteen years old, its most recent entry of any substance having been entered during the fall of 1992.

"You've gotta be yanking me," he said, gritting his teeth as he opened the case file. Of particular note was the fact that while it had lain dormant for more than a decade, the file was last updated near the end of 2004, flagged with a new instruction to apprise Deputy Director Nicholas McFarland should any new information come to light.

Okay, so much for another boring day trapped in my hole. Assuming this new update amounted to anything, it was very possible that Brian might see actual daylight as he left the cubicle farm on this floor to go inform McFarland of what he had found.

Using his mouse, Brian clicked on the alert-box and opened the file indicated by the message's embedded link. A new screen opened on his monitor as fresh information was routed to his workstation, updating his copy of the affected file. According to the transaction log forwarded to him, a funds transfer had taken place within the hour, routing money from a bank in Switzerland, the account number for which was one of several listed in the case file. The transfer log displayed a list of several nodes and other banks through which the funds had been routed and rerouted, sometimes three or four times. Within a span of ten minutes, the money—more than one million

dollars—had moved through banks in Europe and the
United States.

Then it vanished.

"What the hell?" The question echoed off the walls
of Brian's cubicle as he pounded his keyboard, searching
through the string of screens and pop-ups in a frantic attempt to backtrack to where he might have lost the trail.
It took nearly twenty minutes before he realized he had
been duped, and it had happened rather early in the transfer process, to boot. Somehow, whoever was behind the
movement of money between banks and other financial
institutions around the world also had launched a feint
as a way of covering their tracks, as though they expected
their activities to trigger alarms and summon scrutiny. The
two sets of transactions had both separated and converged,
racing alongside and even overlapping one another within
the chaos formed by millions of other transactions taking
place at the same time. From what Brian was able to tell
in the short time he had invested to this point, the money
actually had stopped moving after only the first few transfers, with the rest of the following transactions executed
simply for show.

McFarland's gonna love this.

"What the hell do you mean you lost it?" asked Nicholas
McFarland, his eyes boring into Brian's with such intensity
that Brian thought he might just burst into flames.

He now stood before the deputy director's desk, his
laptop cradled in the crook of his left arm, having indeed
seen daylight thanks to the summons to report to Mc-

Farland's office on the top floor. Glancing past the man himself and through the large windows that formed the office's back wall, Brian noted the cloudless blue sky and the lush green forest surrounding the Agency complex. Right now, the idea of hiding himself amid the dense foliage seemed quite tempting.

"To be honest, sir," Brian said after taking a moment to force down the lump that had lodged in his throat, "I never actually *had* it." As quickly as possible, he described the process by which the funds were removed from the Swiss bank account. "It took me some time to figure out, but what actually happened was that the electronic transfers were a wild goose chase. The money was actually withdrawn by someone with access to the account who physically visited the bank. Nearly one point five million dollars in a briefcase, just like that."

"What about the transfers?" McFarland asked, tapping the fingers of his right hand along the top of his large mahogany desk.

Brian replied, "All a ruse, sir." Holding up his laptop, he waited until the director nodded his approval before stepping closer to the desk and placing the portable computer atop its polished surface. "We've got some footage from the bank's security cameras, but it's not very helpful." To save time, he already had set up the video playback software and advanced the clip of footage to the appropriate point. "It was a woman who made the withdrawal," he said, pointing to the figure standing at the teller counter. "Watch how she keeps her face turned away from the camera. I only caught her for a few frames." Freezing the image, he enhanced it so that McFarland could get a better look, but frowned when the director seemed to register no emotional reaction as he studied the woman's face.

"Anything else?" McFarland asked.

Nodding, Brian advanced the video file until the image shifted to that displayed by another camera. "I tried to isolate footage of her entering and leaving the bank, but something weird happened there, too." He said nothing more as he allowed the video to play. On the laptop's monitor, the woman was walking toward the camera, but then the image seemed to jump forward to where she passed out of the frame.

"Watch the time stamp, sir," he added as he replayed the footage. "It doesn't shift like you'd think it should. It stays steady, but she just seems to flash forward. I don't get it." He cast his eyes down toward the beige carpet of McFarland's office. "Not that it really matters. She kept us chasing our tails while she walked out of there with the money. It's like she knew we'd be watching when she went after it. Whoever she is, she's good, sir. Damned good."

Maybe we'll hire her. There's bound to be an empty cube on my floor by lunchtime.

To Brian's surprise, McFarland did not offer any sort of denigrating retort. Instead, he merely nodded as he reached to open his desk's center drawer. He extracted a pack of cigarettes along with a lighter, not of the disposable variety but instead one of those old-school stainless steel jobs with the flip-top and that needed fluid. Not a smoker himself, Brian felt an urge to remind the director of the building's smoking policy, but discretion won out over righteous indignation as McFarland fired up his cigarette. Instead, Brian noted that the side of the lighter was emblazoned with the emblem of the United States Marine Corps, and remembered that the director had once served in that branch of the armed forces.

Taking a drag from the cigarette, McFarland tilted his head back and blew smoke into the air above him. After a moment, he said, "She *is* good, Mr. Hicks. Very good. She may not have possessed the technical skill to accomplish what she did, but it's obvious she still has access to resources and personnel to help her with this kind of thing." He shook his head as he pulled again on the cigarette. "Damn."

Brian frowned again. "You know her, sir?" The smoke now had reached him, and though it stung his eyes he made a conscious effort to refrain from wiping them. He began to feel a tickle in his throat and fought the impulse to cough.

Though he seemed to recognize the discomfort he was causing, McFarland said nothing, instead simply taking the partially smoked cigarette and snuffing it out in the ashtray near the corner of his desk. "Yes, I know her. She used to work for us, on a freelance basis, several years ago. The name she used at the bank in Switzerland is . . . was . . . an alias of hers in the early nineties. As for the account itself, it was one she used as a transfer point for money she received from us for . . . services rendered. The account's been dormant for more than ten years, but it was never closed."

Brian said, "Sir, you updated the file with a notation to alert you should something like this happen. Prior to that, the case had been cold for more than a decade. You knew last year that someone would try to access that account, even though so much time had passed." Frowning again, he asked, "What kind of work did she do?" Even as he spoke the words, Brian knew what answer he would receive.

Shaking his head, McFarland said, "That's way above your pay grade, Hicks. For now, I want you to concentrate on monitoring the other accounts listed in that case file. If another nickel moves from any of them, I want to know about it."

"Yes, sir," Brian said. "Will there be anything else?"

"Just that you're not to discuss any detail of this assignment with *anyone*. That includes your immediate supervisors. I'll make sure they're briefed appropriately, and that you're given the latitude you need." He paused, grunting in mild exasperation. "To be honest, Hicks, this is a long shot. The person we're talking about was very—*very*— effective at staying off radar screens. My gut reaction to what you showed me is that she wanted us to see her pulling this money, just to show us that she could do it and get away clean. I don't expect her to do it again anytime soon. If she holds to pattern, she's lying low somewhere, for whatever reason. But, you were still on the ball enough today to catch her in real time. You keep up whatever computer voodoo it is you do down there, and you might get a bit luckier next time."

It was as close to a compliment as he was likely to get

from the director, Brian knew. "Assuming there is a next time, sir."

McFarland nodded, and for the first time Brian noted the fatigue that seemed to cloud the other man's eyes. "Something tells me we'd better hope there is."

TWELVE

ATLANTA, GEORGIA

IF THERE WAS a downside to a mild Sunday morning during any summer in northern Georgia, Frederick Morehouse was convinced that it had nothing at all to do with the merciful weather gods, and everything to do with the increased number of golfers on his favorite course. They always seemed to beat him to the best tee times.

"I'm being punished for sins in a past life," he said, casting a look of disgust over his shoulder toward his three companions and their caddies and shaking his head. They had been standing a respectful distance from the starting point of the first hole, waiting for the group ahead of them. Three of the four golfers in the other party already had teed off, but the final member of the quartet, a man Morehouse knew was a local district judge as well as a pompous jackass of the first order, apparently was making a career out of his first swing. Dressed in a pink pullover and white pin-striped slacks that matched the color of his well-coiffed hair, the judge appeared to be talking to his golf ball as he lowered the head of his club to the grass in slow, deliberate movements, only to raise the club in order to repeat the steps all over again.

"Maybe we'll get lucky, and he'll take a slice to the nuts." Grunting in irritation, Morehouse turned toward his caddy, a teenager dressed in khaki shorts along with an orange T-shirt and matching cap. Nodding to his golf bag, Morehouse said, "Hand me one of those water bottles from that outer pocket, would you, son? I'm thinking we're going to be here a while."

It was while the caddy was fumbling with the bag that Morehouse felt his cell phone vibrating in his pocket. Retrieving the phone, he studied its digital display and immediately recognized the calling number. Even if he did not know who was calling him, the 703 area code was clue enough: Virginia, probably Langley. Course etiquette usually frowned upon the use of cellular phones, and Morehouse observed that courtesy except in the most extreme or unusual of circumstances.

Today, this call fell into that category.

Flipping open the phone, he brought the compact unit to his ear. "Hello?"

"Have you figured out how to hit it through that little windmill yet?" asked the voice of Nicholas McFarland, longtime friend and former co-worker.

Chuckling in spite of himself, Morehouse replied, "Thanks for getting back to me, but that joke doesn't get any funnier, no matter how many times you try it."

Since retiring from his position as a CIA deputy director nearly a decade ago, Morehouse's contact with McFarland had been sporadic—holidays, get-togethers during vacations or when the occasional consulting job took him to Washington. Those infrequent exchanges and meetings had undergone considerable change during the last year, since McFarland had told him of Lona Callahan's incredible return from supposed oblivion.

"What have you found?" McFarland asked, dispensing with the jocularity and getting down to business.

Morehouse grunted, stepping away from his friends and keeping his voice low. "Nothing. Everyone I've got on the case has come up dry," he replied. Since hearing from McFarland about Callahan's brazen visit to one of the banks she once had used as a transfer point for the Agency funds she received, Morehouse had contacted several government and private sector associates, gaining access to a small pool of talented computer specialists who could be relied upon to carry out discreet investigations for a handsome freelancer's fee. The efforts of those individuals had yielded only slightly more information than McFarland already knew, essentially confirming that Callahan had to have employed her own computer gurus in order to cover her tracks with such skill. While Morehouse's people were able to determine the starting point for the string of faked money transfers, it only had angered McFarland to learn that she or her accomplices apparently initiated the diversion from somewhere inside the bank, utilizing the building's own local area network.

"There's been nothing new for weeks," McFarland's voice growled through the phone. "On one hand, it's like it always was, but considering everything that's happened since we started this up again, I don't like it."

Morehouse nodded in understanding, knowing that no verbal acknowledgment was required. Old habits had taken over during these increasingly frequent conversations, with both men leaving out specific references to Callahan or her activities as they talked over the open phone line. After all, one never knew who might be eavesdropping. "What do you want me to do?"

"I've already got my people going through every file we have," McFarland replied, "looking for anything we might have overlooked or forgotten. I don't expect to have much luck, though. You remember how this used to work."

Indeed, Morehouse thought. Lona Callahan always had been disciplined and effective at maintaining her anonymity, to the point that it used to be a point of debate about whether she ever had provided her real identity to her employers. For years, Morehouse was convinced she had, refusing to believe that even her formidable talents were a match for the Agency's all but unlimited resources.

Now, however, he had to wonder.

"I'll have my people keep digging," Morehouse said, reaching up to wipe the first beads of sweat from his forehead. The pleasant temperatures of the morning were giving way to the more traditional heat and humidity characteristic of Georgia summers. "We might still get lucky." Even as he spoke the words, he felt a tinge of doubt that irritated him. Computer technology and its usefulness to law enforcement and intelligence agencies had increased a hundredfold during the twelve years that Lona

Callahan had been away. "Sooner or later, our people will find something, or someone."

"You think there may be others?" McFarland asked.

"Absolutely." While Morehouse found it unlikely that Callahan could have closed her learning gap in such a short time to the point where she could stand toe-to-toe with the best experts employed by the Agency, it was obvious that she still commanded formidable resources despite her long absence. This suggested close friends or partners for whom time would not have been a factor with regard to loyalty, and it was a thought that troubled Morehouse.

Behind him, he heard the sound of someone clearing his throat, and Morehouse turned to see his friend, Geoffrey Thorne, pointing to his watch and then toward the tee-off for the first hole. The other group had finally moved off, making their way down the fairway at a modest pace.

Thank Christ for small favors, he mused, looking at his own watch and realizing that it had taken the judge almost five minutes to tee off. *Arrogant prick.*

"I've got to go, Nick," Morehouse said, "but I'll call you later this afternoon, or sooner if something turns up." There would be plenty of time later to worry about Lona Callahan.

McFarland replied, "Sounds good, Fred. Good talking to you. Wish it could be more often, and under better circumstances. Try not to hit any innocent bystanders."

Ending the call, Morehouse returned the cell phone to his pocket before turning back to the rest of his group. "Okay," he said, smiling as he clapped his hands together and rubbed them in a gesture of anticipation. "Who's first?"

"That would be you, old man," Thorne replied. The muscled African-American man smiled as he stepped closer and clapped Morehouse on the shoulder. "And I don't want any excuses out of you when we kick your ass all over this course."

Morehouse laughed, pulling a white leather golf glove onto his left hand before selecting his club. "Promises, promises," he said, grabbing a ball and tee from his bag.

"Sounds like we still have time to up the bet," said his friend and partner for this game, Allyn Gibson, offering his trademark leering grin which almost always assured some manner of mischief. "What do you think, Fred?" To the rest of the group, he asked, "Any takers?"

Thorne's partner, Bill Leisner, nodded in agreement. "Okay, Mouth. Double it," he said, smiling like a college freshman invited to his first sorority party. "But don't say we didn't warn you."

"Works for me," Morehouse said, offering a good-natured wave as he placed his ball on its tee and adjusted his grip on his club, setting his feet in preparation for his swing. "Just be sure to remember where you hid your wallets when we get back to the clubhouse."

Morehouse flexed his fingers and rolled his shoulders, straightening his posture to stretch the muscles in his back before settling into his stance. He raised his head, closing his eyes and enjoying the warmth of the morning sun on his face.

* * *

Through the crosshairs of her rifle scope, Lona Callahan observed the better portion of Frederick Morehouse's head disappear. The sound of the lone rifle shot echoed across the well-manicured golf course as Morehouse's limp body fell to the grass.

From her concealed position more than four hundred yards away and from several feet deep into a line of dense undergrowth, Lona refocused her attention and watched as chaos gripped the rest of Morehouse's group. The caddies scrambled for the meager cover offered by nearby trees or in depressions along the sides of the fairway, their heads or the occasional limb visible from behind their places of concealment as they fidgeted and trembled in fear. Two of the other players also had dropped to the ground, their heads moving as though on swivels in search of the threat. One of the other players, a large dark-skinned man, rushed to where Morehouse had fallen and crouched beside his friend, seemingly unworried about inviting a similar fate as his expression and body language confirmed to the rest of the group what Lona already knew.

Frederick Morehouse was dead. Mission accomplished.

It was her first kill in thirteen years—or nine months, if she chose to view such things subjectively—and the actual mechanics of carrying out such a task had come back to her with no effort. With the slightest of movements she played the rifle scope over each of Morehouse's friends as well as the caddies. Though she could have dispatched the other seven people within seconds, training and years of experience and self-discipline would not permit such reckless behavior. Her goal was achieved, and anything more would be wasteful. Besides, taking the time to engage additional and unnecessary targets would only give others opportunity to determine her location. She was well concealed, of course, and while her extraction would be executed with the same efficiency as her infiltration, one could not always discount random chance or simple luck.

Even as her right forefinger moved away from the weapon's trigger, Lona felt her body shudder, not from a chill or even from adrenaline. This was different, and she closed her eyes for a moment and allowed the sensation to wash over her. It was a warm, almost pleasurable glow radiating through her, not at all dissimilar to what she experienced while locked in a lover's passionate embrace. In a word, it was *fulfillment*. This was new, and something in her mind told her it felt as though she somehow was being rewarded for her actions.

Pondering that thought as she remained motionless, nestled in the sniper's nest she had created within the thick brush, Lona could not help but be troubled. While she had designed and implemented the plan to kill Frederick Morehouse with all the expertise and patience used throughout her infamous "career," what had differed on this occasion was the reason behind the actions. No one had explicitly hired or ordered her to carry out the assassination, nor did she possess any personal motive for wanting Morehouse killed. Still, she had felt a drive—a *compulsion*—to carry out the task. In the past, her motivation had been the large sums of money she was paid for her work, and the opportunities such payments allowed for her to live an opulent, if more than a bit reclusive, lifestyle.

This was no longer the case.

Now, it seemed that her thoughts increasingly were influenced with a new sense of purpose, a *larger* purpose. While the urge to pursue this objective was strong, Lona had tried and failed on numerous occasions over the past months to understand specific details or reasons behind what now drove her. The answers to her many questions seemed to hover just inside or perhaps behind a strange fog clouding her thoughts, which only intensified the harder she tried to penetrate it. Was her own mind conspiring to keep the truth from her? If so, why? Was she suffering from the onset of mental illness, or was this apparent secrecy within herself deliberate? As always, the queries brought forth no responses.

Naturally, Lona suspected that it had something to do with whatever had happened during her time spent in "the future," as incredible a notion as that still sounded to her. If the claims of Jordan Collier, the self-proclaimed envoy for the 4400, were to be believed, then Lona and the other returnees were instruments, taken and perhaps even modified by people living years or decades from now, and for reasons as yet unexplained. According to Collier, she and the others had been returned to this point in time in order to somehow prevent a devastating event which—if true—ultimately would result in the collapse of human civilization.

It remained to be seen how the 4400 would succeed in averting "the catastrophe," as it was called in news reports, websites devoted to the returnees and the mystery surrounding them, and Collier's own recently published book.

As such, Lona had no idea as to the nature or scope of her role in such momentous actions. She even had considered seeking out Collier for guidance in the hopes that he might provide some insight, but that notion was shattered a week ago when he fell to the bullets of his own assassin.

I wonder if McFarland thinks that was me. It was a likely possibility, Lona knew, but what bothered her more was the idea that Collier's murder and what she had just done here were somehow connected. Were both events part of a larger plan put into motion by whoever had abducted the returnees? If so, what other events might be in play, about which she knew nothing?

Continuing to watch the scene on the golf course, with the rest of Morehouse's party still crouching in terror as they waited for something to happen, Lona once again asked herself why she had opted for a sniper attack as the means to eliminate Morehouse. It was the same method she had used to take out Miraj al-Diladi during her last contracted assignment, and surely Nicholas McFarland, as the Agency official who had sanctioned that previous action, would surmise that she was the one responsible for his friend's murder. The only reason that Lona could summon was that she wanted to make a statement of sorts, to inform McFarland, Norton, and anyone else who might know of her existence that while she might be back in action, it was not on their terms—and would never be again.

She already had taken steps that Reiko considered unwarranted risks, namely the visit to the Swiss bank. While obtaining the money had not truly been necessary, given the sizable "retirement fund" she had accumulated prior to her disappearance and to which Reiko had attended during her absence, it was a test to gauge the authorities she knew must be looking for her. The experiment had proven valuable, in that the computer techs Reiko hired to plan and execute the diversionary funds transfers were able to determine the level of pursuit and investigation launched by Agency assets. It was enough to tell Lona that similar actions on her part were inadvisable, and that revisiting other aspects of her former support network would give her hunters the edge they sought to capture her. From this point forward, she would have to discard or eliminate all facets of her previous life. This, of course, included Nicholas McFarland and others like him.

Does it also include Reiko?

The question erupted from the haze enveloping her mind. How had she not considered this before? Reiko was the only person in the world Lona trusted without exception or qualification. If Lona had any authentic emotional attachment for anyone at all, it was Reiko. The months since their reunion in Seattle had shown that the passage of years from Reiko's point of view had not dimmed her own love or loyalty to Lona, and within only a short time it seemed as though they never had been apart. In addition to the passion they shared and the invaluable logistical support she always had provided, Reiko also offered yet another invaluable service by acting as Lona's counsel and conscience. The very idea of seeing her as a threat to be eliminated was anathema to everything Lona held dear.

Is that still true? Will it always be so?

Forcing away the errant questions and the discomfort they conjured, Lona returned her attention to the golf course, eyeing the scene through her rifle scope. It had become apparent that Morehouse's companions believed they were not in danger. Lona watched through the scope as the caddies emerged from cover, still scanning the surrounding area while two of the other golf players talked excitedly into their cellular phones. In the distance, she heard the faint whines of sirens, of police and ambulances. It only had been a few minutes since Morehouse had fallen, though Lona had factored a quick response into her exit strategy. She was not worried, as no one on the golf course even had hinted at pointing or looking in her direction. Besides, having spent months perfecting her control over the strange ability she now possessed, getting away from "normal" humans would be so simple as to be embarrassing.

Still, now seemed like as good a time as any to make her escape. With unhurried, simple movements born from years of experience and habit, Lona eased herself back from her sniper's nest, withdrawing even deeper into the underbrush. As she moved—ever conscious to avoid even the most minute disturbance of the vegetation that concealed her—she used her free hand to rearrange the bed of leaves she had used, eliminating any obvious signs that a human body had lain there. A slow scan of the nest ensured she left nothing behind. Even the shell casing from the single shot she had taken remained in her rifle's chamber.

She continued her retreat for twenty yards, until she was well within the tree line that formed the outer perimeter of the small forested area bordering the golf course's northern boundary. It was the ideal location for a sniper to stage a covert attack, and any law enforcement personnel with functioning brain stems soon would order the area cordoned in an attempt to corral any suspect who might still be hiding in the woods. Lona had no plans to be here when someone finally made that call. Satisfied that she had obtained enough cover to mask her departure, she rose to her feet and began jogging up the slight incline, deeper into the forest where she had hidden her mode of escape, a four-wheeled all-terrain vehicle.

Even as she broke down her sniper rifle and returned its components to the travel case strapped to the back of the ATV, Lona could not help but notice the lingering sensation of contentment that still seemed to course through her body, as though commending her for a job well done.

It felt *good*.

THIRTEEN

NTAC
SEATTLE, WASHINGTON

TOM BALDWIN GLANCED at his watch, 9:45 in the morning, and already he was frustrated. It normally took until at least midafternoon before he started to feel this level of irritation. Today, he decided, would be another in what was becoming a series of long days.

"I need coffee," he said, dropping the file he was reading onto the pile occupying the center of his desk and rising from his chair.

At the desk situated opposite his, Diana Skouris smiled, but did not look up from her computer monitor. "I know that tone, so let me guess. You've read the files again, and didn't find anything hiding in them that we missed the previous three or four times you went through them?"

"Something like that," Baldwin replied, pausing before the oversized corkboard dominating the wall behind his desk. Stretching the muscles in his back and shoulders, he took in the array of photographs, newspaper clippings, note cards, maps, and other assorted scraps of paper that had collected there. Some of the material dated back to the day the 4400 had returned, though a good portion of what he now studied only had been placed there since the assassination of Jordan Collier, the mysterious man who had become the charismatic as well as controversial face and voice of the 4400.

Almost two weeks had passed since Collier's murder and, with few exceptions, the case had been the focus of nearly every waking moment for Baldwin, Skouris, and a task force of other NTAC agents. The FBI, which had taken the lead on the manhunt, was doing its level best to assure the media that it was making strides and that its pursuit of the killer was intensifying with each day. The truth was that those few clues that had been dredged up in the tragedy's aftermath already were dying on the vine. Even the sketch created from a description of the suspect as provided by a lone witness had yet to generate any tangible new leads.

Baldwin's frustration grew with each day that failed to yield any progress. He had lost count of the number of times he had berated himself for nearly having the suspect—no, the *killer*—in custody. He had been there, at The 4400 Center, mere feet from where the pair of bullets had torn into Collier's chest. It was he who had spotted the shooter on an adjacent roof and was the first to engage the suspect while he attempted to flee the scene. Baldwin had chased him back into the building, where the other man scrambled to the roof and barely escaped through a security grating, which he locked behind him and blocked Baldwin from continuing the chase. The suspect also evaded the hastily erected cordon around The 4400 Center, and disappeared into the surrounding Seattle suburbs.

While brief, every moment of that encounter had been seared into Baldwin's memory. He recalled every detail about the shooter—his black sweatshirt and camouflage pants, the black combat boots and the gloves and dark watch cap, and, slung over his shoulder, the satchel bag that undoubtedly had carried the murder weapon. The only thing Baldwin had never managed to get a good look at was the assailant's face.

Nice job with that, in case I forgot to remind you this morning.

"Tom, you've got to quit riding yourself."

Turning from the board, Baldwin cast an annoyed look toward his partner, but nodded in acknowledgment. She had been telling him the same thing for days, and he knew she was right, but he was not prepared to let himself off the hook so easily. "I know, I know, but as mad as I am now, imagine how pissed I'll be if the FBI hauls that guy in after I let him get away. They'll be eating that one up for years." Interagency rivalry came in many forms, some of it good-natured while other aspects were far more sinister. When it came to the ever-narrowing slice of pie that was the budget allocated to intelligence gathering and security agencies, the gap between success and failure when it came to assigned missions might mean the difference between existence and oblivion. NTAC was in place for the express purpose of investigating the 4400 and handling any issues that might arise regarding them, a move that other parties, most notably the FBI, had protested with much vehemence. If it could be demonstrated that the upstart agency was incapable of fulfilling its mandate, then detractors undoubtedly would use that to convince congressional leaders that NTAC's functions—and more important, its budget—would be better utilized when folded into their own organizations.

Hopefully not before I get my coffee.

Releasing an annoyed grunt, Baldwin turned from the board. "I'll be right back," he said to Skouris as he moved toward the door on his way to the kitchen and salvation. Before he could get there, his path was blocked by their boss and the regional director for NTAC's Northwest Division, Nina Jarvis. Dressed in dark blue slacks and matching jacket over an indigo silk blouse, her straight brown hair falling to rest atop her shoulders, she presented the appearance of someone who held no illusions or doubts about her authority, which Baldwin knew was an apt description for her.

"Morning, kids," Jarvis said, crossing her arms and offering Baldwin her trademark no-nonsense glower. "Anything new?" The expression was rumored in hushed circles to be capable of making the knees of lesser men tremble, but Baldwin knew it as simply the default expression of a straightforward, confident leader who prized hard work and effectiveness while not suffering those fools who blocked the way of getting the job done. Though he and Jarvis had disagreed and butted heads on many occasions,

Baldwin still respected her as a more than able replacement for Dennis Ryland, who had recommended her for the job after being promoted to the position of NTAC's deputy director and transferred to the agency's headquarters in Washington, D.C.

Baldwin offered a mock groan. "Still going back over witness statements from the 4400 reunion, and we've got techs combing through the video footage taken by the cameras at the Center. So far, nothing new is jumping out and no new witnesses have come forward. But hey, the FBI's on the case, so I thought I'd get some coffee."

"Forget it," Jarvis countered, indicating with a nod of her head for both Baldwin and Skouris to follow her. "I've got something that'll wake you right up."

As though sensing where this might be going, Skouris shared a quick glance with Baldwin as she rose from her chair and moved to follow. "You're not pulling us off the Collier case again, are you?" It would be the second time since the assassination that the agents had been reassigned. Last week, they had been tasked with hunting down Jean DeLynn Baker, a 4400 with severe psychological problems who for reasons unknown had been modified by her abductors from the future to serve as a living biological weapon. Her body capable of releasing a deadly, fast-acting virus whenever she became upset, angry, or scared, Baker had already decimated the small town of Granite Pass before setting out for Portland. She had come within a hairbreadth of unleashing the virus in the heart of a crowded downtown district before Skouris was forced to kill her.

"In my defense," Jarvis said, "it wasn't my idea." She cast a look over her shoulder that told Baldwin she really could not care less about any explanation others might feel she should offer on her own behalf. "This is from way upstairs, and you two were specifically requested."

"Us?" Baldwin asked. "Why?"

Jarvis shrugged as she led the way into her office. "We're all about to find out. All I know is that it's high priority."

Like the director herself, her workplace was a model of understatement and efficiency. The walls were painted a light gray, except for the one behind her desk, which sported a rich red tint. A modest assortment of personal keepsakes and curios intermingled with the ordered collection of books, binders, and folders adorning her desk as well as shelves and cabinets. Her cherrywood desk and its matching credenzas were of simple, sleek design, and the office was rounded out with the usual accessories of an American flag affixed to a flagpole in one rear corner and a large bronze version of the NTAC seal on the rear wall.

"Sit down," Jarvis said as she moved behind her desk and dropped into her ergonomic office chair. "Something tells me this is going to be interesting." Reaching for a multifunction remote control, she aimed it at the medium-sized flat-screen monitor sitting atop the credenza positioned opposite her desk. Baldwin and Skouris lowered themselves into the pair of matching black chairs situated in front of Jarvis, turning to face the monitor as it flared to life and coalesced into the image of Dennis

Ryland, staring out from the screen from what Baldwin figured was the NTAC deputy director's office.

"Dennis," Baldwin said by way of greeting, smiling at the sight of his longtime friend. Ryland was sitting in a high-backed leather chair, has hands clasped in his lap. He was dressed in a dark suit with a white shirt and a muted blue tie, and there was more gray around the man's temples than the last time Baldwin had seen him. New creases were visible along his forehead and there were bags under his eyes. "Don't they let you sleep in Washington?"

"I get by. Good to see you again. How're things on the front lines?"

"As well as could probably be expected," Skouris replied, glancing to Tom as she settled into her chair. "To what do we owe the pleasure?"

On the screen, Ryland said, "I wish this was a social call, but the truth is I need you two, and I need you now. Nina's already told you that we've got a situation here. What she doesn't know yet is that it's high visibility and high security, and it's coming at us from none other than the CIA."

"What?" Baldwin asked, hardly believing his ears. From experience, he knew that while the Central Intelligence Agency was many things, flattering adjectives typically did not include "cooperative" or "forthcoming" when it came to dealing with other agencies. "*They're* coming to *us*?"

"Don't worry, I checked," Ryland said, holding up a hand. "Hell hasn't frozen over. Not yet, anyway. Before we go any further, you all need to understand that this operation is classified. The case doesn't exist, so far as anyone else is concerned. Chances are we'd never have heard anything about it, but the Agency is coming to us because it looks like it involves a 4400. You're on this because you're still our best investigative team, but the big reason is because of what Tom can bring to the case."

Baldwin frowned at that. "I don't understand."

"You know that a retired CIA officer, Frederick Morehouse, was killed this past weekend in Atlanta, right? Shot by a sniper, and that the killer remains at large?"

"Of course," Skouris replied. "We even wondered if that case and Collier's might be related, but the MO's are different enough that we're not giving it serious consideration. Are you telling us that they *are* related?"

Ryland shook his head. "Not so far as we know. The CIA believes that Morehouse was killed by a former freelance operator they used to contract for various covert assignments. We're talking real dirty work here, people, things the Agency would prefer never see the light of day."

"Assassination, obviously," Jarvis said. "What does this have to do with us? Are they thinking Morehouse's killer is a 4400?"

"They don't have any hard evidence as to the killer's identity, but they're absolutely certain that their prime suspect is a returnee."

Ryland reached for something on his desk that was not in the camera's view, and Baldwin heard a clicking sound before the image on the monitor split into two windows, one containing the feed from Ryland's office and the other what Baldwin recognized as an extract from a government employee's personnel record. A photograph dominated the image's upper-right-hand quadrant, depicting a woman in her early to middle thirties, with dark red hair cut in what experience told him was a short yet outdated style. Something about the woman was familiar, he decided. Glancing at the dates accompanying the photo, he noted that her file—or at least the version released by the CIA—had not been updated since 1992.

"NTAC's database on the 4400 lists her as Alicia Colbern," Ryland said, "though the CIA has since told us that's an alias, one they didn't have on file from when she was still an active asset. According to them, her real name is Lona Callahan."

"Alicia Colbern," Baldwin said again. "I know that name."

"The day the returnees were released," Skouris replied. "Remember, that incident near the bank? A 4400 was attacked, but disappeared?" Looking to Ryland, she asked, "This is who we're talking about?"

Ryland nodded. "That's her. Long story short, she did wet work for the CIA for more than a decade. She's responsible for dozens of assassinations—political leaders, heads of business, known and suspected terrorists—every one sanctioned by the Agency, and she was the target of a global, interagency manhunt in the '80s and '90s. Her last known authorized assignment took place on June 23, 1992."

Hearing the date spoken aloud jolted Baldwin as though he had just touched a live wire. "You can't be serious."

"Tom?" Skouris asked, her expression one of concern. "What is it?"

Ignoring her question, Baldwin leaned forward in his seat, closer to the monitor. "Dennis, are you telling us that this woman is, I mean was . . . ?"

"Yes," Ryland replied before Baldwin could complete the question. "According to the CIA, Lona Callahan was the Wraith."

"Jesus," Jarvis said, her expression of shock mirroring Baldwin's. "I haven't heard that name in years." She looked to Tom. "Wait, you were involved in that case when you were with the FBI?"

Nodding, Baldwin said, "I was in Baltimore when Miraj al-Diladi was shot. I was a junior agent, one of hundreds working the case all over the country. It'd been going on for years before I even got there." Feeling anger beginning to boil in his gut, he rose from his chair and began to pace the office's narrow width.

"Dennis," Skouris said, "all this time, it was a CIA freelancer?"

Shaking his head as though unwilling to believe what he was saying, Ryland answered, "The whole Wraith persona was a smoke screen put out by the Agency, to keep everyone else busy and throw them off the scent of it being one of their own people. They leaked information to the media to fuel the fire, and even left bogus evidence at some of the scenes to control the situation. Chances are, whatever leads the Bureau was following from case to case, it was thanks to something the CIA fed them."

They played us for chumps, Baldwin groused, and the thought only furthered his mounting irritation.

Still pacing, he shook his head. "At least now we know how she got away. Damn it." He released a frustrated sigh as he recalled the events of that day. "The Bureau spent months working with the Behavioral Analysis Unit at Quantico, drawing up a profile. We researched every high-visibility event on U.S. soil, looking for targets that might fall into what we knew about the Wraith's MO, but the only patterns we'd ever established were incomplete, because details changed from victim to victim. He . . . *she . . .* used different methods—sniper rifles, car bombs, all sorts of IEDs, even poison. She killed a Middle Eastern arms dealer with a black mamba she tossed into his Jacuzzi while he was in it."

"I read about that one," Jarvis said. "Very stylish."

Baldwin grunted. "Yeah. Anyway, al-Diladi's visit to Baltimore was determined to be a high-percentage target." He and the senior agents who had invested far more time and sweat had come closer than they knew, and he still felt a degree of guilt with regard to his role in the failure to capture her.

Sounds familiar, doesn't it?

"Remember," Ryland said, "pretty much every assignment they gave Callahan was illegal. You can bet that, somewhere in a drawer at Langley, is a file with copies of all the paperwork necessary to exonerate them and her. As for the assassinations she carried out, you could maybe argue that everyone she killed deserved it, but that's not our concern. The fact that she's a 4400 puts her in our wheelhouse."

"Has she demonstrated an ability yet?" Skouris asked.

Shaking his head, Ryland replied, "Not so far as we know, but that's just one more thing to worry about. The idea of a trained assassin with a 4400 ability has a lot of folks running scared. They want us to find her, fast, and they're willing to provide whatever resources and support we need."

"Of course they will," Jarvis countered, shaking her head. "If this ever gets out, heads will roll, no matter what sort of Get Out of Jail Free cards the Agency has in its pocket. And that doesn't even take into consideration terrorist organizations or other governments who might be pissed that we put hits on their leaders."

Ryland leaned forward, resting his clasped hands atop his desk. "Give the lady a cigar."

"What about Morehouse?" Skouris asked. "Obviously they're saying he wasn't an authorized target. So what's their story? Has she gone rogue?"

"That's the current theory," Ryland replied. "They tried to make contact with her after she was released from quarantine, but their efforts were unsuccessful."

Baldwin and Skouris exchanged looks. "Yeah, we saw." He recalled the steps taken in the days following the incident at the bank. Alerts had been posted, warning other returnees that they might be targeted by persons or parties unknown, and to be watchful. Attempts to contact "Alicia Colbern" in the hopes of learning more about what she encountered were unsuccessful, and as the case turned cold it eventually was put in the inactive queue as Baldwin and Skouris's attention was drawn to some of the higher-profile cases involving other returnees.

Yeah, like saving humanity from the great future catastrophe, and so on.

"So, what do they want us to do?" he asked.

"Callahan's dropped off the grid," Ryland said. "The address she gave for where she was planning to settle after she left quarantine was a dead end, and she's never reported to an NTAC office for weekly check-ins."

Skouris said, "After we logged the incident at the bank, the southeast regional office picked up the ball and tried to track her down based on the address she gave us. I don't remember the details, but we did get a report saying they never found her." Shrugging, she added, "After that, well you know what it's been like. We've had our hands full with the 4400s in this part of the country."

"What's the CIA's take on this?" Jarvis asked. "What do they think she's up to?"

Ryland replied, "Current thinking is that she's tying up loose ends from her former life, wanting to disappear and retire." He shrugged. "If what I was told about the money she was paid is true, she'd have a pretty nice life on a beach somewhere. Anyway, the Agency is keeping the lead on this, of course, but now you know why they want you, Tom. In addition to you and Diana being our foremost investigators on the 4400, you're also one of the few assets still on active duty with an in-depth knowledge of the Wraith case file."

"In-depth?" Baldwin repeated. "Dennis, it's been twelve years since I even looked at that stuff, and the evidence we collected wasn't exactly earth-shattering, and now you're saying at least some of that was crap fed to us by the Agency."

"The Bureau's already sending everything they've got," Ryland replied, "and it's being run through the Agency to filter out anything generated by whatever false leads were followed. You'll have it by the end of the day. Most of the profile information created by the BAU is still valid, and we'll have access to their people, as well. The CIA will also make available their own information on Callahan, though I'd count on a lot of the usual interagency stick-fighting before we start to see anything useful." He paused, reaching up to stroke his chin as he regarded Baldwin through the screen. "What do you say, Tom? A chance to catch the one that got away?"

Despite his mood, Baldwin could not help the small, humorless chuckle that escaped his lips. Of the cases he had worked during his time with the FBI, "the Wraith" was the lone unsolved mystery. Still, there was something about this new wrinkle that troubled him, something he could not bring into focus. The CIA's apparent readiness to work so openly with another organization was odd enough, of course, but then there was Ryland's seeming willingness to subordinate NTAC to them. Was something more going on here than met the eye?

There always is, he reminded himself, *and it's way over your head. Dennis knows what he's doing. Just do your own job.*

Turning to Skouris, he asked, "You in?"

She answered without hesitation. "Absolutely."

Nodding with new conviction, Baldwin looked first to Jarvis and then to Ryland. "Okay, then. Let's go." Then, as he and Diana moved toward the door, he held up a hand. "But first, I get my coffee."

FOURTEEN

SEATTLE, WASHINGTON

"WHEN YOU SIGH loud enough that I can hear you in here, I think that means you can use a break."

Alana Mareva's gently maternal tone made Baldwin smile, even as he removed his reading glasses and closed his eyes, reaching up to rub the bridge of his nose. He could feel the headache coming on but just the sound of Alana's voice was enough to chase away the discomfort, even if only for a short while.

Hunched over his dining room table, he sighed as he regarded the disheveled mess arrayed before him. FBI and CIA case files, some of them dating back nearly twenty years, littered the tabletop. Reports detailing scenes of the Wraith's numerous alleged victims sat alongside psychological profiles supplied by the FBI's Behavioral Analysis Unit—only some of which had proven to be off the mark by varying degrees. He recognized his own handwriting in some of the files, but none of it offered anything he did not already know about Lona Callahan or her media-supplied moniker. Indeed, Baldwin decided as he leaned back in his chair and ran one hand through his hair, he was certain that the disorganized papers might even be mocking his efforts to glean any helpful information from them. His tired mind offered taunting imagery of the files conspiring with one another to continue hiding any useful data from him—like some twisted game of Keep Away—so long as he insisted on sifting through them and disturbing the slumber they likely had enjoyed for more than a decade.

Okay, he commanded himself. *Definitely break time.*

"How about something to eat?" Alana said from behind him, at the same time he heard her making her way from the kitchen.

Raising his arms over his head and interlocking his fingers, he stretched the muscles in his back, emitting a groan of satisfaction around which he fashioned a reply. "Sounds great. How about one of your famous meat loaf san—"

The words died in his throat as Alana stepped into his line of sight, long dark hair framing her elegant features and highlighting her ever-present knowing smile as she stepped up to the table and set down a steaming mug of coffee and a small plate containing a sandwich, cut in half.

"Why do I even bother asking?" Baldwin tilted his head to greet her with a kiss before she took a seat in the chair to his right. Reaching for the sandwich, he peeked under one slice of bread and laughed. "Damn, it *is* meat loaf."

Alana replied, "With lettuce, two thin slices of tomato,

and not too much mayonnaise." With a teasing smile, she added, "After eight years, I think I know by now how you like them."

Baldwin could not help the small chuckle that escaped his lips as he took a bite of the sandwich. In moments such as these, he seemed almost surprised by his own ability to rationalize and accept what his life had become since the return of the 4400, particularly in regard to the woman who now reached over to stroke his cheek. Sure, she would know how he liked his sandwiches. She knew a damned sight more about him than that, thanks to the unique nature of their relationship.

Herself a 4400, Alana had been given the extraordinary ability to construct a complete "virtual reality" within her own mind. More than a daydream or fantasy, this imaginary existence could be tailored to her most stringent specification and in accordance with her most far-flung desire. She could create or re-create surroundings and events, conjure people from true existence or the depths of her imagination. Further, with a simple touch she was able to bring another person's consciousness into the virtual world she had created, manipulating every aspect of that person's physical and emotional reactions. The illusion could be so convincing that while under her influence, a person might become lost within this new life to the point of losing their mental grip on actual reality, accumulating years' worth of manufactured memories and experiences that did not truly exist apart from Alana's projected reality.

Tom Baldwin had spent eight years there.

In reality it had only been a handful of minutes, during which Alana immersed Baldwin into a life of utter happiness. She had created a world in which there never were 4,400 people abducted from different points in time and returned to Seattle in 2004. As a consequence, his son, Kyle, never lapsed into a three-year coma but instead was accepted to medical school. Baldwin's reputation with NTAC was of a scope approaching heroic proportions. Topping it all, he found himself married to a beautiful woman he was convinced he had never met—Alana herself. As time passed within this imaginary world, Kyle would realize his dreams of a career in medicine, and Baldwin himself would fall completely in love with Alana.

Eventually, Baldwin was able to figure out that it was all an illusion created by her, and return them both to the real world. As Alana explained it, her connection to him was as designed by the people responsible for creating the 4400. She had been sent to provide him support, her abilities offering sanctuary; a temporary respite from the stresses of trials and obstacles he would face as the reasons for the 4400's presence here became clear, along with the truth behind the fight they were to wage.

Was Alana Mareva his destiny? His reward for future challenges he had no means of foreseeing? Did she represent nothing more than further manipulation of the past by those from the future? If all of that was true, Baldwin did not especially care. The reality of what he felt for her lay in these small moments of just-right sandwiches and smiles hinting at how much she knew about him, inside and out. For these and so many other reasons, Baldwin was secure in his decision to pursue a relationship with Alana here and now, despite the initial confusion and skepticism of those around him.

"You've got that thousand-yard stare going," Alana said after a moment, breaking through his reverie. "You're not trying to create your own make-believe world, are you?"

It was only then that Baldwin realized he had just swallowed the last bite of the sandwich in his hand, and he looked down to see that the other half remained on the otherwise empty plate before him. "Guess I was hungrier than I thought," he said. "Thanks."

"My pleasure," she replied, every word she spoke possessing an almost lyrical quality owing to her Tahitian accent. Swiping his coffee mug for a quick sip, she turned her attention to the files littering the dining table. "Making any progress on this?"

"Not really," Baldwin said, shaking his head as some of his frustration returned. "I can't really talk too much about it."

Alana shrugged. "I'm not asking for details, Thomas. I was speaking to the process of your investigation, not the content."

Snorting, Baldwin replied, "That's just it. The content is the biggest stumbling block." He paused, taking a drink from his coffee. "When Ryland told me I'd have access to every bit of information, I figured there'd be boxes of papers to sort through and there'd be no way I'd get through it in a week." He gestured toward the paperwork before him. "Instead, I get this, most of which I read twelve years ago." Picking up one of the folders he had been reading earlier, he held it up for her to see. "Hell, I *wrote* some if it twelve years ago."

Alana frowned. "So, none of it's of any use to you?"

"Nothing I don't already know," he replied, dropping the file back onto the table. He reached up to rub his face. "Well, nothing that I'm not remembering once I read it again." At the moment, it was as much about reminding himself what the files no longer contained. Before being transferred to NTAC, all of the FBI files had been reviewed by someone from the CIA, assisting Bureau record keepers to eliminate information stemming from fabricated evidence, false leads, and other such distractions perpetrated by the Agency in its bid to keep secret Lona Callahan's true identity. The downside was that Baldwin remembered as much of the FBI reports created from that falsified data as he did the few pieces of actual, relevant evidence, and trying to filter it out as he refreshed his memory was proving more difficult than he had anticipated. As for the files from the CIA itself, they were little more than official dossiers and after-action reports, all brief and terse, with little to assist Baldwin in further understanding the fugitive he sought, though NTAC had been promised additional information as it was cleared by Agency officials.

Yeah. This is me, holding my breath.

"I see," Alana said after a moment. "At least, I think I see."

Baldwin blew out his breath between pursed lips, leaning back in his chair and once more stretching tired muscles. "It probably doesn't help that I haven't really thought about this case in I don't know how long. I know some agents can't let old jobs go, but this was one of my first cases, and when it went cold I was transferred to other assignments." He shrugged. "I know it's an open case, but the truth is I never thought it would be solved, and I damned sure didn't think I'd be the one trying to solve it. Not after all this time."

"That may have been true once," Alana said, "but I can see the fire in your eyes."

Baldwin nodded, taking another drink from the coffee mug. "It's like one of those old spy movies, where the hero gets sent on this special mission and he thinks he's doing the right thing, then he finds that they sent him to kill one of his own guys." He reached again for one of the files, spinning it on the table beneath his finger. "We've just been told that hundreds of us were kept from doing our jobs by people we thought were working with us, not against us. The only reason we're involved now and still not getting fed a CIA smoke screen is that Callahan's a 4400. That puts NTAC in charge, and me under the gun to find her. I want to get her this time, and put the case to bed for good." He rubbed his temples. "I just hope I can do it before I drive myself blind from the paperwork."

Reaching across the table, Alana took his hand in hers. "You need a break, Thomas." She squeezed his hand. "I can help with that, if you let me, even if it's just for a short while."

They had talked about experimenting with Alana's abilities, but never had actually explored doing so since that fateful first encounter. Baldwin had wondered just how far she could immerse them in their shared world before his rational mind lost all connection to reality. How long could it last? In theory, she could take his hand for just a few moments and provide him the restorative mental rest of a week's stay at a tropical resort. She might whisk them both to medieval Scotland, or even a space station with a wondrous view of Saturn's rings. His mind reeled at the possibilities.

"Tempting," he said. "Very tempting." He looked into her eyes, mulling over what fantasy they might try first, until he heard the telltale sound of the back door opening and slamming shut, followed by familiar footsteps crossing the kitchen. "Maybe later."

Alana regarded him with a wistful smile as she leaned closer to whisper. "I'll hold you to that."

Any response Baldwin might offer faded as he looked up to see his son emerging from the kitchen. "Hey, Kyle."

Entering the dining room, Kyle Baldwin peeled himself out of his gray hooded sweatshirt. "Hey, guys," he said, offering a mild, almost lifeless wave. Baldwin was struck yet again at how his son had grown into a healthy young man of twenty-one, something he feared would never happen during the three agonizing years Kyle spent comatose in a hospital bed. Of all the miracles that had accompanied the return of the 4400, Baldwin was most thankful for Kyle's revival, which came thanks to Shawn Farrell, a returnee and Baldwin's own nephew. Shawn had returned possessing incredible powers of healing, and used them to free Kyle from the grip of his coma. Given a second chance to right some of the mistakes he had made when Kyle was younger, Baldwin had rededicated himself to maintaining a connected and honest relationship with the son he feared lost forever.

For a moment, Kyle stood there looking at the two of them as though he knew he should say something but just could not come up with the words. Baldwin offered a smile and a way out of the situation. "How was the movie?" When Kyle's unreadable expression did not change in response to the question, Baldwin wondered whether he had actually paid attention when Kyle left the house earlier in the evening. "You did say you were going to a movie, right?"

Kyle nodded, clearing his throat. "Yeah. I did, but I didn't."

Laughing at that, Baldwin asked, "Help your old man out, will you? You did, or you didn't?"

"No, sorry," Kyle said. "I did say I was going, but I ended up not going." He shrugged as he moved to drape his sweatshirt over the back of one of the dining chairs. "I ended up driving around instead."

Alana started to rise from her seat. "Are you hungry? I can fix something."

"No," Kyle replied, rather sharply, then looked as surprised by his own outburst as Baldwin felt. "I mean, no, thank you, Alana. Don't go to the trouble. I'm really not hungry."

Baldwin frowned, paternal instinct rearing its head. "You okay, Kyle? Something on your mind?"

"Dad, it's—" Kyle started to answer, then shook his

head. "I'm fine, really." Stepping away from the table, he grabbed his sweatshirt and headed toward the living room. "I didn't mean to interrupt you guys. I'm sorry."

"You're not an interruption, Kyle," Baldwin said, calling out as he heard his son heading upstairs. "Kyle?"

"Thomas," Alana said, putting her hand on his arm, "maybe he just needs a little space tonight. It's okay."

"Space? Space from what?" Baldwin scowled as she looked upward and shrugged in a self-deprecating manner. "From *you*?"

She nodded. "Well, you said it was hard enough for you to fully accept. Imagine what it must be like for him to adjust to the new woman in his father's life."

"You're hardly new," Baldwin said automatically, before catching himself. Holding up a hand, he added, "Okay, point taken, but I thought the two of you were hitting it off, and I know from . . . from our time together how much you love and support him. He'll come around, sooner or later."

Alana smiled, patting his hand. "He might come around sooner if his father helps him out a bit." She nodded toward the table. "Maybe you could set this aside for tonight and go spend some time with your son. I'll clean up here and be upstairs in a little while."

"Thanks," he said, leaning in again for a soft kiss. Her hair brushed against his cheek as he pressed his lips to hers, feeling her warmth.

Pulling away, she rose from her chair and nodded toward his plate. "And be a good dad. Take him something to eat."

Baldwin snatched the remaining half of his sandwich, shoving nearly a third of it into his mouth. "Hey, the kid said he wasn't hungry," he countered, smiling around the wad of meat loaf and bread.

Bounding up the stairs, he saw the door to Kyle's room shut with no light showing from beneath it. He frowned, wondering if the inroads he had made with his son in recent months might again be starting to slip away. With that in mind, he rapped softly on the door, then opened it. Light from the hallway split the room and illuminated Kyle as he lay on his bed, his back to the door.

He can't be asleep already.

Baldwin entered the room, making his way to the edge of the bed. "Kyle?" He reached out to place his hand on his son's shoulder, and in that instant his son spun around, a startled look on his face.

"Whoa!" Baldwin said, jerking back his hand.

"What?" Kyle's expression shifted from surprise to frustration as he gripped a pair of white wires lying along his chest and pulled the speaker buds from his ears.

"Sorry," Baldwin said, trying to force a smile. "You scared the crap out of me, too. We're even, okay?"

"Okay, I'm sorry, too," Kyle said, catching his breath. "What's up?"

Baldwin shrugged. "I just wanted to check in, see how you're doing."

"Thanks, Dad," Kyle replied. "I'm just tired, is all."

Taking a seat on the edge of the bed as Kyle swung his legs to one side to make room, Baldwin said, "Look, I'm also sorry about all the late nights. Things are pretty crazy at work right now."

"I figured," Kyle said, his fingers playing with the wires

connecting the earbuds to his portable music player. "Jordan Collier, right?" He lowered his gaze to look at the floor. "You any closer to finding who did it?"

Baldwin released a tired snort. "Truthfully, no, but something's going to break soon. No one wants this thing to go cold. It's just a matter of finding the right lead or talking to the right person." If experience had taught him anything it was that one lucky break, one seemingly innocuous clue, might be all he needed to break the whole thing wide open.

"Yeah," Kyle said, his voice almost a mumble.

Sensing that his son was keeping something to himself, Baldwin said, "Don't think for a minute that I'm not here for you if something's bugging you, okay? You know you're my first priority, Kyle. You always have been, even if I did a lousy job of showing it a lot of the time."

Kyle nodded. "I know, Dad. I know," he said, still not looking up.

"Want to try that once more with some feeling?" Baldwin asked, smiling and hoping a lighter tone might break through the tension he still felt between them. Patting Kyle's leg, he said, "Seriously, if there's something you want to talk about, hit me with it."

Kyle looked up, shaking his head. "I'm just tired, Dad. Honest."

Take the hint, Dad.

"Gotcha," Baldwin said, rising from the bed. "If I miss you tomorrow, remember that Alana's here. I know everything with her is pretty damned strange, but trust me when I say she loves you, okay?"

Kyle smiled in a way that Baldwin could sense was a little forced. "I know. It's just taking a bit of getting used to, you know? You have to admit the whole thing's kinda weird."

"Welcome to my world," Baldwin said as he stepped to the door. "Weird is pretty much my whole job these days." Now back in the hallway, he was about to pull the door shut behind him when he heard his son call out one more time.

"Dad?"

"Yeah?"

"Seriously," Kyle said. "Thanks. I do trust you, you know."

Baldwin turned to look in the room, a sliver of light from the hall illuminating his son's face. "I know," he said. "Get some sleep."

"Good night, Dad."

Baldwin pulled the door closed, feeling secure with the knowledge that Kyle did trust him and would come to him with whatever problems he might be experiencing. Baldwin only hoped for his own sake that it would be sooner rather than later.

Whoever said parenting only gets easier over time, he thought as he walked back to the stairs, *was never a parent.*

FIFTEEN

"Hey, check it out! Looks like it's finally going down."

Diana Skouris started at the sound of Marco Pacella's voice echoing across the dimly lit Theory Room, causing her to look up from the notes she was taking during their conversation about Lona Callahan. "What?" she asked, irritated by the interruption. It was barely after ten in the morning, and already she felt exhausted. The late night spent studying Callahan's less than helpful CIA files had not added to her good cheer, and the last thing she needed was Marco going after whichever half-dozen things might attract his attention at any given moment.

You *called* us *down here, remember?*

Pulling away from the conference table situated at the center of the room, Marco now was focusing on the over-sized projection screen dominating the far wall. Displayed upon the screen was an image of a young woman, smartly dressed in a blue jacket and matching skirt and with her blond hair pulled back from her face in a ponytail. She was talking into a handheld microphone, though Skouris could not hear what she might be saying.

"Turn it up," Marco said.

Skouris frowned as she looked about the cluttered table, the top of which was hidden beneath a layer of file folders, computer disks and printouts, empty coffee cups, and a half-consumed box of doughnuts, but she saw no remote control or other device to adjust the volume on the screen. "How do you find anything in here?" she asked. The table and its detritus fit right in with the rest of the Theory Room. Located on the basement level of the NTAC headquarters building, the office was an amalgam of transparent marker boards bearing scrawled and all but illegible computations she had no hope of understanding, computer workstations connected by four times the wiring than looked necessary for the job, and racks of metal shelves crammed full with surplus electronic equipment and numerous other items Skouris did not recognize.

"Hello, volume please?" Marco said, turning back to the table and shuffling aside files and other debris until he located a compact remote control unit beneath the box of doughnuts and thumbed one of its buttons. In response, the voice of the woman on the screen promptly blared through the suite of recessed speakers installed around the room.

"—hind me is the rural cabin outside Golden, Colorado, where law enforcement officers and agents from the National Threat Assessment Command have focused their efforts and attention for six days. However, this morning, it appears that their standoff with 4400 returnee Eric Wheaton might be nearing an end."

Good Lord, Skouris thought, wincing as she realized what this was about. *How the hell did I forget about this?*

"What are we watching?" she asked.

"A network affiliate from Denver," Marco replied. "It's the raw feed direct from the scene, not the broadcast signal. We'll see everything they're sending to the station."

On the screen, the journalist said, "NTAC agents had been searching for Wheaton for the past several months. A returnee from 1982, Wheaton disappeared shortly after being released from quarantine, and failed to report for his regular scheduled medical screenings with the regional NTAC office once he settled here in Golden. However, when Homeland Security agents began linking Wheaton to a series of terrorist threats against government facilities— including the delivery of a crude improvised explosive device to the Federal Reserve Bank in Kansas City—NTAC took a definite interest in assisting with his apprehension."

The reporter was walking now, and a whitewashed log-style cabin with a corrugated metal roof was coming into focus several dozen yards behind her, well beyond a cordon of yellow caution tape. Skouris shook her head, part of her feeling sorry for Wheaton. She did not begrudge him his choice of reclusive lifestyle; she knew that a number of the 4400 had found acclimation to their new world a challenge and had taken similar routes of retreat. His later actions, however, served to deflect any sympathy she might hold for him.

She heard the door open behind her and turned to see Tom Baldwin entering the room, a cup of coffee in each hand, having ended his brief respite from Marco's rapid-fire litany of theories and questions about Lona Callahan and how she might fit into the ever-growing web of mystery surrounding the 4400. Walking around the table, he offered one of the cups to Skouris as he nodded toward the screen.

"Wheaton?" he asked.

Marco looked over his shoulder. "Yeah. Looks like he's finally giving up." Noting the fresh coffee both Baldwin and Skouris were drinking, he added, "I'm good, but thanks for asking."

Ignoring the jab, Baldwin asked, "Surrendering without a fight? Not what I'd expect from him, but I'll take it."

Skouris nodded in agreement, also hoping for an uneventful conclusion to these events, which even now were being carried on the airwaves and Internet streams to uncounted viewers across the country and around the world. "Who's on-site from the Denver office?"

"I thought I saw Garcia and Gapczynski," Marco replied, waving toward the screen, "but they've probably got half the regional office there by now."

"We have confirmed that NTAC agents entered Wheaton's cabin just before sunrise this morning," said the reporter on the screen, "after the latest round of negotiations that lasted more than nine hours. From what I've been told by NTAC spokespeople on-site, we might see them come out with suspected 4400 terrorist Eric Wheaton in federal custody."

Shaking her head, Skouris said, "'Suspected 4400 terrorist.' That's perfect. Just the kind of thing we need to make sure the public stops trusting any returnee."

"Assuming the public ever really trusted any of them in the first place," Marco said, sighing as he ran a hand through his unkempt dark brown hair. "Besides, it's local TV news. They're just filling the air and hoping people don't flip to CNN or the Playboy Channel." He reached up to adjust his thick, black-rimmed glasses, which Diana thought should have made him appear as the quintessential nerd but instead lent him an air of intelligence tempered with a vulnerability she somehow found comforting.

Just don't tell him that, she chided herself.

From behind her, Skouris heard a muffled snicker, and looked over her shoulder in time to see Brady Wingate, one of Marco's Theory Room team members, lean away from the computer workstation on his desk and tap his companion, P.J., on the shoulder.

"No channel surfing here," she heard Wingate say in hushed tones. "She does it for me."

"It's the blazer," P.J. replied. "You're all about women who look like they're in charge."

Both men were regular denizens of this overcluttered hovel, each perpetrating the time-tested cliché of the classic science geek: glasses, horrendous fashion sense, and high-pitched, nasally voices. Wingate's shock of brown hair likely had not interacted with a comb in months, whereas P.J. was bald save for a ring of close-shaved stubble around the sides and back of his head. Had she not known P.J. to be married, Skouris would have bet a year's salary that neither agent had left this room since the beginning of the current presidential administration. When they nodded to each other before turning to stare at her, Skouris realized that her chosen attire for the day was not all that dissimilar from that of the journalist on the TV.

"I'll bet she's not carrying a gun," she said, smiling as both men responded by taking a profound new interest in whatever lay before them on their desks.

"Here we go," Marco said, pointing to the screen.

Skouris returned her attention to the TV, on which she saw the cabin's weathered front door swing open. "There's Garcia and Gapczynski," she said as two female agents, each dressed in jeans and a dark blue Windbreaker bearing the NTAC seal over the left breast came out of the cabin. Following after them was a pair of burly police officers— sheriff's deputies from the color and cut of their uniform, Skouris surmised—escorting a handcuffed man.

"And you can see Eric Wheaton being escorted out of the cabin now by local law enforcement officers," the journalist said, stepping out of the frame in order to provide an unobstructed view of the proceedings. Wheaton was dressed in dirty khaki trousers and a worn red flannel shirt, his chin darkened by several days' beard growth while his dirty black and gray hair dangled in strings before his expressionless face. Another officer exited the cabin behind him, reaching out to grasp the bedraggled returnee by his other arm. The local reporter's photographer kept his camera on the three of them as they stepped off the cabin's porch and began making their way toward a line of police vehicles parked a few dozen yards ahead of them.

"Wow," Marco said, speaking over the journalist's ongoing commentary. "They let the locals make the arrest. Someone must have called in a favor."

Skouris sighed as she watched Wheaton march toward the waiting SUVs. "He looks more like a drowned rat than a real threat. He's not making any trouble."

"I can live with that," Baldwin said, draining the last of his coffee. "Considering what he's supposed to have done, this could've gone a lot worse. Score another one for the good guys." Nodding toward the screen, he asked, "The real question now is, how many more Eric Wheatons are out there, out of step and pissed off that the world's passed them by?"

"Hopefully we'll find out when the Denver NTAC questions him," Skouris replied. She was about to turn from the TV and reach for her portfolio on the table when, on the screen, Wheaton stopped in his tracks. The local news camera had zoomed in on the man's face, and his expression had changed from apparent resignation to shock.

"What the hell . . . ?" Baldwin started to ask, but the words seemed to die in his throat as Skouris watched Wheaton's head cock to one side before sliding free from the rest of his body. A geyser of blood spouted from his neck, dousing the deputies supporting his now-slack form. The picture jerked and lost focus, the photographer obviously stumbling as he pulled back the camera's view of Wheaton's limp body. Then the frame shifted to track his decapitated head, which rolled down the hill until it stopped at the feet of the heretofore staid and composed news reporter, who promptly vomited.

"Hoooly . . . shit," Brady called out, his voice rising an octave.

"That's gonna leave a mark," added P.J.

His fingers scrambling over the keys on the remote control he still held, Marco shouted, "Tell me the DVR's working." He stabbed at button after button. "*Tell* me the DVR's *working*!"

"It's working, it's working," P.J. replied, his own voice heightened by surprise and unexpected anxiety as he worked his computer keyboard. "You've got the wrong remote. Just give me a second! Sheesh."

Skouris watched the image on the screen reverse and accelerate, resetting the picture to those last few moments before Wheaton's grisly end. P.J. tapped another few keys, and the scene began once more to play forward in normal fashion.

"What just happened?" she asked, feeling her heart pounding in her chest.

"Damn if I know," Marco replied, coming around the table and moving toward the TV. "P.J., slow it down," he said, before looking to Skouris and Baldwin. "I don't know how clear this will be." He stepped close enough to the screen that he now was bathed in the colors of the overhead projector, seeming almost to blend in with the image before him. "Hold it right there!" As the screen froze, he pointed to the image of Wheaton, his finger lingering near the pasty white skin of the ill-fated man's neck. "Right there. You see it?"

"Right where?" Baldwin asked, and Skouris could hear the confusion in his voice. "What are we looking at, Marco?"

Tapping the screen with his forefinger, Marco replied, "The slice." He looked around the conference table, grunting as he failed to locate whatever it was he sought, before nodding in satisfaction as Wingate offered him a different remote control. His thumb sliding over its keypad, Marco used it to cycle the halted image back and forth between two frames of footage. Skouris could see the first frame depicting Wheaton's unsullied neck, while in the second frame a thin, dark line appeared along the exposed skin just beneath his jawline.

"What is it?" she asked.

Marco shook his head. "I have no idea."

From behind them, P.J. called out, "Get out of the way. You're making it all blurry."

"That's not me," Marco snapped as he stepped out of the picture and pointed to a hazy area just behind Wheaton's head. "See? It's a glitch in the recording or something." He waved his hands in capitulation. "This isn't Hollywood-grade equipment, you know. Government-issue, courtesy of the lowest bidder and all that."

A glitch? It took Skouris a moment to realize why that phrasing seemed important. "Tom," she said, "remember last year, after the 4400 were released from quarantine? Lona Callahan and those CIA agents near the bank?"

Baldwin nodded, frowning. "Yeah?" Then his eyes widened as realization dawned. "Oh, wait a minute." He looked back at the screen, waving a finger at it as though it had just given up some harbored secret. Turning back to Skouris, he asked, "Are you thinking what I'm thinking?"

Shrugging, Skouris said, "Well, Callahan is a 4400. Maybe what we've got here is some hint as to whatever ability she may have developed." Invisibility? Super speed? Either of those traits, as ridiculous as they may have sounded a year ago, were but the first guesses as she and Baldwin considered a possible new wrinkle in their case.

Behind them, Marco asked, "Wait, you think Callahan killed Wheaton?" He returned his gaze to the frozen picture of Eric Wheaton in apparent mid-decapitation. "Wow. Gotta give her style points."

Skouris nodded in reluctant agreement as she regarded the disturbing image. If this was assassination, it was not a sanitary act by any means, such as those Lona Callahan allegedly had carried out with sniper rifles or furtive poisons. Any of those at least would have allowed the killer some distance from her target. Instead, this was wet work of the old-school variety, the kind of sanction that got an assailant bloodied and afforded that moment of cold clarity found only by staring into a victim's eyes just before the deed was done.

Cold, Skouris mused, swallowing the lump that had formed in her throat.

"Marco," Baldwin said, breaking her reverie, "can you scrub that video? Maybe slow it down even more?"

"I'll need all the footage from every source on the scene," Marco replied, stepping back to the table. "If I can get that, I should be able to create a multi-angle model and show you anything and anyone in the picture. Maybe by tomorrow morning?"

"Get on it," Baldwin said, "and get with Galanter while you're at it. He's got some other footage you can compare it to."

Marco nodded. "Now I remember. Okay, we'll get it going."

"Thanks," Baldwin said, and Skouris watched as he retrieved his portfolio from the conference table before heading for the door. "Come on, Diana, we've got some calls to make."

"Denver?" she asked, falling in step behind him.

"Denver," Baldwin replied. "I want to talk to the on-site agents. Maybe they saw or heard something." He shook his head. "Hell, I don't know."

"Do you really think this might be Callahan?" Skouris asked as they left the Theory Room, with Baldwin leading the way toward the elevator.

Her partner shrugged. "Only one way to find out."

NEAR GOLDEN, COLORADO

As the crisp mountain air played along the beads of sweat spotting her brow, Lona Callahan huddled in a sitting fetal position, gulping water from a transparent plastic bottle and embracing the seductive and fulfilling rush of accomplishment surging through her.

It was just as she remembered, and it engulfed her with the same intensity as she had longed for it to do—maybe even prayed for it to do. The sensation was every bit as euphoric, as consuming, as beyond any other experience to her as it had been the first time it occurred, after she had killed Frederick Morehouse. With this newest taste, Lona knew she could never resist the summons reaching out for her, confident that she always would be rewarded in this manner by whoever or whatever it was that continued to impel her.

Her escape from the area had been effortless, thanks to the weeks spent exploring the remarkable gift she now possessed, this seeming ability to slip free from the constraints of time itself. After much practice, Lona now could move and act in a manner that left her all but unseen to the naked eye, at least for short periods. By focusing her mind on the task, she could stroll through crowds and encounter no interference from people; to them, she simply was not there. She was able to act upon them as well, lifting a wallet as quickly as stealing a kiss, standing before them to stare right into their eyes without their knowledge, or—as she had just done—delivering a fatal blow in front of uncounted witnesses without any of them seeing her, then vanishing back into the ether from whence she had come.

Though she still did not comprehend how she conjured this power, it had not taken long for Lona to realize the physical toll such effort exacted on her. Returning to "normal" time always brought with it an all-but-insatiable thirst, her lungs burning and her heart racing as her metabolism fought to recalibrate itself. Despite this, she had begun to notice her stamina increasing as she continued to practice refining her control over the time-shift. Soon, Lona was certain that she would command greater endurance over her ability just as she enjoyed an overall fitness level improved by her regular exercise regimen.

Soon, but not just yet.

Draining the last drops of water from the bottle she clutched in both hands, Lona still panted from her exertions. Having taken refuge within an abandoned elk hunter's blind more than a mile from Eric Wheaton's cabin and out of sight from anyone at the scene, she dropped the empty bottle into the canvas backpack she had staged here. She retrieved a second, identical container and just as quickly began downing its contents. Then, motivated by the intense hunger she now felt, she reached into the satchel and retrieved an energy snack bar. Barely restraining herself from jamming the entire bar into her mouth, Lona tore away a sizable bite, chewing as she continued to bask in the exhilaration she still felt from what she had just accomplished.

What was fading beyond her ability to retain, however, was the burning intensity of purpose that originally had filled her mind with the image of Eric Wheaton, and that had continued to compel her to the actions she had taken today. Until now, Lona found it difficult to remember when she was not focused on the troubled man to the near exclusion of all else. During her waking hours, Wheaton dominated her thoughts. When she slept, he encroached upon her dreams.

Just as she once had done while preparing to carry out assignments given to her by her former employers, Lona spent considerable time researching Wheaton. With the power of modern-day computers and data retrieval as well as the judicious use of one or two qualified people from Reiko's list of trusted sources, she had tapped public and classified databases to obtain all manner of information about her fellow returnee. His life, his activities, and the crimes he was alleged to have committed all served to define her target.

Tracking him had been far easier, with Lona heeding the force calling out from somewhere in the back of her mind, imploring her to trust it and follow the paths it indicated. How it knew where to find Wheaton remained a mystery, and her attempts to question her unknown benefactors were met with silence and darkness at the edges of her consciousness.

Killing him had been easier still, and in that regard she treated this undertaking just as she had all of her previous targets. Lona had never spent a great deal of time wondering why someone was to be killed, nor had she questioned her employers on the subject. In the past, all the justification she had ever required was transferred to her bank accounts. While she no longer was receiving payment to employ her special skill set, her attitude toward the work remained the same even if those tasking her had changed.

The desire for simple murder was not what drove her. Instinct told her that Wheaton's death would have a purpose, and the manner in which he died must serve as an example to those who would choose to follow him as he pursued his agenda or who might opt to emulate him as they sought their own goals. For her part, Lona felt compelled to demonstrate her newfound physical gifts, almost as a show of appreciation for those who had bestowed upon her such power. After all, it would enable her to dispatch her target with an even greater level of theatricality than she ever had managed to accomplish throughout her previous career.

She looked down at the garrote she had dropped near her feet. This version of the ancient weapon was one of her own making, consisting of a thin strand of high-tensile razor wire, with each end coiled tightly around twin cylinders of wood. It had been a long time since Lona had killed anyone in this manner, having no love for the gruesome mess brought about by such brutal action. With her heightened abilities, however, the act was almost surgical. She had practiced on man-sized dummy targets for days, arrayed in groups and surrounded by motion-detecting booby traps that allowed her to perfect her approach, attack, and escape maneuvers. In short order, she was able to complete practice runs without disturbing the other targets or setting off any of the traps. She was, for all intents and purposes, invisible.

So it had been with Eric Wheaton. At the speed she had been moving, the garrote was as effective as a guillotine, after which she was able to withdraw to a distance of nearly one hundred yards even before the man's severed head touched the ground. Though she had missed seeing the results of her work, Lona knew that in today's sensationalist media-driven culture, video footage of the assassination would be on every news channel and all over the Internet within the hour.

She swallowed the last of her snack bar, sensing her energy level returning—for the moment, at least. Collecting her belongings into the backpack, she slung it over her shoulder before emerging from the blind. A survey of the surrounding trees reassured her that she still was alone and she set off, making her way deeper into the forest.

As she walked, Lona felt a quick stab of regret, not for her actions but for her waning emotional state of bliss. In its place, questions and concerns began to flood her mind. After killing Frederick Morehouse, she knew that other people from her prior life would be stepping up their hunt for her. Given her past history and the flair she often had demonstrated when carrying out other assassinations, it would not take long for one of her former masters to deduce her involvement here.

Likewise, she knew that agents from NTAC, tasked with finding explanations for the 4400, were aware of the capabilities harbored by at least some of the returnees. The nature and extent of such talents in the hands of this enigmatic group was a large part of NTAC's ongoing investigations. It was one of the prime motivations behind the agency's tracking and apprehension of Wheaton in the first place, and it was not unreasonable to assume that they would suspect another 4400 of being complicit in the man's death.

This, of course, raised another question: What might NTAC know about her?

SIXTEEN

LAS VEGAS, NEVADA

"Mornin', Al!"

Alfred Twenter offered a smile and a wave to Shane Bridges as he walked past the middle-aged man's desk in the bank's loan department—this despite his dislike for being called Al. He did not especially enjoy any of the diminutions of his given name that he had received without request from people all his life. Not Fred, Freddie, Alfie—particularly not Alfie, a nickname that his great-aunt Helen had cottoned onto greeting him with when he was a toddler and that had dogged him well into adulthood.

"How's it going, Shane?" Alfred replied, pushing the tortoiseshell frames of his glasses higher up on the bridge of his nose. His question went unanswered, as Shane already had returned his attention to the steaming mug of coffee in his beefy hand and the newspaper lying atop his cluttered desk. Alfred generally assumed the nicknamers in his life were well-meaning. Most of them had been family or classmates or co-workers such as Shane, possibly compensating for his having a name that seemed unnaturally older than his years. Therefore, Alfred interpreted Shane's greeting as a reminder that even at thirty-seven, his appearance remained boyish enough to keep him from fully growing into his name just yet.

His hard-soled wingtip shoes clacking against the marble flooring, Alfred made his way through the spacious lobby of the Federal Commercial Bank of Las Vegas. He walked past the long row of tellers, each separated from the customers by a set of thin, brass bars, and weaved around a succession of well-polished wooden desks. All around him, customers conducted various financial matters with bank employees, their voices hushed yet still echoing slightly within the large, open workplace.

It was the interior of the bank that had charmed him from the moment he first entered its lobby several months earlier, after returning to Las Vegas from Seattle following his prolonged stay there. The bank's traditional décor—"old school," as he had come to learn the current slang for anything society had deemed outdated or passé—made him feel more at home than just about any other location in the city, a sad statement considering he had been born and raised here, long before it exploded into the "Entertainment Capital of the World" sometime during his extended absence. For him, the bank represented a respite from the strange, new world in which he found himself. In his mind, this place was his daily, personal portal back to September 6, 1956, the last day he remembered from his previous life before starting all over again as one of the 4400.

Arriving at his desk, one edge of which hugged a wall near the bank's walk-in vault of safety-deposit boxes, Alfred paused to hang his black fedora on a hook installed on the wall behind his chair. Hat hooks had vanished from the bank over time; taken down, he assumed, as they fell out of fashion. Upon his employment as customer service manager of deposit boxes, he was allowed a few personal modifications to his work area, the first of which was the hook.

"Good morning, Alfred," said Jennifer Martin, the bank manager's young, vivacious secretary—administrative assistant, they were called nowadays—as she walked in his direction on her way to her own desk. Dressed in a cream-colored silk blouse and dark blue skirt that rose higher on her legs than would have been appropriate in Alfred's day, she waved at him as she walked past, eyeing him in approval. "I've gotta say, you sure know how to make that suit work."

Alfred smiled at the compliment, and even felt himself blushing at the younger woman's attention. "Thank you, Jennifer," he replied. While he had chosen to embrace life in this "new" world on many levels, his code for professional dress was one affectation on which he refused to compromise. Looking smart and businesslike never went out of style, he decided, and his appearance seemed to please his customers, particularly the older, conservative types who regularly were steered to him by his superiors.

Among his fellow employees, however, he quickly

learned that his wardrobe had earned him quite a different reputation. His penchant for hats, dark suits, skinny black ties, and crisply starched white shirts lent him an appearance that prompted some of his fellow employees to refer to him behind his back as a "Blues Brother." After searching the Internet and discovering the origin of their assessment, Alfred admittedly agreed with the moniker and played along with the good-natured joke at his expense.

Ah, the Internet, Alfred mused as he dropped into his seat, switching on his desktop computer. Personal computers and the Internet in particular were aspects of life in the twenty-first century that Alfred had embraced with conviction. He was introduced to the wonders of the Internet via acclimation classes provided by NTAC during his time in quarantine, and now relished the conduit of knowledge at his fingertips.

By nature, he was an information gatherer—what folks in his youth used to call a bookworm—and always had immersed himself in reading whatever he could get his hands on. When his 4-F classification blocked him from military service as the United States went to war against Germany and Japan, Alfred worked the night shift at a rubber reclamation center near Las Vegas Army Air Field— later renamed Nellis Air Force Base—keeping his days free to consume every magazine, newspaper, and book that crossed his path. When he returned to the workforce after the war and took a job as an assistant manager of a grocery store, his desire for information was fueled by the store's magazine racks as well as the library down the street.

If it was out there to be learned, Alfred wanted to learn

it. He found himself mesmerized by each new issue of *Popular Science, Popular Mechanics,* and anything else concerning the latest advances in technology. When his mind turned to fanciful applications of such development, he explored the worlds to be found within the pages of pulp science-fiction magazines such as *Amazing Stories, Incredible Tales of Scientific Wonder,* and *Galaxy.* His love for such tales certainly played into his greatest regret about being a 4400: like each of his fellow returnees, Alfred could remember nothing about his time "away," as they called it. He had no idea if he may have spent that time with alien or advanced life forms, as he secretly hoped was the case. Instead, he assumed that one day, the purpose of his abduction would be revealed, and he trusted that the reason would make perfect sense.

His lust for the Internet and what it offered resulted in acquiring a quick affinity for computers, which in turn helped him land his current job. At least, this was what he was told at the time. Later, Alfred learned that his hiring had more to do with his unusual notoriety, and that he was a conversation piece that lent an odd interest to the bank. Alfred was well aware that many of his co-workers, sometimes accompanied by friends or customers, would make obvious detours toward the safety-deposit boxes he managed only to slyly gesture in his direction and whisper among themselves.

Though he usually took such things in stride, there were times when Alfred felt the discomfort of being an object of curiosity for the rest of the world to see. On such occasions, he sought support from other returnees, often finding that solace within the Internet-based message boards and other communities he visited. The time spent with his partners in conversation—he still hesitated to call them "friends," as their presence was anything but physical—brought him a measure of comfort, and reminded him that his experiences in this still-new world were not unique.

Indeed, knowing that he would have time during the usual morning lull before anyone came looking to access their safety-deposit box, Alfred was in the midst of calling up one of his favorite 4400 websites when a voice called out to him.

"Alfred?"

Minimizing the web page on his desktop computer monitor, he looked up to see Matt Dorning, one of the young tellers, approaching his desk and escorting a petite, attractive woman Alfred did not recognize. He caught himself before a look of disapproval crossed his face at the sight of Matt's rumpled state of dress, which consisted of a purple dress shirt and black trousers that each sported matching wrinkles, as though the man had slept in his clothes and then slept through his alarm.

"Hello, Matt," he said, reaching up to adjust his glasses as he rose from his chair and offered a warm smile. "Looks like we have an early bird this morning."

"Uh, yeah," Matt replied, his tone betraying his lack of interest in Alfred's courteous enthusiasm. "She wants to get a safety-deposit box."

"Then I can take it from here," Alfred said, prompting the younger man to return to his duties. When Matt turned and departed with all due haste, Alfred again smiled at the woman while gesturing to a chair alongside his desk. "My name is Alfred Twenter. And you are?"

"Abigail," she replied, leaning forward as she took her seat and affording Alfred an unencumbered view at what he now noticed was the copious amount of cleavage revealed by her tight red dress. He averted his eyes in time to meet hers, hopeful that his sudden interest in her body had gone unnoticed. Her smile suggested it likely had.

"Then, Abigail," he said as he produced an application from one of his desk's side drawers, "let me ask first whether you need a box for your important documents, or perhaps one for larger valuables, such as jewelry."

She paused, apparently thinking over the choices, and Alfred found himself studying her face. He realized that her dark hair, worn in a jagged-banged pageboy style that framed her wide, hazel eyes and her rose-colored lips, reminded him of his favorite photograph of Elizabeth Taylor from a cover of *Movie World* just last year, or, rather, from 1955.

Where does *the time go?* Alfred nearly laughed aloud at his own little joke.

"I'm sorry, Mr. Twenter," Abigail said after a moment, casting her eyes toward her hands, which rested in her lap. "I don't actually need to rent a box." She looked around, as though to ensure she was not being overheard. "I'm here because I wanted to speak with you, personally."

Personally? With me?

Her soft-spoken words piqued his interest, though it also triggered a pang of nervousness as he considered why she might be here. It took physical effort to keep from reaching up to stroke one side of his sandy blond hair, which he had waxed into a modest flattop. Clearing his throat, he said, "I'm all ears. How can I help?"

"I know it's not good to focus on what you hear in the news," Abigail replied, her eyes wide and sincere. "I mean, the press is only looking for the sensational stories, right?"

Alfred shrugged. "Um, sure. I guess," he said, uncertain as to why she had come to him with such concerns, but still curious enough to at least lend a sympathetic ear. "It's what sells these days."

"I can't help watching those reports, the ones they keep showing over and over about that man in Colorado," Abigail said, her hands fidgeting. "That . . . 4400 man."

"Oh." Alfred's voice went flat, as did any interest he held in this faux customer. "So, *that's* why you wanted to talk to me. You could've just come out and said so. I'm more or less used to that type of thing now."

Abigail had the good grace to appear shocked at his reaction. "No, it's not like that. I'm—"

"No, no. Let's just jump right in, shall we?" Alfred countered. Initially discomfited at having been waylaid by her charms, he now allowed that embarrassment to give way to impatience and huffiness. "Shall I just answer the usual questions and get them out of the way? No, I don't have any children who are now older than me. No, I don't remember meeting any bug-eyed space monsters from Planet X. Yes, I know how to use microwave ovens and DVD players and—"

"Stop it!"

Her admonition, hissed through gritted teeth, was sharper than he might have expected from a woman of such small stature, and was more than sufficient to end his frustrated litany. "I said it's not like that." Once more looking around as though to verify that they were alone, she added, "I'm a 4400, too."

"What?" Alfred asked, feeling his brow furrow in confusion along with renewed interest. "You are?" Why had she not simply said so in the first place?

Abigail nodded. "Yes, I'm just like you. The first of December, 1993. That was my last day before whatever it was that happened to us. I wasn't gone for nearly as long as you, but I still feel out of place, just like you."

"Forgive me," Alfred said, clearing his throat and adjusting his glasses. "I haven't encountered any of . . . *us* . . . since leaving quarantine in Seattle. Not in person, anyway." In truth, he had taken steps to avoid coming into contact with other returnees.

"I know, Alfred," Abigail replied, her voice taking on an air of playfulness as she smiled. "You've told me that when we've talked online. I'm ShortStuff93 from the 4400Web room. And when we chat, you're . . ."

"SciFiGuy56," Alfred said, finishing her sentence. He paused, trying to reconcile his mental picture of this fellow 4400 he knew only as a quirky nickname with the woman now sitting before him. The idea that a woman, and a young, attractive one at that, would pursue him from the Internet into his real life raised his excitement as well as his skepticism. Struggling to keep his composure, he hoped he at least appeared polite.

Drawing a deep breath, he weighed what to say next. "ShortStuff . . . I mean, *Abigail* . . . look, it's not that I don't believe you. I do, but, how did you find me? I've never told you who I am or where I live. I never offer that sort of information to anyone."

"Well, I didn't do it by myself," she replied. "That took a little digging with the help of a friend. I wanted to meet you in person, Alfred. Because of our conversations, I happen to think you're a very sweet man. Also, well, I know what you can do."

Hearing this revelation was enough for Alfred to sit bolt upright in his chair. While it was possible that his enthusiasm for companionship and conversation may have caused him to reveal enough fragments of personal information that someone might piece together clues to his actual identity and location, he never—*never*—had discussed with anyone the strange "gift" he seemed to have acquired during his still-unexplained abduction.

While his power was in its earliest form, one Alfred only partially understood and was still learning to control, he discovered NTAC's ongoing research into emerging 4400 abilities. During one of his first medical screenings after relocating to Las Vegas, he had connected to the mind of the NTAC doctor while he suffered through blood tests, blood pressure checks, and other examinations. The contact had revealed to Alfred the nature of the promicin neurotransmitter believed to be active in each returnee, as well as NTAC's concern over how to deal with it. Fearing that he might be subjected to some form of drug or other treatment inhibiting his ability, Alfred had already decided he would forgo his next checkup, currently scheduled for the following month. Since then, he had guarded his secret with utmost care.

"Wh-what I can do? What do you mean by that? What makes you think I can do anything at all?" Pausing, Alfred drew a breath and attempted to regain his composure. "Not all of us have some sort of special power, you know."

Leaning forward in her chair, Abigail lowered her voice. "Maybe not, but *I* have one. I have this way of knowing what we 4400s can do. I'm not sure how I know it or why I know it, but I do, so that lets me help people like us. I like to think of myself as something of a match-maker." She shrugged. "That seems . . . romantic, I guess." Reaching out, she rested her bare arm on Alfred's desk, her palm upturned and open. "Here, let me show you what I mean. Give me your hand."

Alfred looked around to ensure they remained unobserved before resting his hand atop hers, closing his eyes as his fingertips brushed the soft skin of her palm. Almost instantly a jarring rush of vibrant color began filling his mind, and he gasped at the momentary mental hyper-stimulation, just as he always did when physical contact allowed him to peer into the thoughts of another person. His perception of passing time slipped away as he sorted through the blurred bursts of color and guided them to form coherent visual images.

He saw flashes of Abigail's childhood in small-town Michigan, as though he was watching roughly edited Super 8 home movies. Disjointed glimpses of people flashed in his mind, and he recognized them all: her parents, her twin brother, uncles and cousins and pets—all as clear to him as his own memories. Her whole family life—not merely factual information but also her true emotional reactions to those experiences—washed over him, and the more he saw the more Alfred hungered for it to continue.

Just as he always had sated his need to absorb information with hours upon hours of reading, his newfound gift offered instantaneous assimilation of a person's knowledge and experiences—and at a level of satisfaction far higher than anything he might learn through the printed page or even the Internet. Indeed, this need for mental connection with other people had become almost an addiction. Until Abigail, Alfred only had been able to slake this peculiar thirst in all-too-brief moments, such as a casual brush against someone in a restaurant or casino, or a handshake held an extra second or two. Abigail, however, offered her thoughts freely to him.

Then the colors and imagery disappeared.

Abigail pulled her palm from beneath his fingertips and he opened his eyes in surprise, only just realizing that his breathing was labored, as though he had just jogged up several flights of stairs. She was breathing heavier, too, he noticed, as she withdrew her hand and returned it to her lap.

"I want to share myself with you, Alfred," she said. "I really do, but now isn't the time or place." Rising from her seat, she offered him a knowing smile. "We'll have plenty of time for that later."

"Later when?" Alfred asked, jerking to his feet and still

feeling the weight of her thoughts and memories mixing with his own. Whatever she was doing, she was not acting alone. This much he knew from the jumble of thoughts that continued to dance within his own consciousness, but he needed more information. He needed to return to her mind.

"When the time's right," she said. "And don't worry about finding me. I'll find you. It's what I do." Offering a sly wink, she turned on her heel and made her way across the lobby toward the bank's main exit. As the distance between them grew, Alfred sensed the intangible connection between their minds beginning to fade. He tried to grasp the remaining strands of their intense link, which persisted for another moment after she stepped through the front doors. Then it was gone, much to his regret.

Who was this mysterious, alluring woman? Alfred pondered that question, as well as what this strange encounter might mean, to say nothing of what it promised. What was next? When would Abigail choose to reappear in his life?

It could not happen soon enough, Alfred decided.

SEVENTEEN

SEATTLE, WASHINGTON

ALL DIANA SKOURIS wanted was a warm bath and a few moments of blissful silence. She sought nothing less than a soothing environment in which she could let the day's activities and worries melt away and swirl down the drain with the suds and the salts and every other pampering product she could find to pour into her tub.

And wine, she decided. *Yes, wine would be good.*

However, as she navigated the third-floor hallway toward her apartment, Skouris recognized a telltale rhythmic thumping reverberating through her front door, and knew instantly just what was taking place behind it.

So much for quiet time, she thought.

Sliding her key into the door lock, Skouris quietly let herself in. The synthesized drumbeat pulsing through the closed door gave way to a richer spectrum of electronic musical strains as she swung it open. She shook her head at the thought that a team of army rangers could have blown the thing off its hinges and gone equally unnoticed. Quelling her initial instinct to storm the place like the tired and cranky federal agent part of her brain so eagerly wanted to do, Skouris instead smiled, edging herself around the corner of the foyer to get an unobstructed view of her darkened living room and the controlled chaos now erupting within it.

A pair of figures—one taller and one smaller—danced and stomped their feet in unison to hip-hop music while silhouetted in the dizzying bursts of flashing colors and symbols erupting from the television screen. They swung their heads in perfect, synchronous motions, their manes of hair flowing to unseen rhythms as if blown astray by the blaring music itself. Their legs worked like pistons, jamming their stocking feet onto a plastic pad spread across the carpeted floor in front of the television. Rising above it all, their giggles, coming in seemingly endless streams, added a layer of pure joy to the proceedings that Skouris found contagious.

Unwilling to interrupt the moment, she propped herself against the wall, watching her sister, April, and her daughter, Maia, continue their act for several more minutes as the song played out. April's uninhibited dancing—more like flailing—seemed to soften the edginess that had formed around her during her past rough-and-tumble years. Skouris also found herself living vicariously through her younger sister whenever she watched her connect with Maia at a playful and unrestrained level—one that Skouris herself rarely enjoyed with her adopted daughter. At times, she wondered whether that was a reflection of Maia's own preternaturally advanced level of maturity since gaining her 4400 powers of precognition, or evidence that Skouris herself needed to be more encouraging of Maia's outlets for play and whimsy.

Probably a little of both, she decided.

On the television screen, the song reached its crescendo as April and Maia struck exaggerated poses complete with wavering jazz hands. Skouris burst into laughter, applauding as the dancers embraced and collapsed in an exhausted heap onto their plastic dance floor.

"Bravo, ladies! Bravo!" Skouris called out, shouting to be heard over the video game's soundtrack. Her praise at first startled the pair before Maia recognized her adoptive mother's arrival. She scrambled up from the floor in a newfound burst of energy and crossed the floor, wrapping her arms around Skouris's midsection.

"Mommy!" Maia said, propping her chin onto the woman's side and looking up, her face beaming. "When did you get home?"

"Just in time to see the finale of *American Bandstand,* apparently," Skouris replied, rubbing her hands along Maia's back and planting a kiss on the top of her blond head.

Reaching for the remote to mute the television, April bent over and grabbed one corner of the dance mat. She smiled, staring at Skouris and rolling her eyes in mock disgust. "*American Bandstand*?" she repeated. "You've gotta get with the program, big sister."

"Yeah," Maia chimed in. "This is *Dance Dance Revolution*!"

"Wow, my mistake," Skouris said, breaking away from her daughter's embrace but keeping her hands on the girl's shoulders. "But, the revolution is over for tonight, okay? Mommy's had a long day and needs to crash."

"That's okay," Maia said, nodding her head. "Aunt April said we could stay up late and watch a movie, anyway."

Memories of the pair's last late-night movie raced through Skouris's mind, complete with popcorn strewn across the living room floor and repeated reminders to lower the volume. She glanced at April, hoping her sister would correctly interpret her silent plea for a reprieve.

Thankfully, April caught on and offered a surreptitious nod. "How about we back off of that tonight, Maia? All this dancing has kinda worn me out, too."

Maia's momentary expression of disappointment came and went, and she shrugged her shoulders. "Oh, I guess so," she said. "Will you tell me about your day, Mommy?"

Skouris forced herself not to frown as she considered that notion. No, she decided, describing the brutal executions of 4400s by another returnee would not make for a child's bedtime story. Instead, she said, "Well, if I do that, you'll be asleep in no time. I'll be there in a minute to tuck you in. Now, go get ready for bed, okay?"

"Okay," Maia agreed, turning her face up to Skouris as a prompt for a kiss. Once her mother made good on the request, she bolted across the floor for a kiss from April before jogging toward her room.

"And lose the toe socks, Maia," Skouris called after her. "I think you're on day three for those."

"Okay!" the girl's reply echoed from down the hallway.

Tucking the rolled-up dance mat next to the television, April reached up to wipe her brow. "That's a better workout than Pilates. You ought to try it sometime."

"Maybe," Skouris said, crossing toward the foot of the stairs. "It looks like you two are back to normal again. That's nice to see."

April winced, as though wishing Skouris had not broached the topic. She and Maia were fresh off a strain in their newfound bond, after April had attempted to use Maia's clairvoyant abilities in order to win a bet on a sporting event. When the bet failed to pay off, April accused the young girl of deliberately misinforming her of the game's outcome while Maia nursed the hurt of feeling used by her aunt. Skouris, of course, sided with Maia, but nonetheless was pleased that the pair had managed to work out their differences on their own.

"Well, Diana," April said, an edge creeping into her voice, "sometimes young hearts are quicker to forgive and forget. It's a lesson we *all* can learn from, you know?"

Offering a curt nod, Skouris tried to keep her own tone level. "I think I've been more than forgiving lately."

"Yeah, you have," April said, crossing the living room toward the kitchen, "and you've also been really great about reminding me of that as often as you can."

Inside, Skouris felt herself flinch. *Ouch, point taken.*

"All right, that's fair," she said, her sister's remark still poking at her conscience. It was very easy, she knew, for her to fall into the age-old rut of assuming April made nothing but bad choices for herself, rather than trying to see any positive intent behind her sister's actions. "I'm sorry," she said, holding up a hand and shaking her head. "Just chalk it up to me being tired. I'm tired and I'm on edge, and I'll just drop it and go to bed."

April said nothing for a moment, but finally nodded with a tight-lipped smile. "It's cool. This is new for both of us."

"Yeah, it is," Skouris replied. "Honestly, April, thanks for being here for Maia. It means a lot to her, and to me."

"Ah, no biggie," April said, her smile widening. "Being the cool aunt works for me. The cool aunt gets to do the fun stuff that the tight-ass mom never does."

Skouris chuckled, knowing April's jab ultimately was good-natured. "Okay, I deserved that one," she said before heading toward Maia's room, putting aside her fatigue. It was not difficult to do, as this was one of the true highlights of her day. "I'm coming," she called out down the hallway, her tone one of gentle teasing, "and you'd better be in bed."

"I am," came Maia's voice just as Skouris stepped into her daughter's room. As promised, there was the girl in her nightgown and tucked under the bedclothes, lying on one side and working a pencil back and forth against a page in a bound composition book. Skouris paused at the familiar sight, feeling the momentary chill as she recognized that Maia was not merely doodling into a scratch pad, but instead was writing in her diary.

The diary.

"What are you doing, Maia?" she asked.

"Oh, I'm just working on a story," the girl replied, closing the notebook as she looked up at her mother's approach. "It's something I've been thinking about for a while."

"Can I see?" Skouris asked, feeling a sense of trepidation. She knew that "stories" was the term Maia sometimes used to describe the visions she experienced. Her previous encounters with Maia's diary had left her shaken and uncertain as she read the girl's numerous predictions, each written in vague terms as best as Maia was capable of expressing them. Skouris had voiced her initial concerns to Nina Jarvis, who promptly subpoenaed the diary for analysis. Fearing what the journal's contents might lead NTAC to conclude about her adoptive daughter, Skouris instead decided to submit a forged version of the diary as prepared by Marco Pacella.

Maia appeared to weigh the request before replying, "It's not done yet. Can I just tell you about it?"

"Sure, honey," Skouris said, taking a seat on the edge of Maia's bed. "What's it about?"

Maia shrugged. "Well, it's about a girl. A lady, I mean, and she has a very important job, but some people don't want her to do it."

"I see," Skouris said. This seemed innocuous so far, but that discounted the alarm bells sounding in the back of her mind. "So, your lady is a hero and the bad guys are after her?"

Pressing her lips into a tight line, Maia frowned as she considered the question. "I'm not sure yet."

"You're not sure if the bad guys are chasing her?"

"No," the girl replied, shaking her head. "I'm not sure if the lady is the good guy."

The alarms were louder now, but Skouris forced them away, knowing that as long as Maia was in a mood to talk about her visions, she should pursue the conversation. "That's interesting," she said. "Can you tell me more about her?"

Maia closed her eyes for a moment, as though picturing the subject of her visions. "She wears black. That's why I have to scribble her in with my pencil." Shifting in the bed, she adjusted her position so that she could sit up. "And, she's like me."

That gave Skouris pause. "She has visions like you do?"

Shaking her head, Maia said, "I mean, she was brought here like me, with the rest of us."

A 4400, Skouris thought, both anxious and fearful at where this was heading. "What else can you tell me? What kind of important job does she have?"

"I haven't written that part of the story yet," Maia said. "I don't think I like it very much."

Uh-oh.

Leaning forward to place a hand on the girl's arm, Skouris asked, "Why, Maia?"

Another shrug. "She does little things that need to be done so bigger things can happen." Maia paused a moment before adding, "She . . . serves a purpose."

"Well," Skouris said, "it's very important to serve a purpose, Maia. I serve a purpose by working at NTAC. You serve a purpose with your gift to see the future. It's a good thing."

Maia looked at her mother as though she had just smelled something disagreeable. "It's not always a good thing," she said flatly before releasing a tired sigh and lying back down in the bed. "I don't want to talk about it anymore. I'm ready to go to sleep."

Fighting her impulse to prod deeper into the girl's visions, Skouris helped Maia get situated and pulled the blanket up to her shoulders. While she wanted to know whether her daughter was indeed seeing Lona Callahan and if she might gain some insight into the woman's "purpose" with regard to the 4400, she knew that such discussions were best when held on Maia's terms.

"Sleep tight, honey. Happy dreams," Skouris said, kissing Maia's forehead before rising from the bed. She crossed to the door, turning off the overhead light before pulling the door closed behind her.

At least one of us should sleep, she thought, her mind now clouded not only with what Maia had told her, but also anticipation of her daughter's next visions.

That bath, as well as the wine, sounded much more appealing just now.

EIGHTEEN

THE MEDICAL SECTION's basement laboratory was a secluded, quiet place, visited by few who did not have specific business there. It was possible that a good number of personnel employed at the Seattle NTAC facility did not even know of the lab's existence, and that was one of the things Dr. Maxwell Hudson liked about it.

Here, ensconced within the lab's comfortable environs, Hudson was free to work virtually free from disruption. On those days where he was not scheduled to see patients and none arrived for walk-in visits, he would come here. Hours might pass in solitude, his only companions being the sounds of equipment or perhaps the music he piped from the CD player in his office. The privacy was therapeutic, a means for him to shut out the demands of his patient care responsibilities and instead concentrate on the pure research that was his first love and the primary reason for which he had elected a medical career in the first place.

Privacy also carried other benefits, such as being able to conduct a conversation like the one he currently was having.

"Good evening, Max," said the voice of Dennis Ryland as NTAC's deputy director stared out from Hudson's laptop computer monitor. "Working late tonight?" The videoconferencing software on the portable computer seemed to be running a bit slow, Hudson decided as he watched Ryland's image jerk and jump. The drag was likely due to the complex set of calculations with which he had tasked the laptop.

"Hello, Mr. Ryland," Hudson replied. "I could ask you the same question. What can I do for you?"

Leaning closer to the webcam pickup on his own computer, Ryland replied, "We've confirmed that Lona Callahan, or Alicia Colbern, if you prefer, has never reported to any NTAC medical facility since leaving quarantine. For all intents and purposes, she's dropped off the face of the earth. You know what that means?"

Hudson nodded, already feeling a knot forming in his gut. "Of course. She's never received any injections of the inhibitor." Glancing to the bottom left corner of his laptop screen, he confirmed that this conversation was taking place on a secure, encrypted channel, which also meant that no record of the call would be stored on any of the servers residing in NTAC's communications center. He knew that would not stop Ryland from making a recording of the conversation, which was why he had activated his own personal digital recorder before initiating the connection. The small device sat next to the laptop, positioned near one of the computer's built-in speakers and safely out of sight of its webcam receiver.

"To say that's distressing is one hell of an understatement," Ryland said. "You can imagine I've got some worried folks out here in Washington. We know there are other returnees out there who've never reported for medical screenings, and a few of those have proven to be persons of grave concern on the same level as Callahan. If what Baldwin and Skouris are telling me is true, and she does have some kind of invisibility or super speed, then she presents the sort of threat that drove the creation of the inhibitor in the first place."

Hudson nodded in agreement. As part of their conditions for being released from quarantine, each 4400 was required to report to an NTAC medical facility every three months, ostensibly to assess their current conditions and to screen for any change in their physical condition that might be attributable to the time they had spent missing.

Of course, it was only after they were released that the initial reports were received of individual returnees demonstrating extrahuman qualities. NTAC agents investigated these reports, and some of their findings had truly been alarming. Upon examining one of the 4400 who demonstrated such abilities, Hudson had discovered that unlike humans, whose bodies produce four neurotransmitters—chemicals that transfer signals between neurons and other cells within the body—the returnee possessed a fifth such chemical transmitter, which he had dubbed "promicin."

Hudson also found this additional property in other returnees, each of whom had demonstrated a different superhuman capacity, and hypothesized that the presence of promicin allowed use of other areas of the brain not accessible to "ordinary" humans. Such revelations, as well as the mysteries yet to be unearthed about the 4400, had driven Dennis Ryland to order the research and creation of a means to somehow hinder or suppress the promicin neurotransmitter. After months of effort, Hudson developed a compound that, when introduced into the body of a returnee, acted to neutralize promicin.

Suddenly feeling warm even though the lab's thermostat was set to keep the room cooler than other areas of the medical section, Hudson reached up to loosen his tie. "I agree that she's a threat," he said, "but what can I do about it?" Like Ryland, he had seen the preliminary report on Callahan as submitted by agents Baldwin and Skouris. They still were reviewing video footage of her alleged activities in Colorado, but so far the visual evidence pointed to her possessing some kind of cloaking ability, or perhaps an ability to move at incredible speeds.

On the screen, Ryland paused, looking away from the screen as though contemplating a next move. After a moment, he asked, "How's the inhibitor working?"

Hudson shrugged. "I've personally overseen the administration of the drug to more than a hundred returnees, the majority of those who settled in the Seattle area after leaving quarantine. Reports from other NTAC offices show that roughly two-thirds of the entire 4400 population have been given at least one dose, with most receiving additional inoculations during their scheduled checkups. That still leaves around fifteen hundred people out there. So far, there haven't been reports of anything that might be a side effect, but I'm still skeptical. You know I think we rushed deploying this." Hudson had resisted using the compound without further testing, but was overruled by Ryland, who viewed any possible negative consequences as acceptable risks.

"It couldn't be helped," the deputy director replied. "There's too much at stake for us to stand by while returnees all over the world manifest abilities we don't understand and for which we might not have any means of protecting ourselves. The inhibitor is our first line of defense, but it's only a start. What if there are more 4400s out there with abilities like Callahan's? What if they start to organize? We're going to need something bigger and better if we're to have any hope of combating that type of threat. This isn't just a national security issue, Dr. Hudson. The fate of the entire world might be at stake."

Frowning, Hudson leaned closer to his laptop. "You're talking about something more aggressive."

"Absolutely," Ryland said. "The inhibitor works fine for what it is, and that's all thanks to you, Doctor, but we need something we can use in an offensive capacity. We need a means of subduing a 4400 with nonlethal force. Something that could neutralize their ability quickly in a tactical situation. And we need it now."

Hudson did not reply immediately, instead pausing to ponder Ryland's notion. "I suppose there's a possibility that a more potent mixture of the current inhibitor, bonded with a fast-acting tranquilizer compound, could be created, but I'll need to research that in order to better understand any further risks." The idea did little to calm his uncertainty. There still were too many unanswered questions, not only about the inhibitor but also promicin itself. It was still early enough in the inhibitor distribution process that side effects could still manifest themselves in any or all of the returnees. If there was something defective about the drug, creating a more potent strain might exacerbate any potential dangers posed by its current version, or bring about all-new problems. He was traversing dangerous waters here, and there were no charts or maps to guide him. Without thinking, Hudson reached up to scratch his chin, which harbored noticeable stubble.

That's what you get for shaving at four in the damned morning. Get a life, why don't you?

Slim chance of that happening anytime soon, he knew.

"We'll manage whatever risks you might find, Doctor," Ryland said, "but consider this your top priority. We've got agents tracking Callahan right now, and I don't want to lose any of them because they couldn't defend themselves against her ability, or the abilities of any other 4400 who sticks his head up." He tapped his right forefinger on his desk for emphasis. "I want daily updates on your progress, and I don't have to remind you that this is top secret. You're not to discuss this with anyone. Are we clear?"

Resigned to the situation, Hudson nodded. "Yes, Mr. Ryland."

Seemingly pleased with that answer, the deputy director leaned back in his chair, and his expression softened. "I know this isn't easy for you, Max. You're bothered because you're a decent human being, but you have to realize that we're facing extraordinary circumstances here and we need to be ready. We're working toward a greater good, and sometimes the path to such goals is a difficult one to travel. You understand that, right?"

Again, Hudson offered a conciliatory nod. "I do."

"Okay, then. I'm counting on you, Max. Keep me informed." With that, Ryland pressed a control on his computer keyboard, severing the connection.

Satisfied that he once again was alone, Hudson reached for the digital recorder from its place of concealment and pressed the button to halt its covert recording. A quick check of the device's virtual memory confirmed that he had logged the entire conversation.

If things went bad and this project ever saw the light of day or—heaven forbid—something disastrous happened to the 4400 because of what he had been ordered to do, Hudson would have at least one extra card to play once the blame game and the finger-pointing started.

NINETEEN

THE DOOR TO the Theory Room opened, and Baldwin turned to see Skouris enter, favoring as she did so her left foot.

"What happened to you?" he asked.

Skouris scowled as she made her way to the cluttered conference table at the center of the room and took a seat in one of the empty chairs. "I was working out this morning, and twisted my ankle on the treadmill." She shook her head in disgust. "I think I need new running shoes."

Moving from behind his desk, Marco Pacella crossed the room toward Skouris, grabbing an empty chair and sliding it across the floor next to her. "Elevation will help any swelling. Here, put your foot up. Ice will help, too. I've got some in the freezer."

"It's really not that bad," Skouris said, though she did raise her leg to rest her foot on the chair. "This'll be fine, thanks." Casting a look over Marco's shoulder, she smiled and added, "Though a cup of coffee sounds good right about now."

"Coming right up," Marco replied, turning and heading to the far corner that was home to the room's coffeemaker, which so far as Baldwin knew had been in constant operation since the day the 4400 arrived. He had to cover his mouth to hide the slight smile tugging at his lips as he watched Marco in action. While the young agent's attraction to Skouris was one of the worst-kept secrets in all of NTAC and possibly even the entire U.S. government, so far as Baldwin knew the feelings were not mutual.

Considering what we do for a living, he mused, *it's not as though it's the weirdest thing going on around here.*

Baldwin waited while Marco handed Skouris a mug of steaming coffee, noting that the theorist without asking had added her preferred amounts of milk and sugar to the brew before bringing it to her. Once that was accomplished and all three of them were seated at the table, he looked to Marco. "Okay, you called us down to the Batcave. What've you got?"

Even as the words left his mouth, Baldwin knew they sounded harsher than he had intended. He still was irritated at what he had read in the preliminary reports submitted by the NTAC teams in Denver, who still were going over every inch of ground around Eric Wheaton's cabin. Other than a bunch of ATV tracks, a few hunting blinds, and a dead coyote, they had yet to find any sign of Lona Callahan or anyone else who might have killed Wheaton. With that in mind, Baldwin was counting on

Marco and his team to glean any kind of useful information from the video footage of the returnee's death, as right now it was their most promising avenue of investigation.

Appearing to ignore the annoyance underlying Baldwin's question, Marco smiled, his features warming with unbridled pride as he reached across the table's assortment of files and fast-food containers to retrieve one of the ubiquitous remote controls. "That glitch on the video feed from Wheaton's cabin was definitely no glitch."

Adjusting her elevated foot, Skouris shifted to a more comfortable position in her chair. "You found something?"

"Oh, yeah. Big-time," Marco said, aiming the remote at the large screen on the back wall. "Check it out. If something occurs once, then it's an anomaly. Twice, well that might be a coincidence, unless you're me, since I don't believe in coincidences. But when it happens three times, then you've got a trend." On the screen, seven different windows opened, each bearing a stilled image of what Baldwin recognized as varying views of Eric Wheaton's cabin and the area surrounding it.

Marco continued. "Between Denver NTAC and the different news affiliates, we ended up with about a dozen different video sources. These are the seven with the best angles of Wheaton as he was escorted out, and our 'glitch' occurred simultaneously on every single source."

Gesturing toward the screen, Baldwin asked, "Same spot? Behind Wheaton?"

"Precisely," Marco replied, nodding. "It took all night to index and time-synch everything and wash it through our image-enhancement software. We've watched this thing a dozen times and we're still not sure what we're looking at."

For the first time, Baldwin noticed that Wingate and P.J. were conspicuous by their absence. Looking around, he asked, "Speaking of Larry and Curly, where are they?"

"I sent them home to grab some sleep," Marco said. "You can tell when they're tired, because they start picking at each other. It's embarrassing to watch, really."

As though sensing the meeting going off the rails, Skouris said, "And we promise you can go home, too, as soon as we're finished here, okay?"

Marco nodded, adjusting his glasses. "Yeah, right. Okay, watch this."

Leaning forward in his seat, Baldwin blinked as Marco dimmed the room lighting in order for them to better see the images on the screen, his eyes adjusting to the depiction of the glorious Colorado morning sky from the previous day. Frozen in place at the center of the screen was Eric Wheaton, just as Baldwin remembered from yesterday but now benefiting from a far greater clarity of video definition thanks to Marco's enhancement efforts. Grimy and stone-faced, Wheaton stood motionless next to a pair of uniformed officers.

"So, start it up," Baldwin said after a moment, reaching to take a sip of his coffee.

Pointing to the screen, Marco replied, "It *is* started. It's playing in super super slo-mo. See how the cop on the left looks like he's asleep? He's midway through a blink."

Skouris said, "This isn't the same footage we saw yesterday."

"Nope, this one comes from a different local affiliate. It's the best of the bunch, but like I said, don't get your hopes up." Several seconds passed before Marco pointed again to the screen. "Okay, here we go. Watch closely. And . . . *now*."

A blur from the left side of the image caught Baldwin's eye, fogging the barely moving figures of Wheaton and the officers as though the camera operator had smudged a greasy thumb across the lens. The haze continued to wipe across the image, stopping only when it reached the edge of the left officer's uniform sleeve. The smudge then reappeared, but only against the background of the projected image, leaving the human figures unsullied.

"What's happening?" Baldwin asked.

"That's the real question," Marco replied. "It's not a technical screwup. That's the actual image."

Watching Wheaton's expressionless face, Baldwin blinked as the blurred mass obscured it for a moment. "Wait," he started.

"Whatever it is," Skouris said, cutting him off, "it's moving closer to him?"

Marco nodded. "You got it. Now, look closely at Wheaton's neck. As soon as that blur goes away, we see the same dark line against his skin that we saw yesterday."

"But it's not a crisp line," Baldwin said. "It's fuzzy. Can you clean that up any?"

"Trust me, this is as good as it gets," Marco said, once more aiming the remote at the TV and pausing the image. "Now, check this out." He pressed a button, and another window opened, settling alongside the current footage of

Wheaton. "This is video of Lona Callahan from that bank ATM last year. The quality's not as good as the Wheaton stuff, but we were still able to clean it up."

On the screen, Baldwin recognized the scene. Lona Callahan, wearing the clothes she had been given prior to leaving NTAC quarantine, standing on the sidewalk talking to the pair of CIA agents. Neither he nor Skouris said anything as Marco advanced the footage, moving the image past the opening moments of Callahan's brief scuffle before freezing it at the point the female agent drew her pistol and aimed it at Callahan.

Pausing for apparent effect, he turned toward Baldwin and Skouris. "Now you see her." He pressed another button on the remote. "Now you don't."

Baldwin watched as the footage resumed advancing. Frame by frame, Callahan began moving toward the female agent, paying no apparent heed to the weapon aimed at her. Now, Baldwin was not surprised when Callahan seemed to vanish, replaced by a smudge or blur not unlike the one in the Wheaton footage.

"Oh, damn," he breathed.

When Callahan appeared to materialize directly in front of the agent—having somehow avoided being shot by the agent—Marco let the footage resume playing, allowing the woman to disarm and put down the agent at normal speed. The video continued playing until Callahan turned and dealt with the agent's male partner in similar expedient fashion, which included another supposed glitch in the footage as she closed the distance to the man in order to disable him. Once that was done, Marco paused the playback before turning back to Baldwin and Skouris.

"Pretty cool, huh?" he asked.

"So, Callahan killed Wheaton," Skouris said, nodding toward the screen. "It has to be her, but I don't even want to guess what's going on there."

His hands gesticulating as though possessed of their own will, Marco said, "Oh, I can *guess* plenty, if nobody else wants to. It could be hyperactive speed, but who knows what kind of physical toll that might take on a person's body. You have to rule out mass hypnosis, because that wouldn't fool a camera lens. Can't really say invisibility because we're seeing something."

When he stopped, Baldwin saw the look of hesitation on his face, and sensed that the younger agent was reluctant to offer his preferred theory. "Or?" he prompted.

"Or," Marco said, shifting in his seat, "I can't completely rule out a manipulation of spacetime."

"Spacetime?" Skouris repeated, her brow furrowing in confusion.

"I really hope you're going to explain this in English," Baldwin said.

Hunching over in his chair, Marco used his hands to indicate an area of space before him. "Okay, every event occurs in a specific three-dimensional space and at a specific time, which we consider as a fourth dimension separate from the others. Kind of like Rod Serling talks about in *The Twilight Zone*." He paused, frowning. "Wait, that was a fifth dimension."

"Sorry to break it to you, Marco," Baldwin said, "but the Fifth Dimension was a band."

Marco smiled. "Oh, right! I'd forgotten about them. Sweet music."

Holding up her hand, Skouris said, "If either of you starts singing 'The Age of Aquarius,' I'll shoot you both."

"It wasn't 'The Age of Aquarius,'" Marco countered, sounding a bit irked. "It was just 'Aquarius,' and was later released on an album called . . ."

"In the kneecaps," Skouris said.

Nodding, Marco said, "And we're done with that." Drawing a calming breath, he resumed his impromptu dissertation. "Without getting into time-dilation theories and a discussion of the four-dimensional manifold of Minkowski space, let's just say it's not beyond the realm of possibility that our suspect here—which we presume is Lona Callahan—is able to move through space without being connected to time, or at least a rate of time that's equal to our own."

"So, she can move back and forth in time?" Baldwin asked, feeling a headache coming on as he did his best to grasp even the essentials of the information Marco was imparting with ease.

Marco shrugged. "I don't think so, but that's not what I said. She'd still experience time, just differently than we do. She might be able to . . . *unstick* herself from normal time and do whatever it is that she does."

"So to her," Skouris said, "we might all be frozen in place, and to us she might appear to be moving incredibly fast." She nodded toward the screen to emphasize her point.

Obviously impressed with her ability to keep up with

the conversation, Marco offered an approving smile. "Exactly."

"Isn't that just perfect," Skouris said, leaning back in her chair. "Not only do we have a 4400 who's a trained assassin and stone-cold killer, but she also comes back with the ability to bend time and space?"

"Well, it's just a theory," Marco said.

Reaching up to rub his temples in a feeble attempt to ward off the ache behind his eyes, Baldwin considered the implication of Marco's hypothesis. Would the people from the future deliberately equip a returnee with an ability in order to further her natural talents as an accomplished assassin? *Yes*, he decided. Of course, Callahan's existence also begged the question of whether there might be others like her, and what agenda they might serve.

He shook his head, trying to clear it of the larger issues. Right now, their only chance at success had to be focusing on Lona Callahan, the fugitive.

Yeah, Baldwin reminded himself. *One problem at a time.*

TWENTY

SAN ANTONIO, TEXAS

"I DON'T CARE what you heard yesterday. Everything's changed. We need to present a counterbid this morning or we'll be out of the running by lunch. If that happens, you'll be out of a job by dinner. Got it?"

Without waiting for a reply from the distressed head of his company's Contracts Negotiation Division, who had by virtue of rank and position been the one to call him with the latest bit of unsettling news, Lynn Norton terminated the call and returned the cell phone to the pocket of his suit jacket. He took a deep breath, trying to force away his irritation if only for a brief moment, knowing that he would spend the better part of the coming day dealing with the information he had just been given. It went without saying that modern business moved at a faster tempo than even five years ago, but now it seemed never to stop. Twenty-four hours a day, seven days a week, weekends, holidays . . . it never relented. Somewhere in the world, someone always wanted something.

As he did each morning, Norton traversed the winding sidewalk from the executive parking garage to the front entrance of the main building that served as the headquarters for his company, McAllister-Norton Industries. The walking path was one of several cutting through the wooded and landscaped areas around the headquarters complex's twelve buildings. It was a ritual he observed without fail, eschewing the notion of being delivered by limousine to the front door; the drive from his home on the outskirts of San Antonio was a peaceful way to start each day. Often, the quiet stroll, and the time it provided him to think without interruption, was all that was needed to help him gain a proper, healthier perspective on the issues he might tackle in the hours ahead. He almost was able to forget the pair of escorts pacing him at a respectful distance as he walked, the newest measure instituted by his head of security.

And to think, you wanted to retire.

It had been his original plan to retire altogether after leaving the CIA, rather than plunging headlong into the private sector, but he had been enticed by his longtime friend from college, Jonathan McAllister, to take a partnership with him in the massive company he had built almost from scratch into one of the nation's leading defense contractors. McAllister had been looking for a trusted colleague to bring on as a partner, his intention being to divide the company in half with respect to oversight of function. McAllister himself would maintain control of most of the longtime contracts the company enjoyed, while Norton would be charged with seeking out new clients in emerging fields and technologies. It was a challenge Norton welcomed, and less than three months after accepting the offer, McAllister Industries was renamed to reflect this new collaboration.

Then McAllister died in late 2001, leaving Norton to oversee everything, with the help of trusted department heads, of course. With the world shifting virtually beneath their feet in the aftermath of the terrorist attacks that had shaken the world on that fateful day in mid-September, and the United States taking bold and even controversial steps onto the altered global stage as it declared "war on terror," the military-industrial complex was soon operating at a tempo unseen since the height of the Cold War. Large defense contractors such as McAllister-Norton and its competitors soon found themselves awash in engineering and manufacturing as well as consulting and support services contracts, to say nothing of the money that came along with them, all courtesy of a battered and bruised yet determined Uncle Sam.

War's good for business, Norton mused, with no small amount of bitterness coloring the errant thought.

"Good morning, Mr. Norton," he heard a voice call out as he emerged from the garden path and crossed the slim expanse of cobblestones toward the building's main entrance. Looking up, he saw one of his assistants, Scott Pearson, walking toward him. A slim man in his early forties, Pearson carried a black leather ledger and was dressed in a well-tailored charcoal-gray suit and maroon loafers, his conservative attire at odds with the long brown hair he wore pulled back into a ponytail. His narrow frameless eyeglasses gave him the appearance of a professor at UC Berkeley. Though Norton usually preferred his senior staff to maintain a more clean-cut appearance, he permitted Pearson a few minor rebellions, owing to the fact that he had—over the years—become his indispensable right-hand man.

"Morning, Scott," Norton said as he drew alongside Pearson. "I take it you know what's going on with the bid?"

Pearson nodded as he fell in step and the two men continued into the building, the pair of glass doors parting at their approach. "Got the word a few hours ago. I've already got people working the phones and crunching the numbers to come up with some counterproposals for you. You should have it before ten o'clock."

"Give me whatever you have at nine," Norton said, feeling the rush of cool air blowing down from air-conditioning vents as he and Pearson entered the head-quarters building's massive main lobby. "I don't want to give the boys in Washington too much time before we come back with something. It's too big a deal to give up that kind of yardage this late in the game." He said nothing else for a few moments as they crossed the floor, nodding greetings to employees as they passed. The lobby itself was designed as an expansive atrium, its ceiling extending to the eighth floor and with open corridors on the outskirts of the upper levels. The morning sun streamed through the high glass windows, highlighting the bustling activity here even at this relatively early hour.

"You're still scheduled to head to the airport at four-thirty this afternoon," Pearson said, reviewing the copy of Norton's daily schedule he kept in his ledger. "Assuming we haven't worked this out by then, I'm sure I can handle the details until tomorrow evening."

Norton offered a small smile of gratitude. "I appreciate that, Scott." He needed to be on a plane to Atlanta tonight, with Fred Morehouse's funeral scheduled for the following afternoon.

His security director, the walking definition of "thorough" if ever Norton had seen one, had implored him to remain in San Antonio, particularly in light of Nick McFarland's warning that Morehouse had likely been killed by Lona Callahan, who might now be gunning for either of them. To that end, security around the corporate campus had been heightened, to include personal escorts accompanying Norton—at a discreet distance—to and from work. Additional security also was present when he was at home, and his car was inspected at frequent, random intervals throughout the day while he was at the office. Despite this concern, Norton had refused to simply stay and hide. Morehouse had been his friend for thirty years, after all, and there still was something to be said for personal loyalty.

Later, he reminded himself. *First things first.*

"Even though I've got everybody jumping through hoops," Norton said, "my gut's telling me the new offer doesn't have much bite. My sources inside tell me that the other group's pulling every favor and 'good old boy' string they've got, hoping to find somebody who'll tell us to pass on this one and wait for the next deal. DCMA's recommending us, not just because we'll be the better bid, but also to help turn around the bad press they've been getting."

The media had spent the past couple of years maligning the current situation with some contractors and the apparent favored status they received from the Defense Contract Management Agency—the organization within the Department of Defense tasked with obtaining materiel and services for the military from civilian vendors. One of the largest such firms was under prolonged scrutiny, accused of benefiting from several "no-bid contracts" handed out by the DoD. Such controversy was only furthered by the common knowledge that members of the current presidential administration had connections to the company. Perhaps most damaging of all were the growing number of accusations related to overcharging for many of the services provided to military forces currently deployed to Iraq and Afghanistan. Congressional review had resulted in new bidding processes for the latest round of contract negotiations, with McAllister-Norton Industries primed to compete. With his company long respected for its integrity and dependability, Norton had no intention of making it easy on his competition.

"If any of what they've been accused of doing is true," Pearson said as they entered the elevator foyer, "DCMA might end up begging us to take the job." He smiled at that. "That'll make a nice addendum to the piece I hear *60 Minutes* is putting together on the DoD's wasteful spending."

Despite the flurry of demands on his attention, which would only worsen as the day progressed, Norton could not help the hearty laugh that escaped his lips. "Remind me to set my VCR, or digital recorder, or whatever damned gadget's sitting on top of the TV in my office."

They reached the bank of eight elevators, four on either side of the foyer. Norton extracted a key card from the inside pocket of his jacket and swiped it across an electronic reader positioned next to the first elevator, the one dedicated to ferrying him directly to and from his executive suite on the building's top floor. Before stepping into the car, he turned once more to Pearson, "Do me a favor, Scott. I forgot to remind my wife about some of the new security arrangements. Let her know a car will be sent to take her to the airport."

Pearson nodded. "Consider it done. Anything else?"

"Find a way to smuggle me to Hawaii for a couple of weeks," Norton replied, stepping into the elevator. The car rose from the lobby floor, its transparent walls allowing him an unhindered view of the atrium and the growing number of employees streaming through the various entrances now as the start of the formal workday approached.

Then the floor lurched beneath his feet and Norton felt the car stop its ascent. Frowning in confusion, he looked up to see that the overhead light was still functioning. He reached out and pressed the button to open the door and it illuminated, though the doors themselves remained closed. The button for the eighth floor lit up when he touched it, as well, but the elevator remained in place.

Grunting now in irritation, Norton reached for the small
access door situated below the buttons and containing
a phone that would connect him with the security desk
down in the lobby.

There was a click and the panel sprung open and he
flinched as something fell from the phone box inside,
dropping to the elevator's carpeted floor and rolling to a
stop at his feet. It was cylindrical, somewhat smaller than
a twelve-ounce beverage can, painted a slate gray with a
yellow band around its center and additional yellow letter-
ing along its surface. Norton had only a few heartbeats to
realize he was staring down at an M15 white phosphorus
grenade, its pin pulled and its safety handle missing.

The flash of scorching white light was like a miniature
sun against the lobby's subdued illumination, followed
by a concussive blast as the grenade exploded. Standing
near the main lobby entrance, her true identity hidden
beneath a blond wig and large-framed glasses, Lona
Callahan flinched as glass and other shrapnel launched
in all directions. All around her, people screamed as they
scrambled for cover, but she ignored those panicked
individuals. Instead, she was drawn to the sight of the
shattered elevator car, suspended four floors above the
lobby and awash in flame. Inside, whatever remained of
Lynn Norton lay on the floor of the car, the fire quickly
consuming that, as well.

The grenade held fifteen ounces of white phosphorus,
and the explosive's burst radius ranged from fourteen to
seventeen meters. Within the elevator's confines, Lona

knew that Norton's chances of surviving the blast were nil. Indeed, he likely had died instantly, spared from suffering a horrific death as the phosphorus continued to burn up to a minute after the grenade's detonation. Smaller fires were burning in the area beneath the elevator now, as pieces of flaming shrapnel rained to the floor and made contact with carpet, plants, scattered papers, or any other flammable surface. The tinge of burning phosphorus as well as scorched flesh was assailing Lona's nostrils as she noticed other people standing transfixed, their expressions masks of mute horror as they watched the sickening scene unfolding above them.

As had happened after killing Frederick Morehouse, Eric Wheaton, and Robert Fields—a 4400 who had been using his newfound gift for pattern recognition to break top secret code ciphers before selling that information to foreign intelligence agencies—Lona once more felt the now-familiar rush of momentary satisfaction and accomplishment. Unlike Wheaton and Fields, whom she was compelled to kill for reasons she still did not understand, Norton's death was a necessary action as she continued her quest to sever all ties to her previous life. No matter the motive, the sense of fulfillment washed over her with the same level of delightful intensity.

The feeling passed and Lona looked about the lobby, relieved to note that there appeared to be no other casualties. Lona was grateful for that, despite the rather dramatic method she had used to dispatch Lynn Norton—an admitted holdover from her previous life. Though the use of notable, even theatrical techniques to carry out her assignments had become something of a signature during her time as an active operator, she always had upheld the unwritten yet time-honored code of the professional assassin. For her, reducing or eliminating altogether the threat to bystanders or anyone else who was not the contracted mark was simply another aspect of whatever task she was contracted to accomplish.

Alarms now blared through the expansive chamber, no doubt a result of the building's security cadre finally reacting to the situation. Lona cast a glance to the main security desk, a circular station situated at the center of the floor, where three uniformed officers worked either phones or computer terminals, no doubt alerting emergency first responders and other appropriate personnel to the gruesome turn of events. Based on the research she had conducted as part of her overall preparation, Lona knew that she had between four and seven minutes before the first law enforcement or medical teams arrived on-site. Even without her own unique means of making an escape, she still would have plenty of time to blend in with other employees who were in the midst of evacuating the building before the scene was locked down.

"You! Don't move!"

Lona turned at the sound of the voice to see another uniformed security officer standing less than twenty feet from her, his pistol drawn and held in a steady two-handed grip as he stared at her down the weapon's barrel. He was well muscled, his brown hair cut close to the skull and with a trace of gray at the temples. The pistol's muzzle was aimed at her chest, and the officer's stance and expression—particularly the way his blue eyes bored into her—communicated a level of self-confidence that told Lona he was not at all inexperienced. Chances were good that he was not just some rental cop, but was either former law enforcement or perhaps even prior military.

None of that gave him any real chance.

"What?" she asked, affecting an expression of doubt and discomfort at the sight of the weapon in the man's grip. "What's going on?" She made a show of moving her hands away from her sides and the oversized purse slung over her left shoulder.

"Just stand where you are," the guard said, "and keep your hands where I can see them." Taking his left hand from his pistol, he reached for the handset draped over his left shoulder, its coiled black cord snaking over and down his back to the radio clipped to his belt. His eyes fixed on Lona, he keyed the mike. "Central, this is Brooks. I've got a woman matching Suspect Callahan's general description. I need backup immediately." There was a pause during which someone on the other end of the radio said something, to which Brooks replied, "Hair's different and she's got glasses, but facial features match the photos they gave us at the briefing." Though nothing about her own expression or body language communicated as such, Lona was impressed by the officer's awareness.

Of greater concern, even though she should have expected it by now, was that photographs of her were being distributed. This was something that might require her attention, but that was a matter for another time.

Escaping would be simple, of course, even though Lona

was not keen on allowing too many witnesses to observe her ability. Better for her to remain an enigma, she knew, especially to those who hunted her. The mystery would fuel their imaginations and perhaps even their fear, all useful weapons as she continued with her mission. Now, however, she had no choice.

"I'm sorry," she said to Brooks, "but I really must be going."

To his credit, the security officer wavered not an iota. "Stand right there. Move and I'll kill you."

"Good luck with that," Lona replied.

Seconds later—at least so far as Brooks and anyone who may have been watching her in the lobby were concerned—Lona stood in the garden ringing the headquarters building, concealed among the trees and smiling at what Brooks must be feeling at this moment after watching her seemingly vanish before his eyes. Even such a brief burst of time bending—as she had come to call it—had made her thirsty, and she reached into her purse to extract a bottle of water. Taking a long drink, Lona glanced around to ensure she was not being observed before walking in a casual manner toward the garden's outer perimeter. Her rental car was parked in a concealed location on the outskirts of the company's property, and she would be well away from here before the security force was able to lock down all of the entrances as well as the parking garages. With the ongoing confusion as well as a bit of luck, she should not even have to use her ability further to assure her escape.

Only one person relevant to her former life remained:

Nicholas McFarland. He likely would be the most difficult to reach, given his continued association with the CIA. That did not guarantee his safety, of course, but Lona knew that the Agency's formidable resources would be brought to bear in order to protect him. Killing him would require careful planning on her part.

Lona now wondered if, once McFarland and the distractions he represented were out of the way, she would be able to focus all of her attention on the other tasks she knew she must fulfill. Would some explanation for the compulsions that drove her finally become apparent, and would those responsible for what now motivated her reveal themselves?

As she walked through the trees and as though in response to her unspoken questions, Lona once more felt her body quiver with that same sense of contentment. While it was no answer, it would do.

For now.

TWENTY-ONE

LAS VEGAS, NEVADA

AMID THE CLATTER of dinner plates, the frantic piano pounding of Jerry Lee Lewis, and the distinctive clacking of roller skates moving across lacquered wood flooring, Alfred Twenter allowed a symphony of sounds from yesteryear to transport him from the glitz and bustle of this new world back to a simpler and more familiar time.

Well, he reminded himself, *at least a reasonable illusion, anyway.*

As had become his habit several times a week since discovering the place, he was treating himself to dinner at Tubby's Drive-In, a Las Vegas–style re-creation of a 1950s diner complete with smiling waitresses wearing the requisite aprons, skirts, and roller skates. Fatty and fried comfort foods littered the menu, the kind that sent modern calorie counters running for their cardiologists, and classic rock-'n'-roll music blared from a vintage Rock-Ola jukebox system that allowed patrons to choose their favorite tunes from chrome and neon consoles installed at each booth.

The joint was not wholly authentic, Alfred knew, starting with the fact that it had swapped the usual rows of outdoor parking slots used by actual drive-in diners for conventional indoor seating that catered more easily to families and guests of advancing years. He chalked that up to knowing and adapting to one's customer base. Judging by most of the people at Tubby's this night, Alfred guessed that a good portion of them had been patronizing such restaurants for decades. With no small amount of isolation, he reminded himself yet again that with their balding heads and wrinkled skin, slow gaits, out-of-date fashions, and orthopedic shoes, they might well be his contemporaries—had he not been afforded the opportunity to skip the previous fifty years.

Even Buck Rogers never had to deal with this.

Finding comfort in routine, Alfred rarely strayed from what the staff at Tubby's now knew as his "usual." It was therefore no surprise when, only a few minutes after sliding into his favorite booth—one close to the kitchen with seats that boasted alternating rolls of turquoise and white Naugahyde that always seemed to catch a day's worth of crumbs within their stitched valleys—that Roxanne, one of his favorite waitresses, skated toward his table while balancing a tray of food on her shoulder.

"Cookie saw you come in," she said in a tinny Bronx accent Alfred was sure she mimicked for the gig. The gum in her mouth crackled as she set before him a club sandwich, a heaping plate of thickly cut steak fries slathered in brown gravy, and two cups for his chocolate malted: one a glass filled to its brim with the drink and topped with whipped cream and a bright red maraschino cherry, and the other a cold, metal mixing cup holding the remaining mixture. He watched her eye the metal cup, seeing the small drip of malted snaking its way down its side toward the tabletop and deftly swiping at it with one finger. Raising the finger to her mouth, she made a show of tasting the chocolaty drink, following it with a bratty but good-natured smile for his benefit.

"Enjoy," she offered before turning and skating back toward the kitchen, leaving him alone in his booth. Reaching for one of the gravy-soaked fries, Alfred took a bite, relishing the flavor. It might be bad for his cholesterol levels—whatever those really were—but that did not stop it from tasting damned good.

He was on his third fry when an unexpected chill swept over him. It was a familiar impression, one he had been anticipating, though perhaps not this soon.

"Oh my God," he started, realizing only when the words passed his lips that he had said them aloud.

She didn't lie to me, Alfred thought. *She found me just like she said she would.*

Craning his neck to see over the booth's high seatback, he looked toward the front of the diner, all the while savoring the adrenaline-like jolt washing over his mind and body. There could be no mistaking the sensation; it could be coming only from one person.

And then, she simply was *there*.

Abigail moved past the other booths with a subtle,

sensual grace that seemed only to fuel the feelings that gripped him. For whatever reason and despite his all-too-brief connection with her during that first encounter at the bank, Alfred apparently was tapping into the same high level of residual energy he previously had experienced only with the handful of lovers he had met since his return.

It was *intoxicating*.

She caught sight of him and he raised his hand to wave her over, smiling as she cut a path between tables and past other patrons on her way toward him.

"Hello, Alfred," she said, sliding without invitation into the booth on the opposite side of the table. "It's good to see you again." She cast an amused glance down at his plate. "And it looks like I got here just in time."

Feeling himself beaming at her, Alfred replied, "Indeed you did. It's nice to see you as well." He tried to keep himself in check, not wanting to appear too enthusiastic about encountering her again. "Would you like anything to eat?" he asked, glancing awkwardly about the restaurant. "I can call back the waitress."

By way of reply, Abigail reached across and plucked one of the steak fries from his plate, swiping it through some of the brown gravy before popping it into her mouth. "What, you're not in a mood to share?"

Alfred slid the plate of fries to the center of the table. "I'm quite willing to share anything with you, Abigail." He almost winced, knowing his words sounded full of innuendo but not caring a whit.

"Good." As if to emphasize her point, she grabbed

the stainless steel tumbler containing the rest of Alfred's chocolate malted. "You know how to pick 'em," she said, looking about the restaurant. "I love places like this. They always give you the extra malt in the mixing cup. Just like the old days, huh?"

Alfred chuckled at that. "Just like the old days. They're not so old to me, though. Remember?"

"You know I remember," Abigail replied, her expression falling a bit. "It's just . . . different for me is all." She frowned, an expression Alfred found adorable. "I guess it's hard to explain."

"We seem to have plenty of time," Alfred offered, picking up a neatly cut quarter of his sandwich. "Try to explain it for me."

Abigail said nothing for a moment, instead chewing on another gravy-coated fry. Just before the silence began to seem awkward, she said, "I'm not trying to sound mean or anything, but it's like when we chat online and you tell me what things were like and how people used to be in your time." She shrugged. "Sometimes it feels a little, I don't know, corny, I guess."

"Corny? Wow," Alfred said, the comment stinging a bit deeper than she obviously had intended. "Nice of you not to mince words."

"No, seriously," she countered, holding up her hand. "Hear me out. When we're talking, I sometimes feel sorry for you, even though I don't miss where I'm from in the same way. I guess it's because for me, things here don't feel all that different, not like they are for you. When you describe how you're feeling, all I can think about are those old fifties black-and-white TV shows or documentaries or those bad, old instructional films they showed us in school. Remember those? They were supposed to teach kids how to treat each other nicely and how it's polite to go places with your hands washed and hair combed and stuff. It doesn't feel real to me is all."

Alfred could sympathize with her, at least to an extent. The wonders of modern home entertainment—cable television and DVDs—had allowed him to revisit TV shows that were current when he left but now were viewed as items of curiosity, if not nostalgia. "My time did exist, you know," he said after a moment. He dropped his sandwich onto the plate, his hunger having fled.

"Sure," Abigail said, "but not like that. From what I've seen, it just feels like all you guys talked about was the right way to act."

Alfred offered a small, sardonic smile. "And that's strange to you? That people cared about how they treated each other?"

"Yeah, I guess it is," she replied. "People now just don't seem to have the time to be overly polite like you say things used to be."

"You mean they don't *take* the time, Shorty," Alfred said, hoping the use of her online nickname would soften his remarks. "It's as though being nice is the exception, rather than the rule. Just last night on the television news, I saw a report about how someone paid for the next person's coffee at a drive-up window. So, that person, instead of just taking the free coffee, keeps it up and pays for the guy behind her, and so on and so on, until people did it for something like seven hundred cars." He shook his head, laughing as he recalled the story.

Frowning, Abigail asked, "Why is that funny?"

"It's funny that it's *news!*" he said, realizing as he did so that his voice level had risen. He paused, looking about the restaurant to see whether anyone had taken notice, but by all appearances no one seemed to care. "I'm used to when people would toss out enough change to cover coffee for the guy next to them and not think twice about it."

"Well, yeah, back when coffee was a dime or something instead of three bucks," she said, releasing her own laugh. It was the kind of laugh Alfred could listen to all day.

"You know what I mean," he said, reaching for his malt.

Abigail nodded. "I do. I was just teasing you."

"I know," Alfred said, feeling her sincerity course through the tenuous mental link they still shared, "but I have to tell you. This . . . *future* is nothing like I always dreamed it would be."

Her brow creased and her nose wrinkled as she regarded him. "What do you mean?"

Alfred shrugged as he watched Roxanne skate by, wielding another tray as she tended to another booth. "I mean, I'm in a world filled with technological wonders. I've got stuff in my apartment that was in the science-fiction stories I was reading up until the day I left. An oven that cooks with microwaves? A television without knobs or antennae that works with a wireless control box? My own personal computer that's no bigger than a notebook and connects me to all the great databases of the world? Incredible.

"But, in my time, what they told us to expect when all these gizmos became reality was that we would live carefree lives. We'd be in a world without crime, without hunger or sickness or poverty." Shaking his head, Alfred removed his glasses and set them down on the table, then reached up to rub his eyes. "I know how all of that must sound so foolish or naïve to you." The truth was that with all of the reading and daydreaming he once had done, he had bought into the grand utopian vision of the future espoused in those magazines. "Here I am, in the future I always wanted to visit, but the future didn't happen. Not like I wanted it to, anyway."

Abigail said, "Maybe it's not what any one of us expected to find, but maybe some of us cope better by looking forward instead of backward."

"Maybe so," Alfred replied as he put on his glasses before releasing a humorless chuckle. "Just how you wanted to spend your evening, right? Hanging out with a sad sack who's nothing like he seems on the Internet."

"Stop that," Abigail said, and Alfred heard the hint of disapproval in her tone. "I don't think that at all." Waving her hand to indicate Tubby's glitzy interior, she asked, "Is that why you come to places like this? To remind yourself of what it was like to be around people who cared about what life was like for everyone else and not just themselves?"

Thinking about that for a moment, Alfred nodded. "Maybe that's one reason, yeah."

Offering a wan smile, Abigail reached for his glass of chocolate malt. "And that's why I wanted to meet you in person, and why I had a feeling you might want to meet me, and others like me." Taking a sip from the glass, she returned it to its place on the table before glancing about, just as she had during their initial encounter at the bank, as though making sure no one might overhear their conversation. Alfred did not see how that was possible, especially considering the Elvis Presley tune blaring through Tubby's sound system. "There's a group of us. A few 4400s, but we also have many supporters, people who want to help us develop our abilities so that we can use them to make this a better world for everyone."

There was something in her words that intrigued him, Alfred decided, even called to him. Might he simply be responding to his ongoing sense of isolation and his longing for the companionship of someone—anyone—who could identify with what he was feeling?

"Who are these friends of yours?" he asked, leaning forward until his elbows rested atop the table.

Abigail shook her head. "Not here. I just . . ." She paused, as though considering what to say next, before finally reaching out with her right hand and resting it in Alfred's palm. "Here."

As her soft skin brushed his, Alfred's mind flooded with a wash of warm colors. He closed his eyes, allowing the rush of visions to coalesce. Unlike the first time he shared this connection with Abigail, he did not see distinct images, such as those of her youth and family. Instead, he was confronted with visions of himself, at the bank, but those were fleeting, pushed aside as Abigail seemed to offer insight into the more remote corners of her own mind. Tenuous wisps reached for him from those recesses, bathing him in the glow of trust and confidence, followed by anticipation and—finally—hope.

He gasped for breath as Abigail withdrew her hand, and released a sigh as the intensity of their contact diminished for lack of their physical touch. Still gripping the lingering thread of their empathic connection, Alfred opened his eyes and saw her looking at him, her face aglow with an expression of wonder.

"Watching you," she said, her voice so soft that he almost could not hear her, "watching your face, I can only imagine what it must feel like to do what you do. When I know about one of us and what he or she can do, I just know it like I read it in a book. What was it like for you—with me—just now?"

Clearing his throat and wishing for the first time that he had asked Roxanne for a glass of water, Alfred replied, "It's actually a little different each time, depending on what people show me and how much I'm able to draw out of them. Sometimes, it's the sort of thing you recognize right away, like images from television or conversations you overhear. Every once in a while, it's not so easy to sort it all out right away, but I'll have realizations about things later." He shifted in his seat. "Regardless of what happens, it can seem very . . . intimate." Even though he felt comfortable with Abigail, it was still difficult to offer these revelations, which he never had shared with anyone before.

Abigail regarded him with a small, mischievous smile. "Alfred, you're blushing a little."

Laughing at that, Alfred nodded, holding out his hands in a gesture of mock surrender. "Guilty, I suppose." He leaned closer to her. "One other thing I saw, was your reassuring me that I could trust you, and your friends."

"You can, Alfred," Abigail replied, "just as I hope you know we . . . I . . . trust you, too. We trust you and we need you, and your gift."

And now we come to it.

"I saw that, too," Alfred said, adjusting his glasses. "The fact that I work at a bank seems important to you, and your friends." Now he was looking around, making sure no one was eavesdropping. "You're thinking I might be able to provide some sort of financial support."

Abigail waited until one of the other waitresses—servers, as Alfred knew they preferred to be called these days—skated past on her way to the kitchen. She leaned even farther over the table. "I won't lie to you, Alfred. We're going to need resources—people and materiel—to help us reach our goals, and that takes money. It's a means to an end, that's all."

Unsure that he liked where this conversation was going, Alfred was beginning to wonder if his judgment might not be clouded from the contact they shared. In the time that had passed since his "return" and subsequent release from quarantine, he never had given serious consideration to using his newfound telepathic gift for personal gain. The very notion unsettled him.

At least, until now.

"I'd need to know more," he said after a moment, "and

getting my hands on a lot of money isn't going to be like they do it on television. I don't know anything about skimming accounts or diverting money from one place to another. It would be easier to start by tapping into something closer to my area of expertise."

"The safety-deposit boxes?" Abigail asked.

Alfred nodded. "I know what's in most of them. It's all people think about when they go into the vault and when they come out, and I shake their hands every time." Before she could respond to that, he held up a hand. "I don't want to hurt anyone, or take anything from people who don't deserve to be robbed, no matter how worthy your cause might be." That said, Alfred was already thinking of that subset of the bank's customer base who were too rich for their own good. Most were rude jackasses with misplaced notions of entitlement, and who took great pains to alert everyone to that fact whenever they deigned to grace the bank with their presence.

Yeah, he decided, *some of those people could stand to make some charitable donations.* The thought made him smile.

"I'll come up with something," he said, wiping his forehead at the sweat that seemed to have appeared from nowhere.

Abigail said, "I'm not asking you to commit to anything. We'll talk about it later, and you'll get a chance to meet my friends before you make any decisions." Reaching for the plate at the center of the table, she offered a sheepish grin as she retrieved the last remaining fry. "Sorry, I guess I was hungrier than I thought."

"It doesn't take a telepath to figure that out," Alfred replied, chuckling.

Using the french fry to trace an outline of her red lips before putting it in her mouth, she regarded him with narrowed eyes. "If you're *that* good, maybe you can tell me what I'm thinking now."

TWENTY-TWO

THE 4400 CENTER
SEATTLE, WASHINGTON

"Hey, Uncle Tommy," said Shawn Farrell by way of greeting, holding out his hand as Baldwin and Skouris crossed the lobby toward him. Dressed in dark slacks and matching blazer over a blue silk shirt, the younger man seemed to have aged—perhaps matured was a better word—just in the couple of weeks that had passed since their last meeting, at Jordan Collier's funeral. Shawn looked almost at home as the new head of The 4400 Center, having inherited the post in keeping with instructions Collier had left in the event of his death.

Most of all, Baldwin decided, Shawn looked tired.

Offering a firm handshake, he reached up with his free hand to clasp his nephew's right shoulder. "Hey, Shawn," Baldwin said. "Thanks for taking the time to see us. I know you're busy." He knew that was something of an understatement. Since Jordan Collier's assassination,

Shawn had found himself hurled into a position of leadership, overseeing the Center and trying to put a good public face on the 4400 as rumors and questions about them continued to mount. It would be a large enough burden for anyone, doubly so for a man barely twenty-two years of age—or even nineteen, if one were to take into account Shawn's "missing time."

Nodding before shaking hands with Skouris, Shawn said, "No, it's okay. I'm actually glad you called. This . . . all the stuff that's going on has a lot of people rattled, you know?" Gesturing for the agents to follow him, he set off back down the large curving hallway leading from the expansive lobby toward the Center's administrative offices. "Anything new on whoever shot Jordan?"

Baldwin felt a twinge of guilt as he offered the only truthful answer. "Not yet. We're still following a few leads, and there may be some new tips coming from the sketch that's gone out, but so far we're not having much luck."

Shaking his head, Shawn released a disapproving sigh. "I can't believe somebody murders Jordan in broad daylight in front of hundreds of people and then just disappears into thin air. How does that happen?" Baldwin's teeth gritted in response to the unspoken accusation.

Yes, I know. I let him get away.

"We're not talking about an amateur here, Shawn," Skouris said, her tone calm and composed. "They knew what they were doing. It was only by sheer luck that Tom got as close as he did. Other people saw him, too. We'll find him."

Now away from the lobby and into one of the corridors

designated as off-limits to Center visitors, Shawn stopped and turned to face the agents. "And you're sure this other person you're after didn't have anything to do with it?"

"So far as we can tell," Baldwin replied, "whoever shot Collier was acting alone, and between me and the janitor who provided the details for the sketch, we're looking for a male suspect." Seeing Shawn's mouth pressing into a tight line, a sure sign of his nephew trying to keep a handle on his mounting irritation, he added, "Shawn, NTAC and the FBI have hundreds of people on this. We'll catch this guy."

Appeased if not satisfied with this answer, Shawn nodded. "Okay. Sorry, Uncle Tommy. It's just . . . it's been rough around here since he died."

Baldwin patted him again on the arm. "It's okay. I get it, Shawn. I really do." In the time since his nephew's return, their relationship had been strained, and Baldwin knew it was due in no small part to his own words and actions. That tension certainly had contributed to Shawn's leaving home and eventually joining Jordan Collier at The 4400 Center, where the older man had taken him under his wing. While Baldwin always had his suspicions about Collier and his true motives, whatever those might have been, he understood that the 4400's controversial figurehead had been uniquely suited to helping Shawn understand and develop the wondrous ability he now possessed.

"You look like you could use a vacation," Baldwin said after a moment.

That actually made Shawn laugh. "Tell me about it."

He paused, and all three of them turned at the sound of approaching footsteps. "In fact, why don't you tell him about it?" Gesturing toward the new arrival, Shawn made introductions. "Uncle Tommy, this is Matthew Ross. He's been helping me with the transition. Matthew, this is my uncle, Tom Baldwin, and his partner, Diana Skouris."

"Yes, of course," Ross said, smiling as he extended his hand. "A pleasure to finally meet you both in person."

Everyone shook hands, with Baldwin taking the opportunity to size up this new addition to the Center. Ross was a slim man, wearing an impeccably tailored tan suit with a black dress shirt and pale yellow tie. His brown hair was styled with gel, and a glance at his hands revealed manicured fingernails. The loafers he wore probably cost more than a typical NTAC agent's monthly salary.

Baldwin distrusted him on the spot.

"Thank you again for helping us to find Jean Baker," Skouris said. "I know our two groups don't always get along, but your decision to share information with us was greatly appreciated."

"I'm only sorry things couldn't have turned out better," Ross replied, speaking in a measured cadence that to Baldwin's ear sounded almost lyrical, "for her and everyone she affected. It's a tragedy, of course, and something of a mystery to boot. We're at a loss as to what role an ability such as hers might have played in . . . well, in whatever it is the 4400 are here to do." Shrugging, he added, "Still, it's nice to know we can work together when we have to."

"Funny you should mention that," Skouris said. "We're actually here about Lona Callahan. Two of the four people she's believed to have killed are 4400s, and she's a returnee herself. We're hoping the Center's database might have information we can use to find a connection or a pattern as to why she chose them. If so, we may be able to narrow a list of possible targets among the 4400 community."

Shawn frowned. "But, what about the other people she killed?"

"Callahan knew them," Baldwin replied. "Both men were part of her former life." He could not go into specifics, of course—at least, not if he wanted to keep the entire CIA from having a collective hissy fit. "There may be some connection to them, too." So far, all attempts by NTAC and FBI investigators to link the four deaths currently attributed to the nebulous Callahan had proven fruitless. Other than the obvious relationship between Frederick Morehouse and her apparent latest target, Lynn Norton, the victims appeared to have nothing in common.

Baldwin saw the uncertainty on Shawn's face, and Ross appeared to recognize it as well. "What is it, Shawn?" the other man asked.

"You know a lot of the returnees don't trust NTAC," Shawn replied, "especially since word about different 4400 abilities got out." He held his hands out, gesturing around him. "This place is supposed to be a sanctuary for 4400s, Uncle Tommy. They won't come here if they think we're just going to sell them out to the government, and that just makes it harder to figure out whatever it is we're supposed to be doing, and how each 4400 is supposed to contribute."

Even if he did not agree with such assertions, Baldwin

could at least understand where his nephew was coming from. Relations between NTAC and The 4400 Center had been less than cordial, particularly while Jordan Collier was still alive. Though the agency's mission was to investigate the returnees and to learn as much as possible about their abduction and why they had been returned to this point in time, there were those in power who did not believe that mandate went far enough. There already had been calls for greater control on the 4400, perhaps even going so far as to return them to quarantine status until more could be learned about them. Baldwin disagreed with such proposals, certain that the best way to solve the mystery behind the returnees was to work with them, through the Center, with Shawn Farrell and those who followed him.

"We're not going to sell out anyone, Shawn," Ross said, his tone gentle yet firm. "We'd be taking action to protect them, taking advantage of resources not normally available to us." He turned back to Baldwin and Skouris. "Jordan didn't listen to your warnings, and he paid for that mistake with his life. I don't want that to ever happen again. We don't always have to agree on everything, but we should be able to trust each other."

Smooth, Baldwin thought. *Very smooth.*

Shawn nodded in agreement. "You're right, Matthew. We'll try to give you everything you need, Uncle Tommy."

"Thank you," Skouris said. "I'll have someone from NTAC contact the Center so that we can coordinate an information exchange. We'll give you as much information as we're authorized to release. Your people might be able to find a connection we overlook, after all." She started to say something else, but was interrupted by the sound of her cell phone ringing. "Excuse me," she said as she stepped away to answer it.

"Thank you, Shawn," Baldwin said. "Both of you." It was a small victory, but success nonetheless. With time, effort, and good fortune, this one accord might be the first step toward a longer-lasting rapport between NTAC and The 4400 Center.

Ross replied, "I only hope your superiors don't misuse the trust we're placing in you, Agent Baldwin."

Well, that was nice while it lasted.

"Tom," Skouris said from behind him, and Baldwin turned to see the concerned expression clouding her features. "That was Nina. We need to get back."

"What's up?" Baldwin asked.

Skouris shook her head. "She wouldn't say. All I got was for us to get back ASAP."

TWENTY-THREE

DIANA SKOURIS KNEW who Nicholas McFarland was, of course. She had seen him several times, as a guest on news programs or during congressional reviews or hearings televised by C-SPAN, always dressed in designer suits, tanned and lean-muscled—excellent condition for a man nearing sixty years of age—and with hair impeccably styled. On those occasions, the deputy director presented the very epitome of calm and control, a man confident in his position, authority, and abilities.

Not so today. Sitting in Nina Jarvis's office, Nicholas McFarland seemed to be anything except in control. Skouris saw the fatigue and fear in the man's eyes, noted the slight tremble in his left hand as he held a half-full glass of water. His composure was nothing like what she had seen on television, with his tie loosened, his hair combed but looking as though it could stand washing, and the day's growth of beard stubble darkening his cheeks and jawline. Why was he here, now, like this?

Take a wild guess.

Sitting behind her desk, Jarvis indicated McFarland with a hand gesture and Skouris and Baldwin stepped into the room. "Agents Tom Baldwin and Diana Skouris, allow me to introduce you to Deputy Director Nicholas McFarland, Central Intelligence Agency. He's very happy to see you."

Frowning as he shook hands with the other man, Baldwin said, "You're a long way from Langley, Director."

"Don't I know it," McFarland replied before shaking hands with Skouris.

"NTAC's gone to a lot of trouble to get him out here," Jarvis said. "Officially, Mr. McFarland has taken a leave of absence for personal reasons, and is on his way to a remote fishing cabin in Minnesota. Unofficially, he's in our protective custody until such time as Lona Callahan is captured or killed."

Adjusting himself in the chair as though seeking a more comfortable position, McFarland said, "Ordinarily, I'd trust my own people to oversee security for something like this, but given your experience dealing with these 4400, coming here seemed the smart move." He paused to drink from his water glass before adding, "I'll admit it, I'm scared. Lona Callahan was a formidable operator when she was working for us. Now that she has this . . . power . . . of hers, I just don't know." Shaking his head, he released a tired laugh. "You know, for as long as the Agency's been around, we've had rooms full of science types—computer nerds, theoretical physicists, you name it—just sitting around dreaming up the kinds of things these people can do, hoping to find some way to make super soldiers or special agents or whatever. A lot of it was crap, the kind of stuff science-fiction writers might even pass over because it sounded so ridiculous."

Skouris could sympathize with the sentiment. Throughout her life and career, she had considered herself a strict follower of scientific principles. Even as the incredible events unfolded in the aftermath of the return of the 4400, she had held on to her ingrained beliefs and need to find plausible, provable explanations for everything she and indeed the world had witnessed. Even now, nearly a year after that fateful day at Mount Rainier and in the face of astonishing events and even more remarkable people, including her own adopted daughter, her beloved Maia, Skouris knew that none of this was due to elements of the fantastic. Rather, all that had transpired was because of things not yet understood, and she longed for the day when those answers were revealed.

Be careful what you wish for, and all that.

"Have you had any contact with Lona Callahan since her return?" Baldwin asked.

McFarland shook his head, his gaze cast downward at the office carpet. "No. We tried to make contact, of course, once we realized that she was one of the 4400 and that you were holding her in quarantine. At the time, I proceeded like we would if we were trying to bring in any covert agent from the field. Hell, we had no reason to believe that she wouldn't *want* us to bring her in." He shrugged.

"Anyway, you all know how that went. We lost track of her after that, well, for a while anyway." Draining the remaining water from his glass, he looked up at Baldwin and Skouris. "Have you learned anything new?"

Baldwin replied, "We're still waiting on a full report from San Antonio. NTAC and the FBI both have teams on-site, collecting whatever evidence there might be, but white phosphorus doesn't leave much to work with."

"I had our data analysts do a search on similar incidents dating back to 1980," Skouris added. "They found one. It was in Benghazi, Libya, in 1987. The known leader of a terror cell with suspected ties to Muammar Gaddafi was killed by a white phosphorus grenade planted in an elevator at a downtown hotel. The incident was later attributed to 'the Wraith' after months of investigation." Studying McFarland with a disapproving eye, she added, "I'm guessing that was your handiwork."

McFarland nodded. "An Agency-sanctioned operation. We paid Callahan three million dollars for that one, and Lynn Norton was her handler. Morehouse oversaw her actions against Miraj al-Diladi in Baltimore in 1992, so I suppose that explains why she killed him the way she did. I can only imagine what she has in store for me."

"She's definitely not shy about pulling out her bag of tricks," Jarvis said, tapping one finger on her desk. "It's like she wants us to know it's her."

"Not you," McFarland countered. "Me. I was the officer in charge of most of her operations from the late 1980s until her disappearance. My predecessor died years ago, so I'm guessing Lona's saving her best trick for me.

Needless to say, I'd just as soon avoid that happening."

Pausing to clear his throat, he placed the empty glass on Jarvis's desk. "Look, we're not used to sharing this kind of information with other agencies. Damn near every mission we assigned to Callahan was black bag, and I quit counting the violations to domestic and international laws about a year after I took over as her handler. Whatever paperwork exists to prove I was acting under orders from higher up the food chain is offset by layers of plausible deniability up to and including the Oval Office. If Callahan's mission history is ever made public, I'll be the one to fall on my sword, mostly because I'm the only one still alive. So, the way I see it, I've got nothing to lose by offering you anything you think you need to know if it'll help catch her."

Skouris folded her arms across her chest. "We've been considering the idea that Callahan was taken *because* she already possessed these skills, with the intention of putting them to use for whatever it is the 4400 are supposed to be doing." Marco, along with the other members of his team, was currently working to factor this notion into his always-evolving "Ripple Effect" theory, trying to discern if and how Callahan's actions might be playing into the larger mystery of the 4400. As always, such efforts begat even more questions, rather than answers.

"Well, that's going to be keeping me up nights," McFarland said, releasing a humorless chuckle.

Skouris shrugged. "Don't mention it."

Rising from her seat, Jarvis said, "Okay, not to be too heartless about this, Mr. McFarland, but if Callahan gets to you, whatever trail she leaves is going to go cold pretty damned fast, so here's what's going to happen. We'll be taking you up on your offer to give us as much info on Callahan as you have, and I suspect that's going to take a while. Therefore, I'm having you moved to a safe house for the duration." Looking to Baldwin and Skouris, she added, "Hopefully, you two can take what he gives us and find a way to get out in front of Callahan."

Sure thing, Skouris mused. *Anything else?*

The conference ended with Jarvis calling for a transport team to prepare for McFarland's relocation. Once she and Baldwin were away from their superior's office and out of earshot, Skouris stopped her partner with a touch on his arm.

"Tom," she said, "there's something else. Maia's been having visions again, and I think they're about Callahan."

Frowning at this revelation, Baldwin looked around to verify that they weren't being overheard. "What has she seen?"

"Nothing specific. She just gets these sensations of a woman tasked with something important; the descriptions seem to match Callahan. Short red hair, weapons like rifles and knives, that sort of thing. Who else could it be?"

"A girl I dated in college?" Baldwin shrugged off his attempt at humor. "I take it you haven't told Jarvis."

"Not yet," Skouris replied. "This is the first vision she's had since I gave Maia's diary to Nina last week." Even as she spoke the words, she reminded herself that—at some point—she needed to tell Baldwin that the diary she had surrendered to Jarvis was a fake. Deciding that now was not the appropriate time to reveal she had defied NTAC directives, she said, "Whatever it is she's seeing, the images have intensified during the last day or so. She sees this woman as being on some kind of crusade."

"Any chance she knows how this is going to play out?" Baldwin asked.

Sighing, Skouris shook her head. "Just that more people are going to die."

TWENTY-FOUR

NEAR CASPER, WYOMING

LONA CALLAHAN FELT the burn in her muscles as she sprinted up the narrow trail, her legs pumping like pistons. Despite having to navigate the winding path's broken, uneven terrain, she forced her breathing to maintain a consistent rhythm, drawing long, deep breaths and exhaling in time with her footsteps. Through the predawn near-darkness, Lona could see the lights of her house ahead of her. She hit the final hill, swinging her arms even harder to help sustain her pace as the grade increased almost to a thirty-degree angle.

Blood rushed in her ears and her heart pounded as though ready to explode from her chest, but she ignored all of that. A quick glance at her watch showed that she was still ahead of the pace she had set during the previous morning's run. Motivated to best that mark by an even wider margin, Lona grunted and leaned into her stride, her feet digging into the soft earth and finding purchase as they propelled her forward.

The first hints of sunlight were playing through the trees as she passed the pile of stones she had set out to designate her start and end point for the measured run. No sooner did she cross that threshold than Lona slowed her steps, dropping from the full sprint to a steady jog and finally to a walk. She kept a brisk step, allowing her pulse rate and breathing to slow, and tapped a button on her watch to halt its timer function. At the same time, she felt the now-comforting warm glow wash over her as the mystifying energy field—the "time bubble," as she liked to call it—evaporated from around her, releasing her from the temporary detachment from "real time" she always experienced when she conjured the field.

Welcome back.

Looking down at her watch, Lona verified that she had completed the six-mile course in just under thirty minutes—subjective time—trimming nearly twenty seconds from yesterday's run. She walked over to the rock pile, retrieving the compact infrared beam emitter she had positioned atop it. Connected to the device was a digital stopwatch, programmed to start and stop in response to the emitter's beam being broken as Lona passed through it at the beginning and ending of her morning runs. The time on the watch read twenty-six seconds, only three seconds faster than yesterday, but still an improvement.

Six miles in twenty-six seconds. Lona smiled, pleased with her continued progress. Within a few weeks, she figured to have that down to an even twenty. Having long since learned to recognize the physical sensations that coursed through her body as the time-bending field manifested itself, it had taken only a bit more time to comprehend the notion of anticipating those responses and even to imagine them as a means of calling forth her power.

"Eat your heart out, Jaime Sommers," she said to any wildlife that might be listening. As expected, she received no responses.

Lona likened the field to a bubble after determining that the effect was limited to the small area immediately surrounding her body, not much more than an arm's length in any direction, she estimated. Anything inside that sphere was subject to the field's influence, within which Lona was able to cause time to move at a rate slower or faster than real time. With her increased control over the field, she also had learned to mitigate its effects on her own body. No longer was she left out of breath, though she still felt the effects of dehydration. As with any physical training regimen, her body had responded to the grueling conditioning she had undertaken, adapting to accept the exertions she placed upon it and to recover from such efforts with ever-increasing efficiency.

Too bad I'll never be able to call Guinness.

Pausing to retrieve the towel and the bottle of water she had left near the rocks, Lona turned and walked the fifty or so yards separating the trailhead and the back porch of her two-story A-frame house. Situated near the center of twenty-one acres of largely undeveloped forest, her only neighbors were the lush blankets of trees covering the rolling hills in all directions. The sun had yet to rise above the horizon, but the sky was lightening with pending dawn, and the temperature was more than comfortable at this hour. A slight breeze wafted through the forest, cooling the sweat on her exposed skin. Early morning was Lona's favorite time of day. It was now that the world and she seemed most at peace, when she was best able—for a time at least—to set aside and almost forget the realities of the life she had chosen.

Or, more recently, the life apparently chosen for her.

Lona reached the back porch and moved to the pair of chairs positioned beneath a bay window, which offered an unfettered view of the property behind the house. In one of the chairs was her cell phone and she picked it up, examining its digital display and finding no new messages. Only Reiko knew the number, anyway, and Lona did not expect her to call except in the event of an emergency or unexpected change relating to her current task. Reiko had gone quiet after first alerting her that she had tracked Nicholas McFarland to Seattle despite the best efforts of the CIA and NTAC.

That Reiko had not called was enough to tell Lona things were still proceeding according to plan. McFarland was in NTAC's protective custody at a safe house in one of Seattle's suburbs, one of several locations being used to keep him hidden until Lona herself was captured or—more likely—she succeeded in killing him. Reiko's assignment, in keeping with the role she always had played as Lona's assistant, consisted of simple surveillance. Though she was capable of handling herself in the field, Reiko's tasks had only rarely called for her to directly engage a mark. During the years they had worked together, it had been but one of the steps taken by Lona to ensure Reiko's anonymity, as much from her government employers as enemies who might be hunting for her. Such was the case now, with Reiko keeping tabs on McFarland until such time as Lona completed her preparations and traveled to Seattle to handle him herself.

As happened with every instance when her thoughts turned to Reiko, Lona found herself longing for her absent lover. She was the lone constant, the one thing she desired from her previous life, and whereas prolonged separation had been the norm during assignments in the past, Lona had come to realize in recent weeks that she now disliked any such measures. Time had very nearly succeeded in taking Reiko from her, and Lona had no intention of ever again tempting such fate.

So finish this business, she chastised herself, *and then get on with life.*

Stripping out of her sweaty running clothes, Lona made her way to the oversized shower in her Asian-styled master bathroom. Open on the side closest to the vanity, the shower itself was thirty-six square feet of emerald green floor tile. Glass walls on two sides provided an unobstructed view of the surrounding forest, while a host of tropical plants and vines dominated the modular cedar panels and shelves comprising the third wall. Two large circular fixtures descended from the ceiling, in short order releasing a cascade onto her as though she were standing in the midst of a gentle tropical rainfall.

While the shower soothed her stressed muscles, it did

little for Lona's restless mind as discipline and training once more asserted control, and she contemplated her final, lingering arrangements. At the same time, she continued to envision variations of the scenario she likely was to encounter in Seattle. Despite her abilities as well as having surprise in her favor, Lona had long ago learned not to take anything for granted, or to put forth any guarantees of success, either to her employers or even to herself. Such proclamations were the purview of amateurs, the ones who almost always ended up being caught or killed. For these reasons, Nicholas McFarland would die.

But not yet.

The single thought came unbidden, repeating and expanding until it pushed away everything else. Lona flinched, the words driving into her brain with the might of a physical blow. She staggered from beneath the shower's tender waterfall, stumbling toward the wooden bench running the length of the cedar wall. Her fingers gripped sections of the thick, lush vines, steadying her as she lowered herself onto the bench.

There is another.

Melodic yet resolute, the voice beseeched her from within her own mind. The feeling was all too familiar, of course, coming as it did each time she was called—more like summoned—to do the bidding of whatever force commanded her. While such compulsions had come with varying degrees of intensity, this was unlike anything she had yet experienced.

"McFarland," she responded, the single word echoing in her ears. "He must die."

Rather than another response she could understand, Lona instead recognized the sensation that came as images and suggestions began spilling forth and faces, each of them blurred and shadowed, danced in her consciousness. Most were people she did not know, and trying to bring any of them into focus was a futile gesture. She could only wait until whatever it was that impelled her brought the indistinct visions into sharp relief, at which time she could begin to comprehend her next task. Struggling against dizziness and the momentary nausea that always gripped her at this time, Lona waited until a single face centered itself in her mind's eye.

A short, stocky man with thinning red hair. Who was he? Lona knew that other answers would only come in time, and only take longer to reveal themselves the harder she willed them to appear. As with most other aspects of her life, patience now was most certainly a virtue.

Still, she knew she had her new target. This man, whoever he was and because of whatever he had done or might do in the future, must die. McFarland, as important as it was to dispatch him, would have to wait a bit longer. For now, Lona had new preparations to make.

Waves of queasiness subsided and Lona realized her wet skin was beginning to chill. Rising from the bench, she turned off the shower before reaching for the oversized terry-cloth towel hanging on a nearby hook and beginning to dry herself. As she turned to step out of the shower, her eyes caught sight of the cedar wall and she stopped, feeling her jaw muscles slacken in shock.

The vines, some of them anyway, were dead. Desiccated

and brown with extreme age, pieces of the once-vibrant plant now fell to the shower floor, the rest of it dissolving to dust as she reached out once more to touch it. How had that happened? She had watered all of the household plants the previous evening before retiring for bed. Had this one fallen victim to some odd disease?

No.

With a start, Lona looked down at her hands, turning them over and examining them as though enlightenment might appear from her very flesh. She had caused this? Uncertainty and even fear reached out for her as Lona contemplated what she had just done, her anxiety only heightening with the knowledge that she would receive no answers.

It's not fair, damn it!

Again, no one replied.

TWENTY-FIVE

THERE YOU ARE. Fishing in Minnesota, my ass.

Reiko Vandeberg smiled as she peered through her binoculars at the backyard of the unassuming sage-green house, nestled among several homes of similar design plotted around the cul-de-sac she had dubbed "Genericville, Suburbia." Through the lenses, she watched as a lean, tanned man—in good shape for someone in his late fifties—stepped through the open sliding glass door and onto the home's wooden patio deck. He was dressed in dark slacks and a white dress shirt with no tie and his sleeves rolled up to a point below his elbows. Reiko noted that his dark, stiff hair did not move despite a decent breeze. He paused momentarily as if to verify that he was alone, then cupped his hands to light the cigarette dangling from his mouth.

Those things'll be the death of you, sir, Reiko thought as she watched CIA Deputy Director Nicholas McFarland take the first drag from the cigarette. *Says so right on the package.*

Reaching into her pocket, Reiko extracted her cellular phone and flipped open its cover. Pressing a speed-dial key, she held the phone to her ear and listened as she heard her call diverted directly to voice mail rather than ringing through to the other end of the line. Shaking her head, she left another message—her fourth—for Lona to call her back before ending the call and slipping the phone back into her pocket. The message was perfunctory and generic, as required when talking on an open line. Reiko sighed as she returned her attention to the house. The number she had called was known only to her and Lona, and Lona had yet to return any of her messages. For her call to route to voice mail without ringing meant only one thing: she had turned off her phone.

She's gone dark, again. Where the hell did she go this time, and why didn't she tell me before she left?

This was not new behavior for Lona, of course. For years, it had been standard procedure for Lona to "go quiet" when on assignment, for Reiko's protection as well as her own. Reiko knew she should not be concerned, but these were not normal circumstances, and Lona most certainly was not acting like herself—the self she had been before her long absence.

Reiko released an exasperated sigh as she shifted to a more comfortable position where she sat at the base of the large oak tree. Other trees along with evergreen bushes and a low-rise rock wall offered an ideal location for surveillance, concealing her both from the houses around her and the residential street to her right. From here, she had an unobstructed view of the house that was anything but the quiet, unassuming suburban domicile it appeared to be. Looking past McFarland into the house, she could see at least two other figures moving about, one wearing a shoulder holster over his blue pullover shirt. Another man wore a dark blue NTAC Windbreaker.

Not very subtle.

Tracking McFarland to this safe house—all while not revealing her own presence—had proven every bit as challenging as following him and his security escort to the prior two locations where he had been secreted. Not for the first time, Reiko wished Lona was here to assist her with this surveillance, or at least was available to share more of the seemingly infallible insight she now harbored.

It was Lona who had put forth the revelation that McFarland would be traveling from Washington, D.C. to Seattle—most likely to meet with NTAC agents— but she had left it to Reiko herself to track the Agency director's movements once he completed his clandestine cross-country flight. Despite that knowledge, following McFarland was no easy task, as the NTAC agents charged with his protection were doing so in effective fashion. Reiko had made initial contact with McFarland as soon as he arrived at Sea-Tac Airport and was whisked away in a government-issue SUV, and followed him to the local NTAC headquarters.

However, it was while attempting to pursue McFarland to one of the Agency's "safe houses" that she realized his protection detail was leaving little to chance. She had followed what she at first believed to be the vehicle transporting McFarland to a condominium located in Yarrow Point, a small town east of Seattle. Keeping watch over the place for several hours while agents came and went, a sneaking suspicion that things were too quiet there soon came over her. Reiko risked a closer inspection of the condo, only to discover it empty. Angry with herself at how easily she had been duped, it had taken several attempts at following vehicles to and from NTAC headquarters before she finally found McFarland's true hiding place.

I know this body's getting slower these days, but I didn't think I was getting dumber.

Stifling a yawn, Reiko reached up to massage her right temple as she watched McFarland pace the deck. Puffs of wispy, white smoke occasionally swirled about his head before being dissipated by the breeze. In a sense, Reiko realized she owed McFarland a debt of thanks for the role he played in placing Lona into her life. That had been nearly twenty years ago now, though for Lona twelve of those years had passed in the blink of an eye.

For Reiko, as the woman left behind, those years had seemed interminable.

It had taken her months to accept that Lona was gone, either captured or killed, or perhaps in hiding and fearing for her own life and unable to contact her. When the months turned to years, Reiko forced herself to accept that her lover was gone, and so she made attempts to piece together something resembling an ordinary life. Putting to use her formidable computer skills as a corporate software analyst, she slowly opened herself to love as well, finding a new life partner dedicated to her and capable of making even the bleakest of days seem hopeful.

Sweet Carmen, Reiko thought. *And I was able to abandon you so quickly, so easily.* She had not even hesitated, not when confronted with Lona standing before her on that street in Seattle, looking exactly as she had the last time she had seen her more than a decade earlier.

Lona's return was indeed a miracle, especially considering the circumstances surrounding her disappearance and long absence. However, Reiko slowly had awakened to the fact that while her life's true love had come back in body, Lona never fully was present in mind and spirit. At first, she wanted to attribute their emotional disconnection to Lona's reentry process. Acclimating to life after being "gone" for so long had to carry unimaginable layers of adjustment. Later, as Reiko discovered the incredible physical ability bestowed upon Lona by whatever powers had spirited her through time and space, she chalked up Lona's distraction to her process of understanding and accepting this wondrous gift.

However, when Lona began talking about her higher calling—this sense of special purpose and destiny that now drove her beyond any other internal motivations—Reiko realized the woman she knew and loved more than any other person had yet to return to her. She was there, but buried beneath layers of other consciousness that seemed to dominate her every waking moment. This new Lona was unpredictable, impulsive, even reckless as she carried out these mysterious assignments, which came not from her former employers but instead from another authority she would or could not identify. She pursued her targets at a far greater pace than she had in the past. Rather than taking months to plan an assassination, Lona had carried out multiple hits in just a few weeks. Her actions carried with them far more risk than she used to undertake, and Reiko feared that her irresponsible approach to the tasks she carried out would soon be her undoing.

Despite all of this, Reiko continued to support her, though now she did so with an emptiness of soul—one she hoped might yet again be filled. She had come to realize that the only thing worse than losing Lona in an instant all those years ago was losing her to whatever it was that now guided her. There had to be some way to reach her, of that Reiko was certain, but it would take time to reach past these drives and compulsions that seemed on the verge of consuming her lover.

Through her binoculars, she saw McFarland turn back toward the open doorway as though responding to a summons. With her left hand she reached for the laser microphone she had brought with her and aimed it for the sliding door's tinted glass surface. Reiko thumbed the switch and the microphone emitted a laser beam that bounced off the glass, picking up the vibrations of sounds from inside the room beyond the door and transferring those sounds to the receiver in her left ear.

". . . word from HQ. Transfer teams are sixty seconds out," said the man with the shoulder holster, whom Reiko watched with the binoculars. "Time to move again."

"Okay," replied McFarland, his voice somewhat muffled

as the microphone picked up his voice from outside the room. "I'm glad I didn't unpack," he said, shaking his head as he lit another cigarette.

Motion to her left drew Reiko's attention away from the house, and she turned to see sunlight glinting off the polished bodies of three black SUVs coming up the street.

Reiko's mind raced. Should the NTAC agents follow their usual pattern, the vehicles would arrive at the safe house, after which each of them would in turn enter and exit the home's attached garage. This action would conceal McFarland's transfer into one of the SUVs, followed by each of them speeding off in one of three different directions. Odds were strong, she knew, that the subject of her attention would disappear into the Seattle metropolis, possibly eluding her for good this time. It had taken her considerable effort to track him to this house. Could she be successful a second time—and without giving away her presence? Would Lona even be able to find him under such circumstances? Once NTAC realized their movements were being tracked, they would redouble their efforts to conceal McFarland, and may well take more aggressive action to thwart her own activities.

There was another option, Reiko concluded, as she put down the laser microphone and binoculars, and reached for the Sig Sauer holstered beneath her left arm. Without Lona to consult, the decision to act was hers.

She will understand, Reiko thought. Only on rare occasions had she ever engaged a target herself, in situations such as this, where there was a danger of losing a target. So far as Reiko was concerned, this was like those other cases. Of course, Lona always had taken issue in those instances, preferring Reiko to avoid risking herself.

Steadying herself against the tree, she raised the Sig and took aim at McFarland. It would be a tricky shot from this distance, but not impossible, particularly as he was leaning against the deck railing as he finished his cigarette. Indeed, allowing him outside to smoke at all had been the first real mistake Reiko had observed by the NTAC agents protecting him. All it took was one mistake.

"Hey!"

The harsh shout shattered the neighborhood's relative tranquility, causing Reiko to flinch at the same instant she caught movement in her peripheral vision. To her right, a man in a blue Windbreaker stepped from the alley between the safe house and the adjacent home. How had he seen her? Had he simply been paying attention to his surroundings and detected her movement among the trees? Whatever the reason, it did not matter as the man's jaw went slack and comprehension dawned, and he reached for his sidearm.

Without hesitation Reiko adjusted her aim and fired at the agent, hitting him in his left shoulder. The Sig's report echoed from within the tree line, and Reiko heard a dog bark in protest from somewhere in the neighborhood. Ahead of her, McFarland whirled at the sound of the gunshot, his eyes widening in horror as he saw the agent fall.

Damn it!

Reiko bolted from her concealed position as McFarland ducked toward the open doorway. She fired on the run, the first shot missing him and burrowing into the wall beside the door. McFarland screamed in terror, throwing himself through the doorway and into the house. An instant later an arm emerged from the doorway wielding a pistol aiming in her direction and Reiko ducked as the first shots whizzed past her. She fired back in retaliation, backpedaling up the slope. Catching movement to her right, she saw two more agents coming around the far side of the house with weapons in hand.

"Federal agents! Drop your weapon!"

Firing to cover her retreat, Reiko reached the tree line and ducked behind the large oak, ejecting the Sig's magazine and loading a replacement. Gunfire echoed off the walls of the neighboring homes and chunks of the tree's bark splintered away as rounds dug into its trunk. Reiko scrambled back, keeping the oak between her and her pursuers. A figure darted between the trees to her left and she fired at it. Another agent lunged to hide behind a tree, and she heard shouts of warning from different directions.

Stupid! Stupid! Stupid! How had she allowed this to spiral so far out of control?

The back of her foot struck something behind her and Reiko lost her balance, tumbling clumsily to the uneven ground. She landed heavily, wincing in pain as something jabbed her side. With her free hand, she pushed herself up and started rolling to her feet when motion flashed through the trees to her left. Reiko saw a blue jacket and fired at it, hearing the cry of pain as the bullet struck soft flesh. Turning away from the fallen agent, she sprinted through the trees, her eyes scanning for an avenue of escape. Voices of alarm and warning called out behind her, accompanied by running footfalls crashing through the forest.

Then fire ignited in her shoulder.

Agony enveloped her as the bullet ripped into her body and Reiko gasped as the air was forced from her lungs and she collapsed face-first to the ground. The pain pushed outward from her damaged shoulder, her right arm hanging limp and useless. Panic began to set in as the sound of footsteps drew closer. From the corner of her eye, Reiko saw her pistol lying in the dirt and she tried to shift her body in an effort to reach it.

"Don't move!"

Jerking her head to her left, she looked up at the muzzle of the Glock pistol, unwavering as it aimed directly at her face. The face of the agent wielding it was dark with determination and restrained anger. He wanted to shoot her; was waiting for her to provide the reason. Around her, Reiko heard the sounds of other agents approaching, some of them repeating the command to not move or calling out on radios for support.

Fresh pain pierced her shoulder and she bit her lip to avoid crying out as her arms were pulled behind her. Then she felt the touch of cold steel as handcuffs closed around her wrists. There was no stopping the grunt that exploded from her lips as she was hauled to her feet, and it was all she could do to maintain consciousness.

"What's your name?" The voice was urgent and firm.

"Who do you work for?"

"How did you find us?"

Reiko ignored the questions, instead concentrating on dealing with the pain in her tortured shoulder. Above it all, she felt ashamed at what she had allowed to happen. She had rushed to regain Lona's favor, only to be betrayed by her own deep feelings for the woman she sincerely loved and who likely had been taken from her by forces she never would understand.

I'm sorry, Lona.

TWENTY-SIX

LAS VEGAS, NEVADA

As THE HEADLIGHTS of Abigail's red Toyota splashed across the front of the two-story prefabricated metal building, Alfred felt his stomach lurch with another twinge of apprehension. He turned to look at his companion behind the wheel, seeing the alabaster skin of her face bathed in a pale blue glow from the car's dashboard instruments. Only when she offered an encouraging smile was he able to relax, if only a bit.

"We're here," Abigail said, shifting the car into park and killing the engine.

"How do you know you found the right place?" he asked, pushing out the attempt at awkward small talk as he fiddled with the envelope in his hand. "This building looks the same as all of the others out here."

"A little disappointed?" she asked. "Maybe you were expecting some old warehouse down by the waterfront or something?" She shrugged. "Well, there's no waterfront around here, but I could knock three times on the door and give the secret code if it'd make you feel better."

Alfred laughed, shaking his head. "That won't be necessary. I'm just a little nervous is all."

"Oh, sweetie," Abigail said, "I know you're nervous, and I know you're taking a huge risk for me . . . for all of us." Leaning over in her seat, she kissed him.

Alfred silently drank in the brief burst of pink that flared in his consciousness as their lips brushed. He and Abigail had been all but inseparable since the night at the diner, and he had relished every moment of their time together. Evenings were spent talking at length about everything and nothing. They explored each other as lovers, allowing him to delve deeper into her mind than he had with anyone since receiving his gift. Her presence was intoxicating, his feelings for her achieving an intensity greater than he had ever experienced—and in such a short time that he barely dared believe it. It was this trust and faith that gave him the courage to help her, and her friends.

While he still was uncomfortable with stealing from anyone, he eventually justified the notion by telling himself he was acting as a sort of twenty-first-century Robin Hood, taking from the well-off and overindulged in order to help those in need. That had helped him to make this journey with Abigail. But now that they were here, he felt his conscience calling into question his actions, those he already had perpetrated as well as what he might do in the days to come. He did not want to leave the car, but instead to beg Abigail to drive away from this place and never look back.

Holding up the envelope, he said, "This will cost me more than my job, Abigail. When people find out—and they will—I'll go to jail."

"Alfred," she said, "no one is going to let you go to jail." She indicated the building with a nod of her head. "The people in there are ready to protect us no matter what happens. That's part of what this is all about. They're ensuring that the 4400 are not forbidden from fulfilling our destiny by those who don't understand or *can't* understand."

"I want to believe that," Alfred said.

Abigail opened her car door, triggering the overhead dome light. "Then let's believe," she said. "Come on, let's go."

Alfred nodded in agreement as he exited the car, returning the envelope to the inside pocket of his jacket. They walked toward the front entrance of the unremarkable building, which sported a waist-high band of beige, rough-hewn rock below its walls of blue metal siding. Abigail reached the glass door first and Alfred was surprised to see that it was unlocked, given that it and the adjacent window bore no signage or other indication of occupancy.

Once inside, he saw a reception desk outfitted with a computer terminal, a telephone, and the expected array of accessories. Behind the desk, a picture window offered a view of what appeared to be a similarly equipped office space, which to Alfred seemed to lend a sense of legitimacy to whatever operation this might be. At the far end of the narrow room, light spilled from an open door leading to the back of the building.

Abigail reached out to take his hand in hers, and once he touched her, his perception of the room brightened with swirling color. She led the way, striding past the rows of desks toward the open door with the confidence of someone familiar with her surroundings. As they drew closer to the rear of the room, Alfred heard the murmurings of muted conversation echoing through the doorway.

They passed through the door and Alfred dropped her hand as he caught sight of a group of four men standing within an open warehouse area. Shipping crates of varying sizes were scattered in several assorted stacks around the room, with others lining the walls. Abigail's and Alfred's footsteps rang out against the concrete floor, and the men turned at their approach. One of them, a shorter man with receding red hair who to Alfred looked to be in his thirties, started walking their way. He was dressed in khaki cargo pants and a dark blue or black shirt, over which he wore a scuffed brown leather jacket, the ensemble giving him the appearance of—as Alfred might once have read in one of his pulp novels—a "man of intrigue."

Or, perhaps he's just dangerous.

"You must be Mr. Twenter," the man said. "Abigail's told us good things about you. I'm Darren Abbott."

Alfred extended his hand in greeting. "Please, call me Alfred." They stood motionless before one another for several seconds before he realized from the look in Abbott's eyes that the man had no intention of shaking hands. Clearing his throat, Alfred instead reached up to adjust his glasses, certain that Abbott's choice was not one of discourtesy but rather because he wished to avoid having his thoughts read. It was a guess, of course, but it was enough to further unsettle Alfred.

As his companions stepped closer, Abbott said, "Abigail also tells me that you're considering joining our effort. I appreciate that." He smiled for the first time. "As you could probably figure out when you walked in, we're just getting started."

Nodding, Alfred asked, "Getting started doing what?" He had posed similar questions to Abigail, of course, but she always deferred, telling him that all would be made known to him when he finally met her friends.

"Right now," Abbott replied, "we're focusing a lot of effort on gathering resources and networking among our fellow gifted returnees, something our friend Abigail has been very helpful with."

Abigail smiled at the compliment. "I'm just doing what I think is right. It's as though everyone's watching whatever we do, and we're not welcome anywhere we go. I'm tired of living like that. A lot of us are."

"That's why it's time for us to work with each other and set common goals," Abbott said, "as we find out more about ourselves and how we now fit into the world."

Frowning, Alfred felt sweat on his palms and wiped them on his pants. "Isn't that the kind of thing The 4400 Center is supposed to be doing?"

Abbott shrugged. "Jordan Collier is dead, and I'm not convinced that place was doing anything to improve our situation while he was alive. Besides, there are advantages to keeping this operation among ourselves, rather than build some massive public testament to our presence. That sort of thing just invites scrutiny and interference, from NTAC on down."

His confusion and apprehension growing with every word Abbott spoke, Alfred asked, "What do we have to hide? Don't we want to build trust among people instead of just sneaking around?"

"We will," Abbott replied, "but we also have to shake off the shackles of our self-appointed masters, such as those at NTAC. Surely you know that they've been working actively to suppress the gifts we've been given?" He held up his right arm for emphasis. "They're injecting us with drugs. I only found out about it after I'd received three doses. I still have no idea what ability I might have. They've taken it from me." Lowering his arm, he stepped closer to Alfred. "We can't allow that to continue, Alfred. We have to organize ourselves and our resources. That's where people like you come in, Alfred." He nodded to Abigail. "I'm told you've already made some preliminary inquiries on our behalf?"

That's my cue.

"Um, yes," Alfred said, reaching into his jacket and retrieving the white envelope. Seeing the wrinkles along its edges, no doubt inflicted by his nervous toying with it during the drive here, he tried to smooth them by rubbing it along his arm. He looked to Abigail, who nodded in encouragement, before he held up the envelope.

"This is a list of names and safety-deposit box numbers from my bank. The boxes contain jewelry, rare coins, and other high-value collectibles. Some of the customers also use their boxes to store various amounts of cash." He never claimed to understand that practice. "All told, it's probably worth a couple hundred thousand dollars." It had taken him all night to review the list of deposit box renters, crossing off those names he felt did not deserve to fall victim to robbery, regardless of whatever cause Abbott was championing. He had made his views on this clear to Abigail, but felt that now was the time to restate his position. "I cannot stress enough the need for you to stick to this list. It's bad enough they'll eventually figure out I was behind this. I don't want to hurt some old widow along the way."

Abigail said, "I told him it wouldn't be a problem, and you'd find a way to work with whatever he could provide."

Nodding, Abbott said, "No problem at all. We'll take care of everything, and I'm glad you feel you can trust us, Alfred."

Alfred, his uncertainty climbing with each passing moment, offered the envelope to Abbott, holding it in such a manner that his fingers extended along its underside. When Abbott moved to take it, his fingers brushed Alfred's, the fleeting contact enough to give Alfred a connection to the other man's mind. Harsh violet exploded in his vision and a chill coursed through his body. Acting on pure instinct, Alfred reached out with his other hand, latching on to Abbott's bare wrist. He gasped as richer, darker colors flooded his mind even as Abbott shouted and struggled to free himself. Alfred ignored that, instead concentrating on the rush of imagery flashing before him, seeping through billowing clouds of purple and black.

There was more here, much more, but then the colors faded to nothingness and Alfred felt himself shoved with brute force to the cold, concrete floor.

"What the hell was that about?" Abbott growled, and Alfred looked up to see the other man eyeing him with menace as he massaged his wrist. One of Abbott's companions approached and picked up the envelope from where it had fallen to the floor, while the other two men moved to pull Alfred to his feet, each of them holding one of his arms in a grip that told him he would not be making an easy exit.

"Abigail!" Alfred shouted even as the men holding him twisted his arms in a bid to hold him still. "He's buying weapons with that money!"

"What?" She stepped forward, an expression of disbelief clouding her features. "That's not true!"

Unable to free himself from the two men holding him, Alfred grunted in mounting anger. "I saw it in his mind," he said, glaring at Abbott.

"Of course we're buying weapons, you moron," the other man said, making no attempt to hide the disdain in his voice. "There may well come a time when we'll be forced to defend ourselves." His voice was urgent, though not angry. "It's not the most desirable of options, of course, but sometimes we must do unpleasant things in order to achieve our goals. Surely you can understand that, Alfred?"

Abigail's expression was one of rage as she balled her fists. "He *lied* to me, Alfred! I swear he never said a word about this!"

"I know," Alfred said, nodding. He tried to free himself

from his new escorts, but it was a useless attempt. "I believe you."

Stepping closer, Abigail pointed an accusatory finger at Abbott. "You said there wouldn't be any violence. You said it wouldn't be like that!"

"And it won't," Abbott replied, "so long as no one forces my hand, but we have to be ready for that possibility."

With renewed strength, Alfred jerked his arms free from Abbott's men, who made no move to restrain him further. "It seems to me as though you're expecting—maybe even hoping—for someone to 'force your hand.' You're just waiting for an excuse to make some kind of 'statement.' And what do you intend to do after that?" His connection with Abbott had been too brief for him to gain a complete reading of the other man's mind. Only the most surface thoughts had been made available to him, but Alfred was certain he sensed something deeper, something far more menacing, than those few clues he had detected before Abbott pulled away.

Abbott regarded Alfred with cold eyes. "You do possess a wondrous gift, Alfred. What else has it told you about me and what I intend to do?"

"Not much," Alfred conceded, "but it's enough to tell me I don't want to be any part of this." Even as he spoke the words, he eyed the envelope one of the other men had given to Abbott. "I'm finished here." He looked toward Abigail, sensing that she wanted to go with him.

"So, that's it?" Abbott asked. "We say our good-byes and you go on about your merry way?" He nodded to his men, who once more took hold of Alfred's arms. The third man grabbed Abigail by her right arm. Alfred tried to loosen the grips of the men holding him, but once again was unsuccessful. Turning his attention back to Abbott, he was distressed to see that the man had produced from his jacket pocket a pistol—a Colt .45 semiautomatic that Alfred recognized as like those once carried by the U.S. military—and was now aiming the weapon at him.

"I'm afraid that's not likely to happen, Alfred," Abbott said, offering a humorless smile. "So, you have a choice to make. Sure you don't want to talk it over?"

Alfred heard Abigail gasp, and looked over to see her face was stained with tears. "Talk what over? How can we believe anything you say now?"

Directing an indifferent gaze toward her, Abbott said, "I'm really only concerned with what Alfred might believe. He needs to understand that I'm quite serious about this, and you can help me convince him."

In the heartbeat that passed before Abbott began to swing the pistol toward her, Alfred saw what was about to happen in his own mind's eye.

"Wait!" he shouted. "You don't have—"

His pistol aimed at Abigail, Abbott pulled the trigger, and the sound of the single shot echoed against the warehouse's walls as the bullet struck Abigail in the chest.

"No!" Alfred cried, watching as she collapsed, dead even before she crumpled to the floor. She lay face up, eyes staring unseeing at the ceiling as blood stained her blouse and started to pool beneath her. At the same time, Alfred flinched as the slight yet still-perceptible mental link— one he had been able to maintain with Abigail whenever in her presence—seemed to rip from his mind, leaving a dark void in his consciousness from which he sensed nothing but his own pain and despair.

Abbott turned back to Alfred. "Don't tell me you didn't see that coming." His expression told Alfred that the man was rather pleased with his own joke.

Grunting in rage, Alfred strained to free himself from the two men holding him, only to wince in pain as one of the men clocked him along the side of his head. Stars danced in his vision and he sagged, coughing. "You son of a bitch," he whispered, the words spilling from his mouth.

"That I am," Abbott said, raising the pistol so that it was once more aimed at Alfred. "So, about our unfinished discussion."

Whatever he said next was lost amid the cacophony of an immense explosion that rocked the entire warehouse. Alfred felt himself thrown to the floor as the blast rattled the metal paneling and white-hot air surged overhead, and he rolled onto his stomach and threw his hands up to protect his head.

A second explosion tore through the warehouse on the heels of the first, sending roils of flame through the air above him and he felt the heat on his exposed skin. Dark smoke rolled through the warehouse and he gasped for breath. All around him, debris from what once had been shipping crates and assorted warehouse detritus littered the floor. Lying among the wreckage were three bodies—Abbott's men—but not Abbott himself.

His ears ringing so loudly that he could not hear even his own wracked coughing, Alfred crawled to Abigail, hoping to drag her body away from the chaos. He paused as he came abreast of her, his heart leaping into his throat as he once more beheld her lifeless eyes and the expression of surprise and pain fixed on her beautiful face.

No.

The single word tore at his soul as he reached out to brush her cheek, emotion overruling logic and reason as his mind searched for some sign, some link, that she might still be alive. He found only nothingness.

Dear, sweet Abigail.

The sound of tortured metal rending from somewhere overhead snapped him from his mournful reverie, and Alfred looked up in time to see the steel beam smashing to the floor close enough to cut through the ringing that still assaulted his ears. As the beam settled onto the floor, he turned his gaze toward the ceiling, feeling his mouth drop open at the sight of the roof's entire network of beams and roofing panels beginning to buckle.

Get out!

The command echoed in his mind as Alfred jerked his head around, searching for a means of escape. To his left, one of the warehouse's walls had collapsed, offering him a way out. Scrambling to his feet, he navigated through the remains of the storage bay and its contents until he found himself in the narrow hallway connecting the warehouse to the building's front offices. Behind him, sections of the roof fell to the floor in a rolling crescendo that echoed through the confined passageway. A fresh burst of dust and other pollutants blew into the hall, enveloping Alfred in a thick cloud.

Gagging on the contaminants clogging his lungs, Alfred huddled along the wall of the hallway, the ringing in his ears only now starting to fade. He peered into what remained of the warehouse, its roof now partially collapsed and shrouding the majority of the room, still not quite believing he had managed to escape with his life. What had caused the explosion? Some unstable munitions or other materiel stored within the warehouse? Was it possible that Abbott and his men had fallen victim to their own carelessness?

Alfred sat huddled against the wall for what seemed like several minutes, listening for signs of any other survivors but hearing nothing. How many people had been in the building? He had not seen Darren Abbott since the explosion, but the man's threats still echoed in Alfred's ears. Had fate not intervened, Alfred was certain he would not have survived the night.

"Twenter."

The single word was hoarse, barely audible, but it chilled Alfred nonetheless. He turned to see Darren Abbott, blood running from a nasty gash on the left side of his head, staring at him with unbridled hatred. His left arm hung limp at his side, but he still carried the .45 in his right hand, the muzzle of which was aimed at Alfred's chest.

Alfred held up his hands, knowing the gesture was useless. How had he failed to detect Abbott's presence? Had the explosion so rattled his senses?

Doesn't really matter now, does it?

In the distance, Alfred could hear sirens. How much

time had passed since the explosion? Long enough for police or the fire department to respond? For a brief moment, he almost allowed himself to hope they might arrive in time.

"There's nothing I can do to hurt you," he said, keeping his hands where Abbott could see them. "If you leave before the police arrive, I'll have no way of knowing where you're going. I'm no threat to you."

Abbott frowned, shaking his head. "I'd like to believe that, but I have no idea how much of my mind you read. I can't take any chances. If it's any consolation, this isn't personal." He even sighed as he raised the .45 until Alfred could stare down its barrel.

Then Alfred felt a rush of air pass him, as though he was on a sidewalk too close to the street as a large car or truck passed him by. An instant later he watched as a huge, red line appeared across Abbott's throat, reaching from side to side. Blood began to pour from it, streaming down his chest and adding a dark, wet stain to his dust-ridden shirt.

What the hell?

Abbott's eyes were wide with surprise, and he dropped the pistol to reach for his throat even as he gasped for breath. Alfred heard nothing but a sick gurgling as the man fell to his knees, blood spattering the dull gray carpet before him. He dropped face-first to the floor, his body continuing to convulse for another few moments before finally becoming still.

Horrified at what he had just witnessed, Alfred lurched away from Abbott's body, backpedaling away from the dead man until he could regain his feet before turning and scrambling up the littered hallway. He had run only half a dozen steps before he felt a hand on his collar, yanking him to a halt. The corridor echoed with his shriek of terror as he was pulled backward and slammed into the nearby wall. A knife pressed against his throat, and Alfred flinched as he got his first look at his attacker. He closed his eyes and waited for the sting of a metal blade.

Nothing happened.

Alfred opened his eyes, beholding Darren Abbott's apparent murderer. It was a woman, shorter than he was and dressed in a black, form-hugging bodysuit that emphasized her lithe, athletic physique. She wore a cap on her head that concealed her hair, and she glared at him with bright green eyes, saying nothing as she kept him pinned against the wall.

"Please." The single word was a hoarse whisper, his vision blurring as tears filled his eyes. A ragged cough shook him, a product of the smoke and dust he had inhaled.

She said nothing, instead reaching up with her other gloved hand to grasp his jaw and turn his head from side to side, as though trying to determine whether she recognized him.

Alfred's body jerked as his mind connected with hers, filling with bursts of red and black, a kaleidoscopic jumble unlike any he had previously encountered. He fought to push past the urgent, primal emotions that drove her, but found himself slamming into some kind of mental barrier. It seemed somehow to be imposed upon her, another separate consciousness infiltrating her own and connecting to her every thought.

Only with effort was Alfred able to circumvent this obstacle, allowing him access to the woman's innermost thoughts. He saw within her the people she had killed—including Darren Abbott and his men—as well as the people she planned to kill in the future. Some of the victims appeared selected based on self-preservation, a desire to protect herself from those she considered a threat. Others were targets for reasons she did not possess or understand. No, he decided, that was not correct. The reasons were there; they simply were not hers. This woman was not acting entirely of her own free will.

My God, his mind screamed. *She's a 4400!*

She was being impelled to seek out these individuals, though Alfred was able to sense the confusion and doubt that troubled her. Despite these concerns she pressed forward, burying her emotions and proceeding as though she were nothing more than an automaton, acting based on the wills of others. *Was she being controlled by the same people who had abducted her, who had taken him?* With horror, Alfred realized this woman might represent a danger much greater than someone like Darren Abbott.

The sirens were getting closer, and it was obvious his assailant wanted to leave before the authorities arrived. She released her grip on his face, and Alfred sensed that she had no intention of killing him. His feeling was verified when she stepped away from him.

"You are not a target," she said simply, before turning to leave.

"Wait! What does that mean?" Alfred shouted, trying to make sense of the jumble of thoughts swimming in his mind from their lingering mental link. Gesturing about the warehouse, he asked, "*You* did all of this? Why?" Outside, he could hear the engines and sirens of fire engines as the huge vehicles pulled up to the building. There were only seconds remaining before firefighters would be here.

She stared at him, her jade eyes cold and all but lifeless. "It does not concern you," she said before stepping away. Then, she just disappeared before his eyes, the only evidence of her presence being pieces of paper and other small detritus kicked up in her wake. Even before the litter began to settle once more to the floor, Alfred realized that the residual connection he felt after linking with someone had dissipated, telling him the mysterious woman was gone.

Incredible.

The word echoed in Alfred's mind even as he collapsed against the wall and allowed himself to sink to the floor, drained as the emotions of the past several minutes returned. Terror, grief, hopelessness, and despair washed over him. His body trembled in anguish and as he thought of Abigail, tears streamed down his cheeks.

She's lost. The single, agonizing thought echoed in his mind. *I've lost her.*

Alfred heard new footsteps in the hallway. Looking to his left, he saw flashlight beams cutting through the near darkness, and bulky, shadowy figures making their way toward him. As they drew closer, he recognized the distinctive helmets and heavy coats of firefighters.

"Sir," one of them said as he came abreast of Alfred and

knelt beside him, "are you all right? Are you injured? Is there anyone else in here?"

"A woman," Alfred said, his voice weak. "She ran inside." Reaching up, he gripped the man by his arm. "You have to stop her."

The firefighter's expression was one of concern. "Stop who? What's going on?" Hooking his hands beneath Alfred's arms, he pulled him to his feet and began directing him toward the exit. As they walked, Alfred heard the crackle of the radio clipped to the other man's equipment harness.

"Building's clear," a voice called out from the radio's speaker. "Captain, we've got four bodies in here. Looks like one of them had his throat slit."

Feeling the firefighter tense as he heard the report, Alfred turned to see the man's features darken, and he sensed his suspicion as his grip tightened on Alfred's bicep. "You know anything about that?" There was no mistaking the accusation lacing the man's words.

Still trying to process everything that had happened to him, Alfred did not even try to answer the blunt question. "I need to talk to someone immediately," he said, now knowing what he had to do. "I need to talk to someone from NTAC."

TWENTY-SEVEN

NTAC
SEATTLE, WASHINGTON

"Good afternoon, Mr. Twenter."

Alfred looked up at the sound of the feminine voice, which tore his attention from the canary yellow legal pad upon which he had been writing details of his official statement to NTAC. He set his pen down upon the wooden tabletop as a man and woman stepped into the room, so engrossed was he on trying to make sense of the jumbled thoughts rattling around in his exhausted mind that he had not heard the interview room's door open. Both new arrivals wore casual business attire—slacks and jackets—and Alfred could see the outline of holstered firearms beneath their jackets. The man was carrying a manila file folder while the woman held a black leather portfolio.

"Good afternoon," Alfred offered as the man closed the door. He restrained an impulse to respond in a less polite manner. Alfred had endured different versions of the greeting since arriving at the NTAC offices earlier in the day and the platitude was wearing thin. After what he had endured the previous evening, there was nothing "good" about the morning or the afternoon, or how he felt about life in general at the moment. "Please, call me Alfred," he said, rising from his chair.

"Fair enough, Alfred," the man said. "I'm Agent Baldwin." He indicated the woman with a gesture. "This is my partner, Agent Skouris. Under the circumstances, I hope you forgive us if we don't shake hands."

Alfred could not help a small, humorless chuckle. "I guess you've read my initial statement."

As she pulled up a chair and took a seat, Skouris replied, "Yes, and we want to thank you again for contacting us, especially considering what you've been through."

The words washed over Alfred but he ignored them. *What he had been through?* All of it was trouble of his own making. He was ashamed at himself for what he nearly had entered into with Darren Abbott and his ilk, and guilt weighed upon him for what had happened to Abigail. That Abbott was dead did not concern him, and had he been thinking more clearly at the time, he might even have thanked the woman responsible for killing him.

As for why he was here, the reason for that was simple: Alfred had seen the woman's mind, the thoughts that tortured her and the strange compulsions that drove her. She was someone NTAC needed to know about. What he had not been prepared to hear was that the federal agents standing before him already knew about her, and had been looking and even hoping for the kind of information Alfred was here to provide.

From where he stood behind his partner, Baldwin said, "Alfred, we don't want to appear insensitive to your loss, but we're a little pressed for time. I hope you'll understand if we cut to the chase." Though the man's tone was casual, Alfred sensed an underlying tension in both agents. They looked tired, as though they had not slept in quite some time. Something was keeping them here rather than allowing them to go home, and it was wearing on them.

"Very well," Alfred said. Pointing to the large mirror dominating the wall behind the agents, he asked, "Are your questions for your own benefit, or for whoever is behind that one-way glass?"

Without batting an eye, Baldwin replied, "Both, actually." Stepping closer to the table, he opened the folder in his hand and extracted what Alfred recognized as a glossy photograph, which he laid on the table. "Is this the woman you encountered last night?"

Alfred gazed down at the photo and could not help the involuntary gasp that caught in his throat. From out of the picture, striking green eyes bored into him. The woman's slim, angular face was framed by short red hair cut in a style that reminded him of his dear Abigail.

"Dear God," he said, bringing his hand to his mouth. "Yes, that's her. Her name is . . . Lona . . . something." Alfred found it odd yet interesting that he had not managed to grasp this simple piece of information from the woman while they were linked.

Leaning forward and allowing her forearms to rest on

the table, Agent Skouris pointed to the photograph. "Her name is Lona Callahan. Do you believe she was part of the group you met at the warehouse?"

Shaking his head, Alfred replied, "Not at all. Indeed, she was the one who put an end to whatever plans they had." His preliminary statement had included quite a bit of information regarding Darren Abbott and the small group of followers who were with him at the warehouse. He also had included his own reprehensible actions in the days leading up to their meeting, and had come to NTAC prepared to accept whatever consequences might result from his admission. However, Baldwin and Skouris seemed not at all interested in hearing about the rogue 4400 and his band.

No, Alfred decided, it was not that they were disinterested. Instead, finding this other woman, the one who had killed Abbott and his men, seemed simply to be a higher priority.

Baldwin leaned toward the table and placed his hands palms down on the table. "Alfred, did you have direct contact with Lona Callahan? Were you able to read her mind?"

His eyes still locked on the photo, Alfred nodded. "Yes, I was." Upon being taken to the NTAC office in Las Vegas, he had informed agents there of his ability, at first thinking they would be skeptical if not a bit surprised to hear such a tale. Of course, he realized in short order that the agents had been dealing with the 4400 for nearly a year. They likely had been hearing about and investigating all manner of bizarre claims and incidents since the release of the returnees from quarantine. It would be much the same for Baldwin and Skouris, who Twenter knew were not only among the agents at the forefront of investigating the 4400 but were also currently trying to solve the murder of Jordan Collier. For them to be here, now, and asking him about this uncanny woman told Alfred that his chance encounter with her was of great importance to them.

Baldwin had taken a seat in one of the other chairs, turning it so that he straddled it and rested his forearms atop its straight back. "Can you tell us what you saw?" he asked.

Frowning, Alfred replied, "I'll do my best, but sorting through another person's thoughts can be quite difficult, even more so when it comes to this woman."

"Just do the best you can," Skouris said, her voice low and calm. "Why is it different with her? Was she able to resist you in some way?"

Alfred shook his head. "No, nothing like that." Pausing, he searched for the right words, frustrated at the effort it took to convey what he had plumbed from the depths of Lona Callahan's mind. He held up both hands, hoping to illustrate what he wanted to say.

"It's almost as though she possesses a dual personality. At first, her mind seemed precisely disciplined. She's a trained killer, an expert at what she does, having learned from the best. I also sensed that she's completing a mission of personal importance, but after filtering through all of that, I found something else." He grimaced, knowing how this next part would sound. "It was like an overriding, unerring sense of larger purpose, one dictated to her by a higher power she is completely dedicated to serve. What I found odd about this was that she doesn't seem to know who or what this other authority might be."

"Like she's on some sort of internal *jihad*?" Baldwin asked. "A holy mission?"

Alfred frowned, not certain if that was an apt description. "I'm not sure, because she seems so conflicted. Much of the time, she's very committed to her personal quest, which I sense is motivated from a standpoint of self-protection or even survival, as though the people she targets represent threats to her." Noting the look Baldwin exchanged with Skouris, he knew his read of Lona Callahan, as muddled as it might be within his own mind, was still accurate.

"You said she was this way much of the time," Skouris said. "What about other times?"

Nodding, Alfred replied, "On those occasions, when this 'higher calling' comes into play, she seems compelled to set aside that goal. As strange as this sounds, it's almost like she's driven by what she considers her . . . destiny, as if she's fulfilling a predetermined role in history. This instills in her a formidable self-confidence, as though she already knows she'll succeed." Unable to interpret the fixed expressions on the faces of both agents, he slumped back in his chair. "I know how crazy this all must sound."

"Not really," Baldwin said, offering a tired smile. "After this past year, nothing sounds crazy to me anymore."

"Well, it gets crazier," Alfred said, before explaining the incredible speed he had seen the woman demonstrate.

"She ran like Mercury," he said, shaking his head. "It was amazing,"

"Par for the course, these days," Baldwin replied. Shaking his head, he added, "When did I start taking this kind of thing for granted? When *exactly* did that happen?"

"About ten minutes after that ball of light showed up," Skouris said, looking up from where she was jotting notes at a furious pace on the pad inside her portfolio. To Alfred, she said, "This higher purpose or calling you mentioned. What do you think it is?"

Alfred reached up to adjust his glasses. "I knew you'd ask me that. This is where it starts to get very jumbled for me." He gritted his teeth, recalling the rapid-fire succession of images that had threatened to engulf him during his connection to Callahan. "In her mind, when she is called to act against a fellow returnee, it's as though she sees herself as an equalizer, an authority charged with maintaining what she understands to be a 'balance' among the returnees." Skouris reacted to that phrasing, blinking several times as though unsure of what she had just heard, or that the words had triggered some other memory. "Agent Skouris? Is something wrong?"

Shaking her head, she replied, "No. It's nothing." Her eyes narrowed as she regarded him. "A balance? Between what?"

Alfred searched the memories he had collected, those belonging to Callahan as well as whatever other consciousness dwelled within her mind. "Somehow, the force guiding her actions employs her when something is detected that it believes affects whatever social or historical course the returnees are meant to travel, as though scales were being tipped one way or another." Sighing, he added, "I'm afraid it doesn't get much more specific than that, at least so far as she's concerned. It's as though information is compartmentalized, and she's given just what she needs to accomplish her tasks, which are designed either to maintain or restore this balance."

Baldwin said, "Hell of a way to balance a scale."

"She doesn't seem to see it that way," Alfred countered. "I mean, it's how she's trained to respond to a threat. She neutralizes it."

Rising from his chair, Baldwin began to pace the room. "So, any 4400 who steps out of line, Callahan is programmed to take them out? Eric Wheaton and Darren Abbott jumped ship from whatever big plan the 4400 are here to carry out, so they ended up on her radar? What about some of these other splinter groups of 4400s we've been hearing about? Will she go after them? What about Robert Fields? He never made any such threats, so far as we know of, anyway." He pointed to Alfred. "What about you, for that matter? Why didn't she kill you? You're not a threat to her?"

It was a notion Alfred already had considered several times. While he may not have presented a hazard to Lona Callahan during their previous encounter, what did the future hold?

Skouris shrugged. "Maybe he fits into the plan in some other way, something we don't understand yet."

"Yeah, that narrows things down," Baldwin snapped.

Something Skouris had said seemed to resonate with

Alfred or, more accurately, the memories he carried within him. "You may be on to something. I didn't get a sense that she was acting out simply to stop violence, but rather that she was taking whatever action was necessary to protect the greater goal."

Skouris said, "Of course, for all we know, the greater goal might eventually hinge on violence at some point."

The three of them sat silently for a moment, before Baldwin abruptly looked at his wristwatch. "You've been a great help to us, Alfred," he said. "If you don't mind, we'd like you to stay in Seattle until we clear this up, just in case we have additional questions."

Alfred sighed. "I can't say that I'm in a hurry to get home." There was nothing—no one—waiting for him. "Do you know what will happen to me?"

"I don't know," Skouris replied. "There may be more questions, and the NTAC offices in Las Vegas will certainly want to talk to you about Darren Abbott and his people."

"And after that?" Alfred asked. He knew he likely would have to answer for some of his actions, but would the cooperation he had shown here place him in good stead? The idea of using his abilities to help others, perhaps even helping law enforcement or agencies such as NTAC to do their jobs better, carried an appeal he could not ignore, he decided. While the future he had envisioned all those years ago had not yet come to pass, Alfred now was thinking that perhaps there was something he could do to help bring it about.

Baldwin said, "Hard to say, Alfred. A lot of it will depend on . . ." He paused, as though unwilling to complete his sentence.

Nodding, Alfred knew what he was about to say.

"A lot of it depends on what Lona Callahan does next."

TWENTY-EIGHT

"WATCH YOUR HEAD."

Reiko felt the female guard's hand on the back of her neck as she was guided up the step and into the back of the gray prisoner transport van. She entered the rear of the armored vehicle, surprised by the uniformed woman's politeness as she carried out her duties. The guard's demeanor was notably out of place, particularly when contrasted against that of her partner, who stood watch over the proceedings with a shotgun cradled in his muscled arms.

Her soft-soled shoes still made enough noise against the metal floor of the passenger compartment to echo within it, and the odor of industrial-strength cleanser stung her nostrils. Reiko settled herself onto a bench running the length of the transport's left side, moving somewhat gingerly to compensate for the lack of mobility in her right arm—now in a sling to favor her aching shoulder. She leaned her left side into the cool steel, rather than sitting with her back flat against it, trying to keep from irritating her wounded shoulder.

"We're headed to the Sea-Tac Federal Detention Center," the guard offered as she reached over to chain Reiko's ankles to the floor at the base of the steel bench seat, then secured the manacles around her wrists to an eyebolt on the bench next to her right leg. "You're looking at about thirty minutes in here." Over her shoulder, Reiko saw the guard's partner scowling at her, the shotgun in his hands gleaming in the late-afternoon sun.

Reiko nodded in mute reply. Thirty minutes, even a solid day in the small, cramped transport would be a respite from her time in federal custody. Her questioning had been relentless almost from the moment of her capture. When she awakened in an NTAC medical center following treatment of her gunshot wound, agents were there. When she was released and taken to a holding cell, agents waited for her. Every moment of every day, when she ate, when she was allowed brief periods to rest, when she used the toilet, an agent was present. As the woman guard secured her restraints before taking her own seat on the opposite bench, Reiko gave silent thanks as her partner shut the transport door, locking her and the woman guard inside. It prevented yet another NTAC agent from jumping aboard and joining her for the trip.

Her eyes still were adjusting to the low level of illumination allowed by the transport's small, louvered window slits as the van's diesel engine rumbled to life and the vehicle lurched forward. Across from her, the female guard sat in silence. Though she had treated her with decency if not compassion, the woman now seemed content to undertake the journey to the detention center without saying another word, leaving Reiko alone with her thoughts.

She reflected on her time in custody, her guilt weighing on her as she felt the van's movements reverberate through the bench. The questions she faced while in custody had run the gamut, beginning with the usual inquiries as to her own identity before moving with all due haste to focus on Lona. One agent in particular, a man named Baldwin, had possessed a definite edge, and he questioned her at length about her relationship to Lona, how long she had known her, her past history and her current mission. The demands for information about Lona's newfound abilities carried a particular intensity, even though Reiko sensed that Baldwin already knew almost as much as she did herself.

The agent struck her as very driven, as though he held a personal stake in finding and capturing Lona. In a way, Reiko admired this facet of the man. Baldwin's obvious passion to know more, and his willingness to press her as hard and as far as he felt was necessary to get what he wanted, reminded Reiko in some ways of Lona herself. Reiko also derived some small amount of satisfaction from the way Baldwin grew more frustrated each time she told him that. She made sure to tell him that a lot.

Baldwin's partner, the slim, angular-faced woman named Skouris, was not nearly as aggressive, though she had been no less determined. Still, there had been a quality to her that reminded Reiko of her former lover, Carmen. Maybe it was the agent's demeanor during the questioning, her ability to be businesslike yet personable at the same time. Reiko felt almost compelled to like her, to trust her, even though she was well aware of this attempted connection between captor and prisoner as a time-honored interrogation technique. Still, she had sensed in Skouris an empathy, almost as though she might understand what it was like to know a 4400 returnee—to *love* a 4400 returnee—and the special challenges brought about by such love.

Despite this supposed connection, artificial though Reiko knew it was, she had resisted all attempts to glean information about Lona from her. When their efforts failed, Baldwin and Skouris had wasted little time in altering their approach. With time very much an issue, Reiko would now be handed over to "interrogation specialists," who she knew would administer to her all manner of drugs, compounds that would make her mind pliable and agreeable to suggestion.

Why they had not done so from the outset was a mystery. Reiko knew she only would be able to resist for a short time before the drugs that soon would course through her body compelled her to reveal everything she guarded within the depths of her mind. However, she could at least take some satisfaction from knowing that she had withstood all of the previous interrogation attempts. Whatever happened next would be beyond her control. Lona would understand.

Something slammed into the van, the impact jostling

her and the guard as the vehicle jerked to the right. The violent motion shoved Reiko against the bulkhead and she grunted as pain racked her wounded shoulder. With her hands secured to the bench her center of gravity was compromised, and she had to brace her feet to maintain her balance as the transport was struck a second time.

"What the hell?" the guard shouted, holding on to the bench to avoid being tossed to the floor of the compartment. Reaching for the radio clipped to her belt, she brought the unit to her mouth. "What's going on up there?"

The only response was another impact, forceful enough to tilt the van up on its right wheels. Reiko pitched forward, crying out as her motion was arrested by the restraints pulling on her injured arm. The guard was thrown into the bulkhead behind her, wincing and groaning in protest as her head struck the metal. Her radio fell from her hand, clattering to the deck as the van fell back to the left.

"Jesus," the guard croaked as she reached up to rub her injured head. "Hang on," she said, and Reiko felt the van rock as the driver pumped the brakes before stomping on the accelerator. The transport's engine began to howl as the vehicle surged forward.

Hang on. The words rang in her ears. *Like I have a choice.*

There was an audible popping sound from somewhere outside the van and when the vehicle lurched to the left, this time it kept going. Reiko fell flat against the bulkhead as the transport rolled onto its side, tossing the guard across the open space until she struck the wall. She screamed and Reiko heard bone snap just as the compartment was filled with the sounds of scraping, rending metal as the van slid along the pavement. Several seconds passed before the transport came to a stop, its engine still running. Reiko heard the van's engine die. Inside the passenger compartment, the overhead light was broken, the only illumination now coming through the window slats on the van's right side, which now looked up toward the sky.

Reiko lay on her back against the van's left bulkhead, her entire body awash in pain, her pulse pounding in her ears and her breaths coming in deep, ragged gasps. To her right, the guard lay unmoving near the rear doors, a line of blood streaming from her head across the bulkhead's polished metal surface.

"Hello?" she called out to her, though Reiko could tell by the unusual tilt to her neck that the other woman likely was dead. The woman had treated her with decency and humanity, simply doing her job and taking no apparent pleasure in lording her authority over those in her charge. For that reason alone, Reiko felt a momentary pang of remorse.

Something smacked against the transport van's rear door, and Reiko jerked her head in that direction an instant before white-hot light overloaded her vision and a thunderous hammer blow clapped her ears. She squeezed her eyes closed and turned her head as the concussion rocked the wrecked transport yet again. Her ears rang in the wake of the blast as the doors fell away from their hinges. Sunlight pierced the compartment's shadowy interior, illuminating the haze of smoke and dust. Through all of that, Reiko was able to make out a silhouette creeping through the open doorway. Even through unfocused eyes she recognized the figure that moved quickly and with practiced grace into the compartment.

"Lona?" Reiko called out, her voice a hoarse croak that she barely could hear through the dull ringing in her ears.

Stepping over the guard's motionless body, Lona maneuvered deeper into the van until she stood over Reiko. Their eyes met, yet Lona did not smile, offered no expression of relief upon seeing her. Instead she stood all but motionless, her features unreadable in the filtered sunlight streaming in through the open door. Then, Reiko saw a single tear streaming down her lover's left cheek.

No.

Realization dawned and Reiko gasped, feeling tears stinging her own eyes. There was no mistaking the conflict raging within her lover's mind, the decision she already had weighed and chosen. Lona had to know that Reiko, if left to the machinations of her captors, eventually would break under the stresses of interrogation. From a pure, tactical standpoint, there could be only one option. Reiko, free or in custody, remained a liability now that her identity was known.

Lona knelt beside her, reaching out with one gloved hand to caress Reiko's cheek, tears now flowing freely down her face. Whatever it was that now guided her, it obviously allowed no quarter for anything that did not benefit the mission she pursued or the goals of those who tasked her. Reiko supposed she should at least be thankful that Lona only seemed to have arrived at her choice after much painful contemplation, and she willed herself to say nothing as Lona bent forward and kissed her.

Then Reiko saw sunlight reflect off the knife's polished blade even as she heard the words on Lona's lips.

"I'm sorry."

TWENTY-NINE

Skouris watched through the observation port as Alfred Twenter sat at the table in the interview room, talking in hushed tones with Dr. Max Hudson. For privacy's sake, the audio feeds from the room had been turned off while they discussed Twenter's 4400 ability, the effect on the man's life since his return, and what his gifts might mean for his future. Skouris had neither official need nor personal desire to eavesdrop on the conversation. Twenter had been more than cooperative since his arrival, and this private meeting was one small gesture of gratitude she felt the government could live with.

Behind her, she heard the door open and glanced over her shoulder to see Baldwin enter the room before crossing to stand next to her. Gazing through the window, he released a tired sigh.

"A 4400 who can read minds," he said. "Just another

day at the office, right?" He offered a tired laugh at his own weak joke. "Well, he certainly seems to know enough about Callahan. A lot of what he gave us checks with what little Reiko Vandeberg's been nice enough to give us. If even half of what he says he read from her mind is right, we've got big problems." Then he frowned, as though just remembering something. "What about the visions Maia's been having? Does any of that tie to this?"

"Oh, I think he's hitting pretty close to the mark," Skouris replied, folding her arms across her chest. During the previous evening, Maia had come to her with new stories of what she had seen since the last time she had talked about her visions. Recalling the vague, fleeting images her adopted daughter had described to her, she added, "Some of the things she's been telling me are definitely starting to make sense."

Baldwin said, "Yeah, well, let's keep that to ourselves for the time being. If Jarvis finds out Maia's having visions again, she'll want her brought in."

Skouris shook her head. "Not if I can help it." Remembering one thing Maia had said in particular, she added, "Maia did say something about the end being near and that somehow balance will be restored. Maybe this is close to being over."

"Yeah, but over *how*?" Baldwin asked. "McFarland getting killed, along with how many others?"

Before Skouris could reply, the door opened again and they turned to see Nicholas McFarland enter the room. The CIA officer looked tired, she decided. His suit was rumpled, his hair looked to have been combed with his fingers, and he needed a shave. Skouris also could smell the odor of cigarette smoke in his clothes and hair.

"Director McFarland," Baldwin said by way of greeting. "I take it you've seen the video from the interviews?"

McFarland nodded. "To be honest, I still don't know that I believe all this nonsense that these 4400 have super powers, or whatever." He pointed toward the window. "But, if it is true, that man's a walking, talking security risk. I shudder to think what he might know from having read Callahan's mind."

"He seems able to speak primarily to her state of mind," Skouris replied. "I'm not sure how much actual information he may have learned about her specific activities."

"So he says," countered the CIA director. "He might say anything to keep us from looking too deeply into what he knows."

"If you mean what he knows about Callahan's former employment," Baldwin said, and Skouris heard the slight edge in his voice as he stressed that last word, "I don't think that's our biggest concern right now. His coming here could be just what we're missing. If we can get him to make sense out of whatever else he pulled from her mind, we might be able to get ahead of her."

Weighing this, McFarland finally nodded. "Fair enough, but it's something that needs to be revisited once this is resolved."

Assuming Callahan doesn't find you first. Skouris felt only a small pang of guilt as the errant thought wafted through her mind.

"What about that stuff he was saying about her maintaining balance?" McFarland asked. "Does that make any sense to you?"

Abruptly, Baldwin said, "She's a watchdog."

"What?" McFarland's brow knit in confusion, and Skouris had to admit that she was not sure what her partner might mean.

"A watchdog," Baldwin repeated. "She's like one of those groups who go after TV networks for putting on too many violent shows, or who keep tabs on politicians to make sure they campaign fairly, or hold to the promises they make in order to get elected. Somehow, she knows when one of the 4400 has strayed from the master plan—whatever the hell that is—and rights the wrong."

"Actually," Skouris said, now running with what Baldwin was proposing, "she's more like software designed to make sure a computer doesn't use too many resources, or that protects against viruses." Shrugging, she added, "Come to think of it, if we're going with the idea that the 4400 really are following some sort of programming they've been given—something they're not even aware of themselves—they might not even know when they go off the rails."

"So somebody like Callahan is sent to make a correction before the margin for error against the end result becomes too high," Baldwin said. "A little brutal, but pretty effective." He blew out a breath, shaking his head. "Marco and the guys are going to have a field day with this."

Skouris nodded, almost able to see the young agent drooling at the chance to incorporate all she and Baldwin had learned about Callahan into the team's ever-evolving theories about the 4400.

Can't wait to see what this does to the Ripple Effect.

As though reading her mind, McFarland asked, "Do you think Callahan may have the whole secret to the 4400 locked away in her brain?"

She shrugged. "Maybe, but I doubt it. I mean, that'd be too easy, wouldn't it? From what Alfred said, it's like she's responding to some kind of subconscious trigger. More mystery from our friends in the future, I suppose."

"The whole idea of someone killing 4400s who don't comply with the big picture is disturbing to say the least," Baldwin said, "but you've got to admit it makes a sort of sense to program a failsafe like this."

Nodding, Skouris said, "Looks like they picked a hell of a failsafe, too." If only a portion of what she had read about Lona Callahan's past covert assignments was any indication, the woman was a formidable weapon, even more so now that she had been augmented by the supposed benefactors who had taken her along with the rest of the 4400.

McFarland said, "That doesn't explain everyone she's targeted since she got back in the game. What about Fred Morehouse and Lynn Norton? They weren't 4400s."

"No, but they seem simple enough to explain now," Baldwin said. "In addition to whatever she's doing as a 4400, she's also severing ties to her past life."

"And once she finishes with that," Skouris said, "she'll be all but impossible to find. We have to get her girlfriend to talk." The woman, Reiko Vandeberg, had already been questioned, but she had offered little useful information. Dennis Ryland had broached the notion of "alternative interrogation techniques," but it was not a popular notion. Jarvis had managed to keep it off the table to this point, but Skouris knew the director likely would be overruled if this situation continued to drag out.

The door to the observation room opened yet again, this time admitting Nina Jarvis. Skouris noted the lines around the director's eyes and the set to her jaw, deducing that Jarvis was not bearing good news.

"What's up?" Baldwin asked.

Sighing, Jarvis said, "We just got a report from Washington State Patrol. The armored truck transporting Reiko Vandeberg was ambushed. It was run off the road, and the door was blown with C-4. Everyone inside was killed, including Vandeberg. Her throat was cut."

"Good God," McFarland gasped. "Callahan?"

Jarvis replied, "That's where I'd put my chips."

"Well, there you go," Baldwin said. "Severing ties, and all that."

Of course, Skouris thought. Everyone had known it was a possibility, though she doubted anyone believed it would happen so quickly and in such brutal fashion. "Vandeberg was Callahan's lover." She eyed McFarland. "I think we can assume she won't be pulling punches for people she knows."

"Then it's time for me to stop hiding," McFarland said, "and come out where she can see me. That's how we'll catch her."

Skouris recognized the resignation in the man's voice. He was tired of living in fear and uncertainty, waiting for Callahan to find him. It seemed obvious that the assassin could strike at will, her already impressive skills only enhanced by her extrahuman ability. McFarland wanted to take charge of the situation, in any way he was able. If nothing else, he preferred to die on his feet, at a time and place of his choosing, rather than being hunted down like an animal.

"There's got to be a better way than putting you in the line of fire," she said. "That just seems foolish."

McFarland said, "This needs to end here, and given that I had a hand in starting all of this in the first place, I need to take responsibility and help put a stop to it."

Jarvis frowned. "I don't like it, either. At least, not until we learn more about what she can do. For now, I think it's best if we stick to the current plan and keep you under wraps, Director."

Any reply McFarland might have offered was drowned out as Klaxons began wailing, echoing in the small room. An alert-light positioned over the door began pulsing in bright red, and Skouris heard the sound of running feet from beyond the door, responding to whatever emergency appeared to be unfolding.

"What the hell is that?" McFarland asked.

Already drawing his weapon, Baldwin said, "Intrusion alarm."

THIRTY

SIRENS ECHOED IN the narrow, utilitarian passageways and frantic voices bellowed from recessed intercom speakers. The primary lighting had been extinguished, leaving backup lamps to illuminate areas over doorways and at intersections. Rotating bulbs flashed crimson in the darkened spaces, providing an eerie, frantic atmosphere to the scene around her.

Lona ignored all of it.

Dressed in a black bodysuit complete with gloves and a hood that covered everything but a narrow slit across her eyes, she made her way down the corridor at something more than normal human speed but still far less than what her abilities allowed. It was still fast enough to avoid the building's network of security cameras as well as anyone she might encounter as she navigated deeper into the complex. Doing so in this manner allowed her to better regulate the energy she expended by maintaining the time bubble.

"Security procedure enabled," said a computer-generated voice, bellowing through the intercom speakers and cutting off the other cross-chatter that seemed on the verge of overloading the system. The diversion Lona had created by tripping an intrusion alarm near one of the building's rear entrances before darting away using her time-bending ability was drawing the attention of nearly everyone inside, but Lona knew the ruse would work only for a time. NTAC agents quickly would realize that she had to be the intruder and would begin an extensive search of the entire complex. Lockdown protocols were already being deployed, sealing all entrances to prevent anyone from entering or exiting and limiting access to NTAC's computer network. Lona was only somewhat concerned about the former, setting that aside in order to concentrate on the latter.

She had expected this development and had planned for it from the beginning, to include contingencies in the event she was unable to gain direct admittance to the computer system and the information she sought. Still, she was impressed at how fast NTAC had responded to whatever threat they had detected. It made sense that the agency would be on elevated alert following her attack on the convoy transporting Reiko. Perhaps she inadvertently had tripped some hidden alarm, or been seen by a vigilant security guard.

"You! Stop right there!"

Lona turned and saw a man in a dark uniform wearing

an NTAC badge and an empty holster on his belt. His pistol was drawn and aimed at her, and she read the uncertainty in his eyes as he beheld the mysterious, black-clad figure before him. For an instant she considered her own pistol, strapped in its holster along her right thigh, but quickly discarded the notion. In spite of everything that had occurred to this point, including Reiko's unfortunate yet necessary death, Lona still had no desire to kill anyone who was not a designated mark so long as she possessed other options.

Thankfully, such alternatives were available.

It took her less than a heartbeat to cross the distance to the security guard, her left arm sweeping his weapon up and away from her as she drove the heel of her right hand into his jaw. His knees buckled and he collapsed to the floor, an unconscious heap at her feet. Retrieving his fallen pistol, Lona stuck it in the rucksack slung to her back before noticing that the guard was also wired with a portable communications unit clipped to his waist at the small of his back and connected via a coiled cord to a receiver in his left ear. She took this from him as well, affixing the unit to her own waistband. One final check of the man's pockets found a magnetic key card, which she pocketed before moving off once more down the corridor.

Signage on the walls made it easy to keep track of where she was, and within seconds Lona found a stairwell. She descended to Sub-Basement Level 5, the lowest level of the complex, using her ability to make the transit in less than three seconds and encountering no one along the way. A camera was perched near the ceiling at the far end of the passageway, aimed down another leg off an intersection as she emerged from the stairwell. She conjured the bubble and flashed down the corridor fast enough to avoid the camera's watchful eye, repeating the process to negotiate the intersection and down another hall until she found a room that looked promising. The sign next to the door was labeled "Archives," and beneath it was a magnetic card reader.

She heard footsteps behind her and turned in time to see another agent coming around a bend in the corridor. Dressed in street clothes, it was obvious he was not part of any search team. His weapon was holstered and his expression was one of shock as he took in the sight of the ninja-like figure standing before him. He made a move for his pistol but Lona was faster, drawing her .45 semiautomatic pistol from its thigh holster and leveling the muzzle at the man's chest.

"Don't," she said. In response, he raised his hands, showing her that they were empty. His eyes were wide with fear.

Keeping her pistol trained on him, Lona took the guard's stolen key card from her pocket and swiped it through the door's reader. A red indicator changed to green and the click of a lock disengaging echoed in the narrow corridor. "Inside," she directed the agent to open the door, following him as they both entered the room. Thankfully, it was empty of occupants, and Lona noted that there were precious few places in which to hide. File cabinets and lockers lined the walls, with a lone desk and computer workstation sandwiched between two sets of bookcases.

"The building's locked down," the man said, his voice betraying more than a hint of fear. "You have to know you're not going anywhere."

Lona shrugged. "Not yet, anyway. Sit down." Locking the door behind them and pressing the control on the keypad to override any further access attempts from the outside, she took the opportunity to relieve him of his weapon before using her own pistol to gesture toward the computer workstation. Reading the name on the ID card hanging around his neck, she said, "Agent Keith Osborne, I want you to get on that thing and log in."

"Network's down," Osborne replied, the first bead of perspiration running from his dark hairline and down the right side of his face. "No one can get in until security lockouts are lifted."

Unimpressed with the man's weak attempt at lying, Lona raised the .45's muzzle until it was pointed at his face. "Then you're of no use to me, are you?" To emphasize her point, she cocked the pistol's hammer.

"Okay. *Okay!*" Reaching up to wipe the sweat from his brow, Osborne turned and moved toward the desk. With Lona directing him, he tapped his access ID and password into the computer's keyboard and the image on its monitor shifted from an NTAC log-on screen to a series of columns featuring directory names. "What do you want?" he asked.

"Nicholas McFarland," she replied. "Everything you have on him." This was not her preferred method of obtaining the information she needed, but circumstances had limited her options. Reiko's capture and NTAC's response to it would without doubt entail a complete revision of whatever protection scheme for McFarland was already in place. Obtaining those amendments directly from NTAC was therefore a necessary step, after which—if everything proceeded according to her plan—Lona would be able to track down and eliminate McFarland before his custodians had a chance to modify their own protocols yet again.

Osborne protested under his breath, but said nothing else as he tapped out a set of instructions. Moments later, a list of file names began streaming across the screen.

Reaching into another pocket, Lona produced a compact flash drive and handed it to the agent. "Copy all of that to this." When he hesitated, she pressed her pistol's muzzle into the back of his neck. Nothing else was said as she observed the files being copied to the portable storage device. As that was being accomplished, she tapped Osborne on the shoulder. "Now, I want a complete roster of the 4400, as well as copies of all case files for those who've demonstrated special abilities." She was not looking for anyone or anything specific at the moment, instead figuring that the information would prove useful in the future.

Lona and Osborne, engrossed as they were in the task at hand, both flinched as a deep male voice boomed from the room's intercom speakers. "Intruder alert. Security teams to S4-6. A guard is down near EWTAC. Be advised that the guard's weapon and access card are missing. Intruder is to be considered armed and dangerous."

"That's me," Lona said, unable to suppress a small chuckle as Osborne handed her the flash drive. She tucked the device back into its pocket on her hip before gesturing to the agent once again. "Now, can you erase any record of what you've done here?" She knew it was a long shot, or perhaps even a temporary measure, but if successful the ploy might buy a crucial bit of extra time to find McFarland.

Before Osborne could answer, the sound of someone attempting to gain entry to the room caught their attention and Lona spun on her heel, leveling her pistol at the door. Her override of the lock had worked and the door remained closed, but she knew that would only alert others that something in here was amiss.

Time's up.

Motion flashed in her peripheral vision an instant before a fist slammed into the side of her head. Lona staggered from the force of the blow as Osborne pounced on her, one hand reaching for the pistol in her hand while the other punched her again, this blow landing just above her left ear. The gun was pulled from her hand and she grunted in pain even as training and reflexes took over, grabbing Osborne's arm and twisting her body in an attempt to pull him off his feet. Another punch struck her right shoulder and she lost her grip on him.

Light glinted off metal and she lashed out at Osborne's hand as he tried to bring her pistol around to aim at her. The gun dropped away, clattering to the floor, and she kicked it out of reach before driving her knee into the agent's groin. Air expelled from his lungs like a punctured tire and he moaned in protest, his knees buckling as he fought to keep his feet. He struck her again, his fist landing a glancing blow along her forehead as he stepped into his attack and attempted to wrap his arms around her. Their combined weight was enough to push Lona off balance, and both of them crashed to the floor. He landed on top, using his larger frame in an attempt to pin her down, but she kicked and squirmed enough to keep her arms free. Her mind was racing, a gentle heat beginning to radiate through her body as she fought for control. The longer this went on, the more likely help would arrive. She had to end this. Now.

The time bubble flared into existence. Osborne seemed to sense that something was happening, his body shifting enough that she was able to reach for him. She grabbed him by the throat, a guttural cry escaping her lips as she pulled him close.

Osborne released a cry of pain and terror, now trying to fight free of Lona's grip. The pitch of his screams changed with each passing second as she watched his skin age and wrinkle and his hair lengthen and whiten. Teeth rotted and fell from his mouth, and his muscles atrophied as his body shrank inside clothing that was fading and fraying. His skin dried and withered until cracks appeared, pushed aside as white bone and shriveled muscle tissue emerged, before it began crumbling to dust that rained down upon her.

The field weakened before disappearing altogether and Lona felt herself slip back into normal time. Her heart racing and her breathing coming in deep, greedy gulps of air, she tossed aside the brown, shrunken skeleton that was all that remained of Agent Osborne. She pulled herself to her feet, aghast at what she had just done. It had been more instinct than anything else, not unlike what had happened with the vines in her bathroom.

"What the hell am I?" Lona cried, her words echoing across the small room.

THIRTY-ONE

NTAC
SEATTLE, WASHINGTON

GRIPPING HIS GLOCK in both hands, Tom Baldwin let the pistol's muzzle guide him down the corridor until he reached the four-way intersection at the center of Sub-Basement Level 5.

Armed entry into an unknown and potentially hostile environment was, like anything else, a learned skill, and as such there was a point when training gave way to instinct and hard-won field experience. Just as he had while progressing every inch since descending from the ground floor into the depths of the NTAC headquarters building, Baldwin scrutinized every doorway, every bend in the passageway, every shadow large enough to conceal a man-sized target. He listened for telltale sounds that would be out of place in an otherwise deserted hallway and even sniffed the air in the hopes of catching the scent of anything abnormal. Without his conscious thought and wherever he looked, the barrel of the Glock followed, his right forefinger confidently resting alongside the weapon's trigger guard yet aching to take up any slack the instant a target became visible. It had been a while since he had faced a similar situation, but all of the old, trusted reflexes were responding as expected.

Just like riding a bike.

Pausing to glance around the corner, Baldwin verified that the passageway ahead of them was empty. He rested against the wall, nodding toward the three security officers making up the rest of his team. "Clear," he said, his voice low and soft. Bringing his left shirt cuff closer to his mouth, he whispered into the radio mike affixed there. "Diana, we're at the main intersection on Five. So far, nothing." He and his team had seen no one else in the passageways, owing to the order issued just minutes earlier for NTAC personnel to evacuate all of the sub-levels.

"We're in the east stairwell, Tom," Skouris replied, her voice sounding tiny as it filtered through his earpiece, "passing Sub-Level 3. We're moving a few stragglers, but we're on our way."

"Okay," Baldwin said, "we're moving. We'll meet you at Archives." Security had detected Agent Osborne's access to NTAC's computer network via the workstation in Archives, and it was Nina Jarvis who quickly pointed out that Osborne had no reason to be in that section today, particularly while lockdown procedures were in effect. Attempts to contact or enter the room had proven ineffective and left Jarvis with precious few options, the least favorable of which was sending teams to try surrounding and containing a fugitive with the apparent ability to move faster than the human eye could follow.

No pressure, right?

Drawing what he hoped was a deep, calming breath, he looked over his shoulder to the other members of his security team. "Let's move," he said, his Glock once more leading the way as he stepped around the corner, hugging the wall to his left and wishing he could see around the next two turns in the corridor.

"Tom, Diana," said the voice of Nina Jarvis in his ear-piece, "heads up. Security network's showing that the door to Archives has just been unlocked."

"Here we go," Baldwin said, more to himself than any-one else, and feeling his grip tightening on the pistol.

Then he flinched at the sounds of gunfire from some-where up the passageway ahead of him.

"Diana?" he called into his mike, muscles tensing as he quickened his pace. More shots echoed in the corridor, followed by shouts of warning. An alarm Klaxon began wailing again, loud enough to drown out everything else. Baldwin broke into a sprint, rounding the first corner on his way toward the intersection that would lead him to Archives. "Diana, are you there? Can you hear me?" He winced when Skouris's voice exploded in his ear.

"I think one of us hit her, Tom! She's running toward you!"

Her warning came an instant before Baldwin de-tected movement at the far end of the hallway near the T-intersection. He stopped short, leveling his pistol at a figure, Callahan, just barely visible in the dim illumination. Dressed from head to toe in black, she staggered into view, hugging the wall, and appeared to be favoring her right arm.

Wounded? Diana thought she or one of her team might have hit her. If she was injured, was it preventing her from using her ability?

"Federal agents!" Baldwin shouted, taking aim at her head. "Drop your weapon and show me your hands!"

Callahan lurched from right to left across the corridor. Whatever had impaired her a moment earlier was either gone or under control, her form now seeming to blur as she moved. Seeing the distinctive silhouette of the pistol in her right hand, Baldwin fired without hesitation.

And missed.

"Don't move!" he warned again, but knew it was a useless gesture. Callahan was moving faster now, gaining speed with every step. Baldwin fired again, this time accompanied by his security team. At this distance someone had to find their mark.

No one did.

The hammer beats of weapons fire consumed the passageway, accentuated by the metallic pings of spent shell casings dropping to the concrete floor. Baldwin's eyes stung from the expended gunpowder, and fear chilled his blood as he watched Lona Callahan, or whatever it was that she had become, dodge, duck, and weave back and forth across the passageway, her body stretching and bending to avoid *every single* bullet Baldwin and his team unleashed upon her.

"Damn it!" Baldwin yelled as he fired his last shot and the Glock's slide locked to the rear. Then the dark blur in front of him disappeared altogether, and he felt the sensation of air moving past him. A grunt of surprise and pain came from behind him, and he turned to see one of the security officers thrown off his feet and flung into the wall, striking a bulletin board and knocking it free of its mounting hooks. Both the man and the board crashed to the floor, but Baldwin ignored them as he exchanged his pistol's empty magazine for a new one, struggling to catch any fleeting glimpse of the escaping figure he knew had to be moving up the corridor. He slammed the magazine home and chambered a round, raising the Glock once more in search of a target.

The passageway was empty.

"Diana," he said into the mike on his wrist, "we lost her. Nina, notify security teams at all exits to be ready. She's got to be making a break for it."

"Too late," replied Jarvis, and Baldwin could hear the frustration in the director's voice. "Network's showing the service entrance on Sub-Level 1's been opened. Nobody at that section is answering us. I've got other teams on the way."

Just how fast could she move, anyway? "Anything on the exterior cameras?" he asked, knowing the answer to the question before the words even finished leaving his mouth.

"We've got nothing," Jarvis said.

Son of a bitch! "Any idea yet what she got away with?"

"Not yet. Looks like she tried to cover her tracks, but

I've got Galanter and his gang going over everything. We should know something in a minute or two."

In the meantime, Baldwin knew, Lona Callahan was still on the loose, with whatever information she had managed to retrieve. "You want to lay odds she was after information on McFarland?" he asked. "That has to be it. Why else would she run the risk of breaking in here?" He almost laughed at that remark, considering the fact that Callahan had walked into a secure government facility as easily as one might stroll up to a roadside hot dog stand.

That's gonna look real *good on the after-action report.*

"Tom!"

Turning at the call, Baldwin saw Skouris and her team coming up the corridor toward him. Though his partner appeared uninjured, one of the security officers accompanying her, a large Latino man whose name tag read "Ortiz," sported a small gash near his left temple, from which a line of blood trickled down the side of his face.

"Are you all right?" Baldwin asked.

Skouris nodded, gesturing to Ortiz. "Julio managed to block her for about a second when she started to run, but that's as close as any of us got." She turned to the security officer. "You fell pretty hard. You should have Dr. Hudson look at that."

"Yes, ma'am," Ortiz replied before turning and heading back down the passageway.

Holstering her pistol, Skouris said, "Tom, we found Osborne, or what was left of him, anyway." She paused, grimacing as though reliving the memory of what she had seen. "There was nothing but a skeleton, in an advanced state of decay. It looks like he's been dead for years."

"What?" Baldwin said, trying to wrap his head around what he had just heard. "How is that possible? Callahan?"

"If so, it's a different facet to her ability than we've seen to this point." Her brow furrowed and she looked away for a moment, seemingly lost in thought, before adding, "You know, we saw her in the hallway, before the shooting started. She wasn't moving fast enough to mask her actions yet, and I could swear the expression on her face was one of shock. What if what she did to Osborne caught her off guard, too?"

Baldwin shrugged. "I guess it could've rattled her, but that's assuming she gives a damn about who she kills."

"She never fired at *us*, Tom," Skouris said. "Not once."

It took Baldwin an extra moment as he recalled his own encounter with Callahan. "She never fired at us, either. She had a weapon, but she never so much as aimed it at us. She wasn't moving at full speed, either, at least not right away. Maybe getting shot hurt her enough to throw off her control of whatever it is she does to move that fast, at least for a minute or so." He shook his head. "It doesn't matter. We can't count on her being so nice to us the next time we run into her."

Before Skouris could say anything else, the voice of Nina Jarvis sounded in their earpieces.

"Galanter just confirmed your guess, Tom. Callahan has everything we've got on McFarland, along with ID information on every 4400 and copies of all our open investigations into those returnees who've shown special abilities."

"That'd make sense," Skouris said. "If she's targeting specific 4400s, it'd probably be helpful to know what they're capable of doing. For all we know it's just part of whatever plan she's following."

Baldwin shook his head. "Let Marco and the guys figure that all out. We don't have that kind of time right now." Into his mike, he said, "Nina, we need to move McFarland now. Full security escort."

"Already on it," Jarvis said. "I've also got Dr. Hudson here. He says he may have come up with a way to deal with Callahan."

"I'm all for that," Baldwin said. So far as he was concerned, he and the entire NTAC staff had shown their asses enough for one day. The idea that anyone, let alone a 4400, could enter a restricted government facility and wreak havoc was unacceptable. An enhanced security presence was needed, possibly even a military contingent whose sole mission would be defending the complex against any such future attacks. That would be his recommendation to Jarvis once all of this was over.

But for now, it's all on us.

"We're on our way," he said into his mike before glancing toward Skouris. "Let's go. I want to be there when they move McFarland." He knew that it would likely be their best opportunity to capture Callahan, while at the same time reminding himself that it could just as easily be a death sentence for McFarland if she found the CIA director before he could be moved to a secure location.

Skouris grabbed his arm, stopping him from jogging up the corridor. "Tom, are you worried about McFarland, or catching Callahan?"

"Both," Baldwin answered, feeling his jaw tighten as he answered. "She's gotten away from me twice now, both times by vanishing into thin air. That's not going to happen again."

Time to put this case to bed for good.

THIRTY-TWO

THE MOSQUITO LANDED on the back of Lona Callahan's left hand, moving about the exposed skin until it found a comfortable spot before plunging its proboscis into her flesh and commencing to gorge itself on its fill of her blood. Watching the insect as it went about its business, she did not flinch, did not react in the slightest fashion. The smallest of movements might attract unwanted attention, and that was unacceptable now, when the situation required her complete focus on the task at hand.

Lona once more had become one with her environment, immersing herself within a line of thick foliage, part of the landscaping that formed the outer perimeter of the recreational park at the center of this quiet, gated subdivision. All of the houses within her lines of sight looked to be cared for in similar meticulous fashion, along with lawns manicured to exacting specifications. The park itself contained a walking path and playground equipment, as well as sufficient open space for field games.

Apparently satiated, the mosquito lifted away from Lona's hand, leaving behind a small, reddening welt as evidence of its visit. She sensed the minor irritation but ignored it, just as she ignored the late-day heat and the oppressive humidity, and the sweat running freely down the insides of her black bodysuit. Putting all of that aside, she instead concentrated on her surroundings.

The public nature of the park had made it somewhat challenging for her to insert herself into the hasty sniper's nest she had prepared, compounded by the fact that she was without all of the gear she might normally employ on such an assignment. Time also had been a factor, given that she was racing NTAC and other assisting law enforcement assets to reach McFarland. Lona knew that the information she had acquired regarding the safe house locations used to hide the CIA director would only be useful for as long as it took NTAC to revise their protection scheme and put into motion a plan for moving him. She suspected that they would not attempt to relocate McFarland without a significant armed presence, owing to their fear of her and the incredible power she wielded.

Power I still don't completely understand, and therefore still can't control.

The vivid imagery of what she had done to the NTAC agent, Osborne, still haunted her, never venturing far from the forefront of her conscious memory. Her ears rang with the anguished cries of pain and terror the man had experienced in his final seconds as her time-bending ability ripped decades from his life. Until that horrifying moment, Lona had believed her extraordinary talents were limited to time's effect on her own body. Of what possible use could such a power be put? What had been the thinking behind that, to say nothing of the motivations of whoever had endowed her with it?

Her heart racing as she recalled Osborne's gruesome death, Lona exhaled slowly in an attempt to bring her breathing under control. She found herself once more dwelling on the constant throbbing in her right bicep, still in pain from the bullet wound inflicted upon her during her escape from NTAC. The discomfort was not helped by her current prone position atop the hard, uneven ground and the grip she maintained on the stock of her rifle. What bothered her more than the injury itself was the momentary effect on her ability to conjure the time-bending field. That power had failed her at a critical moment, nearly resulting in her capture. Survival instinct was all that enabled her to regain her senses and put aside the pain from the wound long enough to make her getaway. It was yet another indication that she still had much to learn about handling her so-called gift.

The bullet from the NTAC agent's weapon had passed cleanly through her flesh, allowing her to treat the wound with the first-aid kit she acquired from a fire station not far from the agency's headquarters building. Pain-reducing medication was out of the question, of course, at least until she completed her mission. For now, she would have to use the pain itself as a means of keeping her head clear. Once McFarland was dead and she was away from this place, she would take the necessary time to heal both her body and her mind. She only hoped that the nameless entity that drove her would allow such a sabbatical before once again calling upon her.

Enough, Lona reminded herself. There were other concerns now warranting her attention, many of which were visible through her rifle's scope. Peering again through the sights, she watched the hive of activity taking place at the opposite end of the park, at the center of which sat a two-story house. Painted an unassuming light blue with dark blue shutters and a wood-shingled roof, there was little to distinguish the home from the dozens of others littering the subdivision—aside from the perimeter of government vehicles arrayed before it.

Though she was able to use her purloined data on McFarland to locate the safe house where he currently was concealed, what Lona had not counted on was the agency's ability to adapt to what had become a fluid, evolving situation. NTAC had mobilized with impressive speed, deploying an armada of black SUVs that now clogged the street.

There barely had been enough time to perform the most cursory reconnoiter of the area, even with the advantage she possessed. Still, it was enough to determine that the only viable avenue of egress from the house would be through the front door to a waiting vehicle. One of the SUVs—armored and equipped with bulletproof glass, Lona surmised—had been backed up to within a few feet of the house's porch, leaving only a small gap of open space from the front door to the back of the vehicle. McFarland had not yet exited the house, but when he did he would only be visible for at most two or three seconds. Lona was not concerned with that. At this distance, it would be more time than she would need.

Other vehicles had arrived on the scene since she had taken up position in her sniper's nest, all of them flashing crimson lights as they added to the gathering before the powder blue house. Lona watched as uniformed NTAC special agents dispersed around the house to form a defensive perimeter, and in the distance she could hear the drone of an approaching helicopter. It seemed that little if anything was being left to chance. There were indications that the uniformed officers, each of them brandishing what looked to be M4A1 carbine assault rifles, might begin spreading out in lines away from the house, perhaps even to conduct a search of the park. If that happened, Lona would be forced to abandon her position, after which finding McFarland again would be difficult if not impossible.

She had considered using her ability to close with McFarland and engage him directly, but had quickly dismissed that idea. After the incident with Agent Osborne, Lona had no desire to mete out a similar fate to anyone else. No one deserved to die in such an appalling fashion, particularly anyone who was not a designated primary mark. For that reason, she had elected to go with the sniper rifle, in the hope that she could eliminate McFarland from a safe distance and disappear before anyone could even begin to react to what she had done.

You might not have a choice, she thought as she watched the NTAC agents continuing to establish their perimeter. *Let's just get this over with.*

Through her scope, Lona recognized the dark-haired female agent she had last seen while escaping NTAC headquarters now wearing a bulletproof vest beneath a dark blue Windbreaker with a white cord running from her left ear beneath her shirt collar. Standing next to her was a man of slight build, with gelled blond hair and dark-rimmed eyeglasses, and Lona realized that she had seen him before. It was the man from Las Vegas, the one she had elected not to kill. Had he somehow assisted the agents in identifying her? How was that possible? What could he know?

For a moment, Lona wondered whether she might somehow have erred by not killing him during their previous encounter. Searching her mind turned up no hint of a directive or impulse driving her to target him. She had seen the faces of Darren Abbott and his little band of misguided renegades, but her unknown masters had for whatever reason not selected this other man for elimination. Might *they* have made some mistake?

Forget it, Lona ordered herself. *Focus on the objective.*

She watched as the female agent held her left wrist close to her mouth, speaking into a radio microphone. Other agents were performing similar actions, and Lona at first was pleased that she had kept the radio set she had taken from the security guard, thinking she might be able to overhear the agents' conversations. The short-lived notion evaporated as she attempted to listen in on the radio's different frequencies and heard nothing but distorted gibberish, an obvious indication of an encryption scheme in effect. Someone at NTAC was thinking, clearly suspecting that she would find McFarland's location and possibly threaten their attempts to relocate him.

Behind her, wood snapped.

In defiance of experience and training, Lona jerked her head toward the sound and saw a man standing less than twenty feet from her. So engrossed was she in the scene at the safe house that she had not heard his approach, and she cursed herself for her lapse. He also wore a blue Windbreaker and was pointing a pistol at her, and Lona realized she had seen him before, during her escape from NTAC.

"No!" The yell was involuntary, born of shock as she pulled herself from her firing position and started to turn toward the new arrival. Already she sensed the energy field forming around her, her metabolism starting to race as she began to accelerate.

Then she felt a sharp stab in her neck. She stopped moving and reached up to her throat, her fingers running over the smooth surface of the projectile the agent had fired at her. An intense, heated sting radiated outward from the point of impact, followed by an immediate loss of focus and sensation of nausea gripping her. Through blurry eyes she saw the NTAC agent moving toward her, arms extended and aiming his weapon at her and shouting something she could not understand. She fell to her knees, her body gripped by whatever substance the dart contained while at the same time struggling to respond to her pleas for the time-bending field to generate.

Despite its own best efforts, Lona's body was failing her.

THIRTY-THREE

THANK YOU, DR. HUDSON.

"I don't . . ." Callahan said, reaching up to pull the dart from her neck and dropping to the ground, her expression one of confusion and disorientation. "How?"

Dropping the now-empty tranquilizer pistol, Baldwin reached for the holstered Glock on his hip and trained the weapon's muzzle at Callahan's head. "Don't move," he said, noting how she watched him with eyes dulled by medication. Only her face was not covered by her black bodysuit, her gloved hands held up and away from her, demonstrating that she was not armed. The sniper rifle lay abandoned on the grass behind her. "Stay on your knees, and keep your hands where I can see them." Raising his left wrist to his mouth, he said into his radio mike, "Diana, I found her. Send backup units to the far end of the park, southwest of the safe house."

"On the way, Tom," came Skouris's reply through his earpiece.

Baldwin nodded in approval. "And tell Twenter he was right on the money."

Both he and Skouris were certain that Callahan would go after McFarland when NTAC attempted to retrieve him for transfer to another safe house. What remained unknown was how or precisely when she might make her move, at which point Skouris proposed the idea of using Twenter and his telepathic abilities to assist in locating the assassin. Baldwin had made clear his skepticism regarding any lingering, tenuous telepathic connection Twenter might retain with Lona Callahan—an apparent result of their encounter in Las Vegas—but with options dwindling he had been open to any ideas, no matter how outlandish. Such doubts were quashed upon arriving in the subdivision, and Twenter quickly reported being able to sense Callahan's presence. From there it was a game of hide and seek, with Twenter directing Baldwin on a search of the surrounding area, hunting the professional killer while avoiding being detected by her.

It was surreal, Baldwin decided, staring down the muzzle of his pistol at Lona Callahan, the Wraith. International assassin and wanted fugitive for nearly twenty years—including the twelve-year gap in her life thanks to her abduction, of course—here she was, ten feet from him and all but in federal custody. Baldwin never had considered the case as any sort of lingering failure on his record from his time with the FBI, mostly in light of the fact that the events leading up to the Wraith's last known assassination in 1992 had occurred so early in his career. He was one of hundreds of agents working the case, nowhere near the links in the chain of command tasked with overseeing the manhunt. Even his onetime mentor, Ted McIntyre, lacked that sort of visibility. After the Wraith's apparent disappearance and the case went cold, and Baldwin was transferred to his next assignment, it was easy to relegate those events to the bottom of his filing cabinet as well as the back of his mind.

Twelve years later, and the case was over, just like that.

McIntyre's going to be pissed.

"What did you do to me?" Callahan asked, her voice barely a whisper.

The noxious potion provided by Max Hudson—a potent, fast-acting, and still-experimental compound developed by the U.S. military as a nonlethal weapon to be employed during urban pacification operations, as the doctor had described it—seemed to be working. Surprisingly, she had not been rendered unconscious, and Baldwin remembered what Hudson had offered about how the tranquilizer targeted a subject's metabolism, and that in time its effects might be mitigated by whatever modifications Callahan's body had received. Still, it had stopped Callahan in her tracks almost from the instant the dart hit her. That was enough for now. She seemed content to obey his instructions, and Baldwin saw her shake her head as though trying to clear it of dizziness.

"Face down on the ground, now," he said, ignoring her question and keeping the pistol aimed at her head while she rolled onto the grass, her hands away from her body. Closing the distance between them, Baldwin retrieved the handcuffs from the holster clipped to the back of his belt, then moved to place his right knee on Callahan's back in order to facilitate restraining her.

When she moved, it was with nowhere near the incredible speed he had seen in the NTAC corridor, but it was still damned fast.

In the instant before his knee made contact with her back, Callahan rolled to her left, shifting her weight and pushing off the ground so that she caught him on the inside of his left leg and forced him off balance. Baldwin swore, dropping the cuffs and reaching for her with his free hand, but by then she was up on one knee. Her right hand moved and Baldwin saw sunlight glint off a knife's polished blade, and he twisted away as she sliced the air just to the right of his ear. He fell to the ground, bringing up his pistol and scrambling for a shot as she regained her feet with surprising flexibility and grace. His first round was wide to the left and she ducked in the opposite direction, and by the time he fired again she already had plunged headlong through the line of foliage that had provided her original place of concealment.

"Son of a bitch!" Baldwin hissed through gritted teeth, pushing to his feet and taking off after her. Breaking through the line of shrubs, he found himself on the sidewalk ringing the park's perimeter. Callahan was already across the street, still moving at normal human speed but well enough that she had a decent head start on him. The sun was low in the sky to the west, the last rays of daylight fading with every passing moment. The approaching darkness would only assist Callahan in her escape. Grunting in growing anger, Baldwin sprinted after her, trying to close the distance. "Diana!" he shouted into his wrist mike. "I've got her. She's on foot, heading into the subdivision on the opposite side of the park. Get that chopper over here now!"

"We heard the shots," Skouris replied in his ear. "I've got SWAT teams headed in your direction, and the chopper's on its way."

Baldwin did not answer, saving his breath for the running. Callahan was still ahead of him but he was beginning to close the gap. He heard the NTAC helicopter approaching, its whirling blades slicing through the air. Police sirens wailed from somewhere ahead of him, echoing between the houses. Now away from the park, which at least could have been surrounded in order to contain anyone within its perimeter, the chances of involving an innocent bystander increased. Based on what Baldwin had seen of Lona Callahan's methods, she seemed reluctant to kill or injure anyone who was not her target unless no other option remained to her, but such a possibility now loomed with great weight as the foot chase evolved.

Thirty yards in front of him, Callahan reached a six-foot-tall wooden fence situated between two houses. In one fluid motion she leaped up and vaulted over, disappearing into the yard beyond. Cursing her agility, Baldwin followed after her, holstering his pistol to have both hands free as he reached for the top of the fence. He jumped up, using his feet to propel him up and over the fence, and as he rolled over the top edge he realized his mistake. Failing to check the other side of the fence before climbing over, he did not see Callahan waiting for him until she grabbed him by his jacket collar, dragging him over and toppling him to the ground.

Baldwin landed heavily, grunting as his holstered Glock dug into his back. He sensed motion and rolled away, narrowly avoiding Callahan's leg as she lashed out at his head, her booted foot slamming into the fence behind him. Regaining his feet, he was in time to see that Callahan had drawn her knife again, holding it low and near her right leg. She lunged at him, the blade coming up, but Baldwin anticipated the move and stepped into the attack. His left arm blocked her knife hand, arresting that motion even as he punched at her with his other fist. Callahan dodged to avoid the worst of the strike, and Baldwin only swiped the side of her head. She slashed with the knife and this time he felt the sting as the blade sliced across his left arm. Growling in anger and pain, Baldwin tried for his Glock but abandoned it when Callahan closed on him.

Damn, she's good. She was younger and faster, and an obvious practitioner of hand-to-hand combat. His own skills were competent, but he knew she was out of his league. Baldwin had to find a way to end this, and damned quick.

The sirens were closer now, and Baldwin was sure he heard voices from somewhere nearby. He also was aware of the helicopter hovering overhead, but none of that mattered as Callahan attacked again. He sidestepped her approach and she overextended her reach just enough to leave her flank exposed. Baldwin seized the opportunity, kicking her in the ribs with his right foot, and was rewarded with a surprised grunt from Callahan. She staggered several steps, off balance for the briefest of moments as she grabbed her midsection. Ignoring his own pain, Baldwin charged her, wrapping her in a bear hug and running both of them into the wooden fence. Wood cracked from the force of the impact.

He reached for her knife hand, his fingers closing around her wrist and pinning it against the fence. Callahan screamed in his ear, refusing to yield. Her other fist smashed the side of his head, and she felt him jerk in an attempt to drive her knee into his groin. He twisted enough to avoid that, but it cost him as he felt her wrench her wrist from his grasp, raising the knife above his head and readying it once more to strike.

Howling in frustration and perhaps even desperation, Baldwin butted her in the face with his forehead and she shrieked with new pain. She sliced blindly with the knife and the blade found him again, this time nicking him across his chest. He staggered backward, reaching for the new wound before stumbling and falling backward to the ground. Already Callahan was moving after him, and Baldwin saw the menace in her eyes as he tried to push himself to his feet.

Then she stopped, staggering to a halt, and Baldwin saw that a thick silver dart with red plumage had appeared in her upper chest. She gasped, her eyes widening with shock as she dropped the knife and dropped to her knees. Her fingers fumbled with the dart, trying to remove it, but her attempts failed and she fell forward to the grass.

Baldwin rolled awkwardly to his feet, putting several

paces between them as he reached for his pistol, and detected movement behind him. He turned to see Skouris approaching, followed by Alfred Twenter and a contingent of uniformed NTAC agents. Skouris's own weapon was drawn and held in front of her, and tucked into her waistband was one of the tranquilizer pistols provided by Dr. Hudson.

"You okay?" she asked, eyeing him as she moved toward Callahan.

Nodding as he fought to regain his breath, Baldwin said, "Yeah, I think so."

Callahan remained still as Skouris knelt next to her, and Baldwin covered her as she locked handcuffs around the other woman's wrists. Even now Callahan was still conscious, an apparent tribute to her extrahuman metabolism or whatever the hell had been done to her.

"She's quite the handful," Skouris said, watching as a trio of uniformed agents took Callahan into custody. The captured assassin was mumbling something, low and unintelligible, and Baldwin frowned as he strained to hear.

"What's she saying?" he asked, moving closer and indicating for the agents to pull her to her feet. As she stood up, Baldwin saw her drugged, bewildered expression, no doubt caused by the tranquilizer. Reaching out, he lifted her chin until he could look into her eyes. "What did you say?"

"Mission," Callahan blurted, her jaw working as she struggled to form other words. "Must . . . complete . . ."

Moving to stand next to him, Skouris asked, "What mission? Whose mission? Who are you working for?"

"She doesn't know, Agent Skouris," said another voice, and Baldwin turned to see Twenter regarding them. "Even taking into account the drugs in her system, her mind is chaos." He closed his eyes, wrinkles deepening on his forehead as his brow furrowed and his lips tightened into a thin line. "She has no idea who's directing her, or why. All she knows is the targets she's selected, but not how or why they're connected. She's struggled to understand the larger picture, and she's experienced much frustration and helplessness at failing to do that." Opening his eyes, he blinked several times before returning his attention to Baldwin and Skouris. "She's a tool, nothing more."

"That's all she ever was," Skouris said, shaking her head, "even before she was abducted."

Baldwin grunted in agreement. "Sounds like the rest of us, doesn't it?" Turning to Twenter, he added, "Thank you for your help, Alfred. I don't know what'll happen to you, and I can't promise anything, but you have my word that your assistance in finding Callahan will be taken into account." He held out his hand. "We couldn't have done this without you."

Taking the proffered hand, Twenter smiled. "Thank you, Agent Baldwin."

"Come on, Tom," Skouris said after a moment. "Let's get you checked out."

"Good plan," Baldwin replied, wincing as his fingers played beneath his torn shirt and over the wound on his chest. "The cuts aren't deep, but they hurt like hell."

Regarding him with a sidelong smirk, Skouris said, "Nothing a little nursing by Alana won't fix, I hope?"

Baldwin snorted, holstering his pistol. "Works for me," he said, nodding to where Callahan was being escorted across the yard to a waiting SUV. "Assuming I live long enough to complete the paperwork you know this case is going to cause."

THIRTY-FOUR

SEATTLE, WASHINGTON

WHAT WAS HAPPENING?

Lona could not understand, could not make her mind focus on what was occurring around her. Dizziness and lethargy seemed to have enveloped her. What had they done to her? Fighting to focus her thoughts, she tried to summon the will to generate the time bubble, but nothing came. She could sense hints of it, tendrils of the mysterious energy she called upon to utilize her incredible gift, but it refused to coalesce around her. Since learning of the power she possessed, Lona had spent a great portion of those months simply coming to terms with it, often wondering if it was something with which she even wanted to cope. It had taken her some time to grow comfortable with this fantastic ability, practicing and honing it until she could command it as easily as she controlled her arms or legs.

That gift had somehow been taken from her, and Lona

now felt the void it left behind. A part of her was gone, and she was weaker for it.

Her mind struggled to clear, if only slightly, and she was able to process what had transpired. The agents had shot her with something, some kind of powerful sedative. Lona suspected it must be affecting her metabolism as well as her nervous system in some fashion. Instead of being able to escape her captors with ease, to kill them all in the blink of an eye, she was laboring simply to remain lucid and on her feet. The effects of the tranquilizer had been severe from the moment the first agent, Baldwin, shot her, but even with that initial impairment she had not been completely incapacitated. She even felt her body beginning to fight the sedative before the second dose, inflicted by Baldwin's partner, compounded the drug's debilitative effects to the point where Lona could no longer resist.

Even now Lona sensed her body laboring to shake off the sedative's grip. Glancing at the uniformed agents escorting her, she knew they were taking her to prison or perhaps even a special holding facility designed to contain her. NTAC surely had a mandate to learn as much about 4400 abilities as possible, and one sure way to do so was to have live specimens in custody. It was obvious that they somehow had learned of her own power and had taken active steps to combat it. The tranquilizer they had employed already had proven most effective, and Lona feared what might be waiting for her if she allowed herself to remain in custody.

You must escape.

Deep within her, the call for her to continue her mission remained, unconcerned with her current predicament. Instead it forced other images into her mind, faces of those who would soon require her unique attention. With so much at stake, there could be no respite. Captivity was not an option.

They were drawing closer to the gate in the wooden fence separating the backyard from the alley between the houses. Lona knew she was running out of time if she was going to act. Whatever drug she had received, her altered metabolism was finally gaining a foothold in the battle to break it down. She could feel control returning to her with every passing second. Using the techniques she had taught herself through months of practice, she attempted once more to summon the energy field, but it still seemed beyond her reach. She needed a few more moments, but it was going to be close.

Ahead of her, the lead agent reached for the metal latch on the gate. The mechanism was rusty and stuck, forcing the man to sling his rifle so that he could apply both hands to unbolting it. The other two guards paused, holding Lona several paces back as they waited for their companion.

In her peripheral vision, she saw something flicker to her left, and she turned in time to catch a fleeting glimpse of a small, moving red dot. It was there only for an instant before it disappeared, but she was certain she had not imagined it.

Lona turned her head to her right, in time to see . . .

* * *

A single rifle shot pierced the air and Baldwin flinched as he saw a cloud of red rain explode from the side of Lona Callahan's head, spattering one of the agents escorting her as well as the section of fence to her left. The trio of agents around her scattered and Baldwin grabbed Skouris, hauling her to the ground before the echo of the shot died. Callahan's body remained upright for an additional moment before collapsing lifeless to the grass.

"Everybody all right?" Baldwin called out, retrieving his pistol. A chorus of acknowledgments answered him, and he exchanged relieved glances with Skouris before both agents rose to their feet, weapons up and in front of them. "That wasn't one of ours, was it?" Raising his wrist, he barked into his radio mike, "This is Baldwin. Who fired at Callahan?" His anger only grew as he received word that, so far as anyone could tell, none of the NTAC or other law enforcement personnel was responsible.

"Where'd it come from?" Skouris asked, looking around in search of a target.

Pointing toward the east, an expanse of hills and forest rather than rows of houses, Baldwin shook his head. "That way, but we'll never find the shooter, not now." He called for search parties to begin combing that area, knowing it likely was a futile gesture. It would be all but impossible to find a single person as sunset gave way to darkness.

"Damn it!"

All around him, he noted shadowy figures peeking out from curtains drawn across windows, trying to see what was happening outside their homes. He could sense the tension permeating the air, understanding and sympathizing with the people whose quiet lives had been disrupted by this unpleasant business. On the other hand, he held no doubts that local courthouses in the coming days would see a flurry of new lawsuits charging emotional distress.

God bless America.

He walked over to join Skouris where she stood over Lona Callahan's body. A single ugly wound desecrated her head, and her eyes stared unseeing toward the evening sky. "What do you think?" he asked. "Another watchdog?"

Skouris released a tired, resigned sigh. "Maybe one day, we'll find out."

Yes, Baldwin decided, that would almost certainly be true.

THIRTY-FIVE

SEATTLE, WASHINGTON

CONCEALED BY THE dense line of trees covering the hillside along with the advancing darkness as nightfall approached, he watched through his rifle scope as Lona Callahan crumpled and fell, dead before she hit the ground. It had been a challenging shot from a distance of nearly eight hundred yards, requiring patience as he waited for a clear line of sight to his target. He had been ready, his finger tense on the rifle's trigger as he watched for his opportunity.

Lona Callahan would have been proud, he decided.

Even as the murdered assassin dropped to the grass, those NTAC agents closest to her lunged for cover, vainly aiming their weapons and searching for the source of the single shot. He observed the proceedings play out for an additional moment, even taking the time to play the crosshairs across the heads of Tom Baldwin and Diana

Skouris. He had no intention of killing them, of course. That was not why he had come here today.

Still, it *was* tempting.

Lifting his chin from the rifle's stock, he glanced down at the luminescent dial of his watch, calculating that as few as two minutes would pass before NTAC forces were redeployed in what would be a fruitless attempt to find him. It would be easy enough to determine from which general area the shot had come, but there was a lot of forest to search along with the broken terrain of the hills, and it would have to be done in the dark. He would be gone long before then, the neoprene suit he wore masking his body's heat from any infrared or thermal imaging cameras carried by the helicopter he could already hear beginning to move in this direction.

Time to go. Already he could feel the summons, his masters calling to him from the depths of his own mind. There still was much work to be done if the future was to be saved.

He disassembled the rifle with methodical yet practiced care and returned its components to their padded case, which also acted as a pack he could carry strapped to his back. It took him less than a minute to secure his weapon and other equipment before taking a final look about his sniper's nest. Certain that he had sanitized the area of any damning evidence, he turned and headed deeper into the tree line, crossing over the hillside and descending to the narrow ravine that would provide effective cover as he made his retreat. Behind him, he heard the helicopter flying low somewhere over the trees, hundreds of yards away.

Satisfied with what he had accomplished and hopeful as to what it might mean for the future, Matthew Ross smiled as he disappeared into the forest.

REFLECTION

JULY 2005

THIRTY-SIX

NTAC
SEATTLE, WASHINGTON

"SOMEBODY DOESN'T LOOK very happy this morning."

Baldwin looked up from his desk and the paperwork piled atop it to see Nina Jarvis entering the office. In one hand she bore a white file folder with an NTAC logo on its cover, which she did not offer either to Baldwin or Skouris as she settled herself on the edge of Baldwin's desk.

Dropping his pen onto the papers, Baldwin leaned back in his chair. "I tend to get cranky when somebody shoots people around me." The anger he now felt had not hit him in the immediate aftermath of Lona Callahan's murder, but instead had festered throughout the night, keeping him from sleeping and finally driving him to head for the office hours before daybreak.

"Well," Jarvis said, holding up the file folder, "if you being mad means you get your after-action reports filed on time, stay mad."

"What do you think makes me mad in the first place?"

Jarvis shrugged. "I've got a teleconference with Ryland, a budget meeting, and a security briefing all scheduled for the same two-hour block. Want to trade jobs?"

"No, thanks," Baldwin said, holding up his hands in mock surrender.

Nodding at her apparent victory, Jarvis asked, "How are you?" She nodded toward his left arm. "Gonna live?"

Baldwin held up the arm, the bandage around the knife wound concealed beneath his shirt sleeve. "Afraid so. It wasn't deep, and didn't hit any veins or tendons." Both it and the cut on his chest largely were superficial wounds. Given Callahan's demonstrated fighting prowess, he was hard-pressed to understand how he had managed to avoid serious injury.

Blind luck. That, and Dr. Hudson mixes a mean cocktail.

Her demeanor turning serious, Jarvis shifted her position so that she also could look at Skouris. "Listen, both of you. No kidding, good work on the Callahan case."

"Well, maybe up to the point where she got killed," Skouris replied.

"The CIA's taking the lead on that," Jarvis said, waving away the dismissal. "They want first crack at whoever killed her. Director McFarland sends his warmest regards and thanks for a job well done, that he appreciates the way our organizations came together in pursuit of a common goal, and so on and so forth. He's sorry about Callahan's loss, but promises the matter will be aggressively investigated and those responsible will be brought to justice." She paused, offering a neutral expression before adding,

"You see how I got through all of that with a straight face just then?"

"Nicely done," Baldwin replied. He had no doubts that McFarland was doing nothing more than putting the final entries in whatever open case files Callahan represented. With her gone, the chances of any details relating to her Agency-approved and still quite classified activities seeing the light of day were remote at best.

Skouris asked, "What if it turns out another 4400 killed her?"

"Then you can bet your ass they'll be back asking for help," Jarvis countered. "Meanwhile, Ryland's putting you both in for commendations, and we get back to work. The media gets a story about the FBI locating the Wraith, and that *he* was killed while attempting to evade capture. Case closed, everybody's happy, life goes on."

"He, huh?" Skouris asked, shaking her head. "Well, that figures."

"Yeah," Baldwin said, "and if it *was* another returnee that killed her, programmed like she was? What if there are more of them like her running around out there? How are we supposed to deal with them?"

Folding her arms across her chest, Jarvis replied, "One of the latest theories from Marco and his boys is that if there are others out there like her, left on their own they might actually provide this 'balance' that Alfred Twenter talked about."

Baldwin glanced toward Skouris and noted the fleeting expression on his partner's face. He knew that Marco Pacella's theorizing had been aided by the visions seen by

Maia Skouris, but had agreed to keep that information to himself. Though he believed the young girl's ability could be a powerful aid to his and her mother's work, Baldwin had no desire to see Maia's already difficult life further complicated by being dragged into NTAC's ongoing investigations.

"Left on their own," Baldwin repeated, tapping his fingers on his desk. "For all we know, there's an army of them, getting ready to wage war with other 4400s."

"Well, unless and until that happens," Jarvis said, "we're not to discuss this aspect of the 4400 with anyone. The public is afraid enough just from what they know already."

Skouris said, "You know Marco's going to be up nights for the next month playing with his Ripple Effect theory and trying to figure out how Callahan or others like her fit in, along with this supposed balance." Shaking her head, she reached up to rub her brow. "I think you might want to increase the coffee budget for the Theory Room."

"I'll bring that up at my meeting," Jarvis said, rising from her perch. "Meanwhile, you two get back to the Collier case. We're getting some new leads from that sketch, so it looks like you're back in business." She departed on that note, leaving Baldwin and Skouris to regard each other across their desks.

"What do you think?" Baldwin asked after a moment.

Rising from her chair, Skouris reached up to rub her temples. "I think I want breakfast. I owe Marco a bagel, anyway. I'll start in on the sketch leads when I get back."

"Deal," Baldwin replied, smiling as she left. *Bringing*

Marco breakfast? Maybe there was something more brewing between those two, after all.

Anyway . . .

Alone in the office, Baldwin found his thoughts returning to Lona Callahan. He was not disappointed that her murder had prevented him from once and for all solving the "Mystery of the Wraith," as he had never truly considered it his case. What he did not like was the host of questions she had left behind, which now taunted him from across time. Only time itself, it seemed, would reveal their answers.

How did a returnee, possessing the motives that had driven her, factor into the purposes for which the 4400 had been sent from the future? If there *were* others like her, what agenda would they be following? What would their intentions and actions mean for the other returnees, to say nothing of everyone else?

For a brief moment, Baldwin heard the haunting words of the late Jordan Collier ringing in his ears. They seemed now to have acquired greater relevance, to say nothing of signaling larger portent than perhaps even Collier himself might have imagined.

The world will have to deal with us.

ACKNOWLEDGMENTS

First and foremost, we'd like to thank Margaret Clark, our editor at Pocket Books for several of our *Star Trek* projects, for inviting us to enter the world of *The 4400*. As we're both fans of the show, it was an opportunity we seized with great relish. Coming in at the beginning of a new tie-in license carried with it challenges we don't normally face with an established property like *Star Trek*. Margaret's patience and guidance was invaluable as we all navigated relatively uncharted waters while producing one of the first entries for this new series of books.

Also deserving of many thanks is Paula Block, Supreme Goddess of All Things Licensing at CBS Consumer Products. She has always offered us great assistance on many of our past projects, and this time was no exception. In addition to keeping us honest with regard to *Wet Work* and making sure it correctly fits within the "mythology" of *The 4400*, she also provided suggestions and advice that absolutely improved our story. People in her position rarely get the recognition they deserve when it comes to collaborative projects like this, but Paula can rest assured that her efforts on our behalf are never forgotten.

Finally, we'd like to thank fans of *The 4400* who reached out to us as they learned we were writing this novel. Their passion and enthusiasm for the series is contagious, and their anticipation as they wait for these new books to be published is heartwarming. Given the uncertain future of *The 4400* on-screen, it's exciting to know that fans are waiting for new stories, and we hope we're able to meet their expectations.

ABOUT THE AUTHORS

DAYTON WARD is a software developer, having become a slave to Corporate America after spending eleven years in the U.S. Marine Corps. When asked, he'll tell you that he joined the military soon after high school because he'd grown tired of people telling him what to do all the time. If you get the chance, be sure to ask him how well that worked out. In addition to the numerous credits he shares with friend and co-writer Kevin Dilmore, he is the author of the *Star Trek* novel *In the Name of Honor* and the science fiction novels *The Last World War* and *The Genesis Protocol* as well as short stories that have appeared in the first three *Star Trek: Strange New Worlds* anthologies, the Yard Dog Press collection *Houston! We've Got Bubbas*, DownInTheCellar.com, *Kansas City Voices* magazine and the *Star Trek: New Frontier* anthology *No Limits*. Though he currently lives in Kansas City with his wife and daughters, Dayton is a Florida native and still maintains a torrid long-distance romance with his beloved Tampa Bay Buccaneers. Visit him on the web at http://www.daytonward.com.

For more than eight years, **KEVIN DILMORE** was a contributing writer to *Star Trek Communicator*, penning news stories and personality profiles for the bimonthly publication of the Official *Star Trek* Fan Club. On the storytelling side of things, his story "The Road to Edos" was published as part of the *Star Trek: New Frontier* anthology *No Limits*. With Dayton Ward, his work includes stories for the anthology *Star Trek: Tales of the Dominion War*, the *Star Trek: The Next Generation* novels *A Time to Sow* and *A Time to Harvest*, the *Star Trek: Vanguard* novel *Summon the Thunder*, the *Star Trek: Enterprise* novel *Age of the Empress*, and ten installments of the original e-book series *Star Trek: S.C.E.* and *Star Trek: Corps of Engineers*. A graduate of the University of Kansas, Kevin works as a senior writer for Hallmark Cards in Kansas City, Missouri.